THE HUNTED

RACHEL BLACKLEDGE

For you Mom, my inspiration and my hero

"How very little can be done under the spirit of fear."
- Florence Nightingale

CHAPTER 1

Mylifemylifemylife.

Okay, now that I've warmed up my fingers I'd like to get started with the day's word count, one thousand on a bad day, two if I'm feeling fine. That gives me a leisurely pace of writing two novels a year including edits. But I don't need to edit much because the only words I put down on a page are publishable.

Virginia likes to hear that anyway, even though it's not true. She's my older sister by three years. Far more outgoing than I could ever hope to be, she handles all of the activities that a bestselling author must do these days. There are regular postings on social media tailored to the day of the week and overall mood of our young, robust community of followers. Or rather, I should say, followers of Amy Mathews.

I'm the wizard behind the pen name. Book one in the *After The End* vampire series sold half a million copies in eight months. Book two sold even more. And book three, the grand finale, had movie producers racing to buy the rights.

I always knew I wanted to be a writer. But did I have fairy dust in my fingertips that could carry dear reader hither and yon? I wasn't sure.

"Leave it to the professionals to decide," Mom told me after I had finished the first draft, crippled with doubt. It was a vampiric portrayal of young love mixed with a healthy dose of coming of age bewilderment.

Before Mom became too sick, we had tidied up the manuscript the best we could, but I didn't have much hope it would find a champion. Virginia put her analytical skills to use and assembled a spreadsheet of agent particulars.

For months she sent out the query package and kept track of the replies. So it was a cause for group celebration when we finally got an offer representing . . . us.

That was Virginia's idea. I couldn't even do the phone interview. During negotiations, when it became clear that writing would be a job filled with speaking events and book signings, Virginia's suggestion to use a pen name seemed like a good idea, keeping me at an arm's length from the glaring visibility.

Then the marketing campaigns kicked in, sales really picked up, and so did the requests for interviews. By then, we'd attracted the attention of a stan. That's what Virginia called him anyway—a stalker fan. I just kept it simple and called him a stalker.

I'd always struggled with social anxiety. But the stalker ordeal turned me into a wreck, and I couldn't even leave the house. So Virginia offered to become the face of Amy Mathews, leaving me free to write and her to socialize on behalf of our fictional fiction author.

And by the time the *After The End* series became a mega bestseller, Amy Mathews was the hottest young author this side of the International Date Line, and I had written myself into oblivion.

But at least I have my books. Growing up, my mom had read aloud to Virginia and I on chilly nights with the wall heater blowing full blast in our latest rental. Daniel Dafoe transported us into a glittering, dangerous world filled with dashing heroes and breathtaking swordplay.

Together with Edmund Hillary and Tenzing Norgay, we struggled up the bleak, blasting face of Mount Everest. We flew to the moon with Buzz Aldrin and explored the deep craters of its lunar face.

In the summer months, we lay on the hood of Froggy, our green Pinto, looking up at pins of light in the deep, dark night sky, imagining ourselves hopping aboard the Enterprise and zooming to outer space, where we met aliens and humanoids, all of whom shared our same hopes and dreams. We fell in love with Heathcliff, felt the wrath of Scarlett O'Hara, had our backs flayed and won our freedom with Frederick Douglass, and we read about people long since dead, brought magically back to the life by the undying spell of words.

Powered by our imaginations, Mom had shown us that magic lives in books and words can carry us anywhere we wanted to go, anytime we wanted to go there.

After Mom had graduated from nursing school and Virginia and I made it through high school, we all moved out to Rhode Island, where we fell in love with thick forests, four seasons, and lots of grounding history.

When we happened upon Glenhaven, a quaint town that looked like a Norman Rockwell painting, we'd started hunting for a place to rent. Mom loved the sharp autumn air tinged with wood smoke and moldering earth. Virginia loved the old-fashioned soda shop in downtown Glenhaven. And I loved the fact that we were two thousand miles away from my old life.

We signed the paperwork on a rental, and Rhenn Larsen, my main vampire character, came to me fleshed out and fully formed. He was a bully slayer. He said things I wished that I had said to my own personal bully, Monica Schaffer, that fateful afternoon she'd played her cruel trick on me.

When my fictional teenyboppers turned cruel and threatening, Rhenn swept over them like a black wraith and sunk his long hollow incisors into their soft yielding necks, silencing them forever.

Then it hit us. The big C. Mom's diagnosis had come right after I'd finished the first draft. We were all in collective denial. People recover from cancer. People beat it. Mom would too.

I'd started working on the second draft, wondering how I'd shape the mess into a good story. I kept working on it, but couldn't really find my footing. The story seemed smaller in scope than I had originally planned and lacked any real depth. I started to worry that I'd never find the story, when Mom's doctor called with her latest test results. Then the 'C' word had turned into the 'M' word: metastasized.

But I can't think about that now. I can't think about that ever. So I get to work instead. Writing has always been my savior. Writing will always be my savior.

I'm sitting in my home office, firing up a new document, getting ready to put in a good day's work. Wood-paneled with floor-to-ceiling bookshelves, my genius cave is where I try to make the magic happen. A soft blue Persian rug sits under my six-legged antique desk. I have views across the backyard through a big picture window and a glass paneled door that opens out to a small patio. And best of all, I have a safe room that we had installed after the stalker saga. That's another thing I try to forget: being hunted.

Mostly, I use the safe room for storage and book overflow, but Virginia stockpiles snacks in case the end of the world arrives sooner than expected.

I open up a document, ready to start fleshing out an idea for a new book that doesn't involve bloodsuckers. I want to exercise my fingers on a modern remake of *Rebecca*, which I cleverly renamed "Rebecca." It's just a working title, but I'm diving right into it, hoping for a wave of inspiration, when the home phone rings.

I look over at the display and don't recognize the number. Why would I? Just wait for it to ring out, I tell myself, turning my attention back to my computer monitor. But what if it's important? I wish Virginia was here to pick it up, but she's out of town on a book signing tour.

The second to last stop on the tour culminated in a knot of adoring fans sitting front and center. I would have expired with fright, but Virginia did our brand good. From an amphitheater at an outdoor book festival, she'd read aloud a cringe-worthy kissing scene out loud that I'd had a hard time writing.

I'd blundered around for about a week, trying to get that scene just right. I'd written it like blind person handling a scorpion: nervous, unsure, and deathly afraid to get it all wrong.

In the end, I think my bumbling effort resonated with dear reader, and I concluded that none of us know what we're doing in the first blush of love, Amy Mathews included.

But the phone. It's still ringing. My heart beats a little bit faster just thinking about actually talking to someone. But curiosity and procrastination overrule. So I pick it up.

"Hello?"

"Hi, is this . . ."—I hear papers rustling—"Virginia Ward?"

"No, this is Eugenia, her sister. Who's this?"

"This is Cody Merrick from Quantum Security. We manage your home security system. Ah ok. Yep, I see right here. You're also on the policy."

"Yes?"

"So we came across some important information that we think you both should know about . . ."

Prickles of foreboding wash over me. "What kind of information?"

"Well, I think it would be best if we talk in person. It's something that I need to show you."

In person? My palms begin to moisten. Personal meetings are my nemesis. I glance over at my monthly calendar that's conspicuously blank. "I'm pretty busy," I tell him.

"The matter is important, Miss Ward," he says. "If meeting in person is too inconvenient, would you be available for a Skype call?"

"Um. Sure, I guess. That seems doable."

"Okay great. What's your user name? I can call you right back."

"Uh . . . that's a little tight. Can I call you back half an hour?"

"Sure," he says and gives me his details.

I spend the next half an hour fidgeting with my hair and biting my nails, while my inner cheerleader tries to bolster me up with chants of: YES YOU CAN! C-A-N!

Then, reluctantly, I call him back on Skype. The screen lights up, showing the face of a man peering into the camera. He looks young and somewhat boyish with mussed hair, wearing what looks like his father's white collared business shirt. Not the typical security type. Maybe he's the computer guy.

"Thanks for calling," Cody says, reaching for something just out of view. "Sorry for the inconvenience. Can I just verify a couple security questions first?"

"Okay."

He asks me for my "DOB" and my mailing address and phone number on file, which I give to him. "Can you tell me what this is about?" I ask.

"Sure. Let me just cut to the chase. Did you receive anything in the mail about our new enhanced security measures?"

"I don't know. My sister usually gets the mail."

"All right. Well, as you know, we take your security very seriously. We're in the process of integrating a facial recognition software program that identifies a database of people who regularly visit your house—we call it your friend circle."

"Sounds proactive. Slightly Orwellian, but okay."

He laughs a little uncomfortably. "Yeah, I guess that's what enhanced security calls for these days."

"Guess so," I say, wondering why his news requires a video call.

"So as a member of our platinum program, your account was one of the first we implemented with the new upgrade." He flips open the cover of his tablet. "We always want to make sure our high value customers are safe and secure . . ."

"Yeah, that's good. We had a little problem a while ago," I say.

That's an understatement. The frightening *stan* saga had ultimately resulted in our current installment of no-breach perimeter walls and the high-tech home security monitoring system that Cody is calling about.

"Mmhm. So part of the implementation process is what we call 'cleaning'," Cody continues. "We scrub all the footage and run checks on everyone who falls outside of the database parameters. Just to make sure the household is safe moving forward." He opens up an app on his tablet. I lean forward, pleased that Quantum is taking our security so seriously. "Miss Ward, we found something that we think you should know about."

Suddenly, I'm not so pleased. He holds up the tablet screen to his computer monitor so I can see. A video starts playing. Instantly, I recognize the camera angle overlooking our backyard. It's in gray relief and uninteresting to the casual observer.

I see Dillon, my sister's boyfriend, walking quickly away from the direction of my office, hands stuffed in his front pockets. I feel a little queasy.

Cody freezes the footage and double-taps on Dillon's pixelated face. A red circle triangulates on Dillon's face, zooms in, and brings his facial features into fine focus.

"Do you know this person?" he asks me.

"Yes," I hear myself saying. "That's my sister's boyfriend."

Cody looks away, his eyes wide with—disbelief?

"What is it?" I ask, skin crawling with suspicion. "What's wrong?"

He taps again on the face, and a police mug shot opens to the right of the frozen video stream. It's Dillon all right, clutching a numbered placard, standing against a height strip. Somehow, I'm not surprised.

In the mug shot, his hair is dark brown, hanging over his forehead like a dirty curtain. I recognize the sullen brown eyes and small crescents of his nostrils.

"Great. What did he do? Rob an old lady?" I ask.

Cody looks up at me, his jaw muscles tense. "Miss Ward, Dillon has a—a violent past." My arm hair stands on end. "He was charged with assault and battery and conspiracy to harm with a deadly weapon. And of course you know about the stalking charge . . ."

I cannot speak.

"Because your prosecution dropped the charges."

My hearing suddenly fails. Virginia was the one commandeering the lawyers. Did she direct them to drop the case? And why, exactly? Cody's brows draw together in concern, while his lips move. He's saying something along the lines of: *I would steer clear if I was you, and definitely don't add him to your friend circle.*

Except that he already is a part of our friend circle. Virginia made sure of it.

CHAPTER 2

I feel sick. Sickened. Totally unwell.

Virginia was the one who had actually seen the stalker. I'd only seen his creepy silhouette. As a first hand witness, she'd gone to all the court trials. Hadn't she?

Cody asks if I'm all right, but I can hardly think.

"Yeah," I mumble, stunned, and cut the video call short. I rise to standing and look around, wondering if Dillon is hiding in a closet. And if so, which one?

Somehow, I get my feet moving through the house, locking every door and window. Then I'm rushing up stairs, down the hallway and into my bedroom. I lock my bedroom door and call Virginia seven consecutive times, but she doesn't pick up.

I send some urgent text messages—*I need to talk to you*— and nervously pace my bedroom, glancing outside, looking for Dillon, who probably has the code to our house, thinking I should have texted—*What the fuck is wrong with you*!

But I need facts from her not a defensive linebacker. How much access does Dillon have to the house? Does he have a spare set of keys? And most importantly, how much does he know about Amy Mathews, our carefully constructed author persona? That's a clean, lucrative shot into the sordid world of blackmail.

But clearly Virginia hadn't considered that when she decided to date him. Is this some sort of twisted Stalker Syndrome? Is dating your stalker even a thing? I sit down on my bed and google "dating my stalker." I need to get to the bottom of Virginia's mind warp. What on earth is she thinking?

Headlines fill my screen: "I fell in love with my stalker and couldn't be happier," "I'm falling for my stalker," "I recently entered a relationship with my stalker," "How I fell in love with my stalker," by lovebug457, who penned an instruction manual about it.

There are more disturbing offerings: "My super-hot stalker," "Stalkers are great in bed," and "Meet my stalker" (in case anyone was interested). There are videos of women gushing about their usual start to a relationship, but what a relationship it is!

There are message boards of women soliciting advice from the dregs of the internet, "Should I date my stalker?" There are even 'romance' books based on hot sex between stalker and stalkee.

I'm appalled. I'm horrified. And I continue reading articles, trying to find out if any of these women had been strangled in their sleep, but the majority of them claim—justify rather—that their stalker's behavior was some sort of shy courting ritual.

Good God. What is wrong with these people exactly? Including my own sister?

I put my phone down, trying to tamp down my anxiety. If I don't get ahold of myself, I'm going to find myself skittering down the slippery slope of yet another panic attack.

Being alone in the house had always given me a wonderful sense of security. Now, I feel a tingling sense of dread knowing that Dillon could be anywhere, making himself at home, helping himself to a beer, and plotting something sinister. Is he here now? Listening? Waiting?

I dare to check my closet. Nothing. Then I examine the lock on my bedroom door, trying to determine if Dillon can pick it. In the movies, dangerous criminals just stick a bobby pin into the hole, rattle it around, and waltz into the room where the victim stands petrified in fear. Mine locks pretty sturdy.

What am I supposed to do now? I'm home alone. I don't even have a dog to hug or sic on stalkers. I do have a security system though, a great big fat one that cost a small fortune.

I'd ponied up the cash without even wincing because I was happy to finally have the backing of state-of-the-art security. I wanted the best money could buy because I was tired of lying in bed at night, watching the shadows, feeling my heart race in my chest.

I'd written book two and three of *After The End* in a state of insomnia and terror and grief. I'll never outrun the grief of losing Mom. Somehow that mix of emotions resonated with a lot of people. Is that a common feeling then?

All I know is that I have an empty house that may or may not be compromised. In my shock, I forgot to ask Cody if Dillon had sneakily entered the property since Virginia left on the publicity tour.

So I huddle in the far corner of my closet, concealed behind my winter coats, and call Quantum. I wait for the automated recording system to rattle off the various options designed to cunningly divert the caller away from a live operator. I push zero eight consecutive times, cursing the automated voice that stutters with confusion and finally puts me through.

"Hi," I whisper when a human answers. "This is Eugenia Ward. I need you to run a surveillance scan on my house and tell me if anyone entered my property in the last week."

"Sure, Miss Ward. Can you give me your account number?"

"Can you look it up by my address?"

"No problem. And that would be?"

I give her my address and wait breathlessly for the results. "Okay, let me just transfer you over to the right department."

My heart sinks. There's a sense of urgency in her voice, maybe after she glimpsed my platinum account status, but I still have to go through the labyrinth. "Can you please hurry?"

"Just a sec."

Some crackly music plays in the background, sounding like Huey Lewis and the News beamed in from outer space. Then someone else comes on the line. Before she makes her introductions and queries my account details again, I blurt, "Hi, this is Eugenia Ward at 1156 Crosshaven Road, Glenhaven Rhode Island. I need you to review my security footage and tell me if anyone has entered my property in the week."

"1156 Crosshaven Road . . ." The woman mumbles as she types in my address. "For security purposes, can you please give me the phone number associated with the account?"

I give her the landline number and answer a few more security questions (Virginia wasn't very imaginative).

"Okay. Great. Here we are. Running scans now . . ."

I pull in one long calming breath.

"How are you doin' today, Miss Ward?"

"Fine."

"You sound a bit tense. Everything okay?"

"Yep, great. Did you get those results?"

"Mmhm. Just working on that now. Can I put you on hold? My computer seems to be a little slow today."

"No, I'd rather wait here on the phone. Will it be much longer?"

"Should take a few more seconds . . ." She starts humming. "Oookay. Here we are. Yup. Looks like nobody has entered the property in the past week."

"Thank God," I mutter.

"You sure you're okay? You want me to send someone out?"

"No, it's okay. Thank you. I just—I had a scare, that's all."

"All right then. You have a good rest of the day, Ms. Ward. And if you have any concerns whatsoever, you just give us a call right back. Or you can always push the red emergency button on your intercom panel. That goes straight to the police."

The technician had described the system when he installed it. Every intercom panel has a red panic button with a little flap installed over the top, to avoid accidental activation and the hefty fine associated with calling out law enforcement for no good reason.

"Okay. Thanks again," I say and hang up.

I have all the empirical evidence I need to feel safe—the house is locked up tight, and Dillon hasn't stopped by—but why do I feel like I'm standing on the edge of cliff? About to fall off?

I pull in some deep calming breaths so I can think clearly and figure out what to do.

In, one two three.

Out, one two three.

I run my hands through my hair, feeling jittery. This isn't working. I need help.

I need my trusty friends.

I need my benzo buddies.

I need my pills.

CHAPTER 3

I stand in my bathroom like I have so many times before, shaking out another pill from an orange vial; anxious to swallow another pill, wondering how I'd gotten here in the first place.

I've always been a bit shy; a wallflower afraid to speak my mind. But writers are introverted, I always told myself. Okay, some. I've never really been the life of the party. My own private Voldemort, Monica Schaffer, hadn't really helped matters in that department, but there was a time when I could at least cope. There was a time when I didn't need my pills.

After we lost Mom, I managed to get through the first tender months of loss on my own steam, but then the stalker arrived. Somewhere between grief and appalling fear, sleep took a permanent departure. So I went to go see Dr. Miller, an

Australian expat, the only doctor I knew, the same doctor who had spotted the first signs of Mom's cancer.

Back in those days, before Mom's health had become too dire, I'd asked him about shrimps on the Barbie, drop bears, and if he'd ridden a kangaroo to work lately.

He'd retired the kangaroo, apparently, but not his prescription pad.

So after my insomnia got worse, I found myself in his office again, trying to stay strong, trying to look "bright-eyed." I didn't want to tell him about my scary new friend. I clung to the irrational belief that if I didn't speak about the stalker problem, maybe it would go away. So I told him that I was having a hard time dealing with . . . everything.

He looked though his spectacles parked on the tip of his nose and gave me a short nod. "Yeah, look, that can all be helped. That's to be expected, Eugenia. You've been through a lot. You've lost your mum. You're still grieving. It's a long process. You need to take it easy, okay? Don't push yourself too hard. And use these quite sparingly . . ."

He prescribed tranquilizers to help with my nerves and Ambien to help me sleep. The benzos helped bring my anxiety levels down, but I still felt like I was going a little crazy. Back when the shadows moved, and the mangled roses kept appearing on our doorstep. Back when the stalker was everywhere and nowhere at the same time.

After I had filled the first prescription, I sat in the Walgreen's parking lot and swallowed a pill dry. I didn't know what to expect, but as I drove away, the chains of anxiety start to loosen.

By the time I veered home, I could breathe again. I could function. And I hung up my car keys for a good few days.

Then came the addiction. I tried to quit. Cold turkey and all that. But anxiety constantly gnawed on my innards, robbing me of strength to rise up and break free.

So I went on with my daily routine, feeling like I needed superhuman feats of courage just to shower. I'd read too many murder mysteries, I told myself as I took another pill. The 'dead woman in the shower' trope took on new meaning. Maybe those authors had done their research. Maybe killing women in the shower wasn't a plot device. Maybe it was accurate reporting.

Then came the depression. Prozac helped me 'manage the blues.' But Prozac made me feel like the walking dead. So Dr. Miller moved me over to Zoloft, explaining that it took time to 'find the right balance.'

Over the following year, I 'tried out' Celexa, Effexor, and Paxil. Some made me feel a little better than awful. But the benzos became my go-to pill during all this upheaval. When I started to get that edgy feeling, I'd just pop another one and try not to feel too bad about it.

"You need to wean yourself off this shit," I kept telling myself. Some days I cut the pills in half and thought positively, hoping for a powerful placebo effect. But The Edge crept up again, its scraggly fingers tearing down my resolve. Well, The Edge is back in a big way now.

If I'm not careful, I'm going to be buried alive in my comfy coffin of pills. A captive in my own house. A slave to my fears forever.

But today isn't a day for personal triumphs. Today is a day for survival. And I shove the vial into my jeans pocket.

CHAPTER 4

One thing is certain: I'm not going to camp out at home and wait for a friendly visit from the stalker turned Virginia's boyfriend. I'm moving out. I pack my clothes in a hurry, trying to figure out where to go, wishing I had a friend or even a boyfriend that I could call for moral support. But my only 'loved one' is Virginia, who caused this whole crisis.

I know her. She'll be angry that Quantum rumbled her carefully constructed backstory. I jam some t-shirts and jeans into a small carryall, along with some underwear and bras and sweaters. I want to clear out of the house in the next few minutes. I have no idea where I'm going exactly, but I'm going to go there until I can figure out my next steps.

Packing done, I zip the carryall closed and dash down the stairs, making a heroic run into the foyer for my car keys. Then I'm in the garage, climbing into my car. As the garage door yawns open, I check the backseat for Dillon, heart hammering in my chest.

No Dillon. I sag into the seat, feeling a little ridiculous. Villains only materialize from thin air in B-rated horror flicks. But I can't help myself. I check under the floor mats just to be sure and reverse out of the garage, watching the bushes for signs of Dillon. Nothing so far.

At the bottom of the driveway, I watch the rear view mirror, while the front gate swings open, just in case Dillon sits up suddenly in the backseat, despite my previous searches. That's impossible, I keep telling myself as I swerve onto Decatur Street and head toward the freeway.

No, I'll tell you what's impossible, comes the reply. *Virginia making a good decision for once in her life. And saying to herself: you know what? Maybe it's kind of a* bad idea *to date my stalker.*

A little less than an hour later, I find myself in downtown Providence, cruising down a wide main avenue. A grand colonial building with a circular entrance catches my eye. The Precedent. It's expensive by the looks of things, and expensive hotels have exactly what I want: very tight security.

I drive into the covered entrance with a grand water fountain on one side and two valets in red livery on the other. I take in a few deliberate breaths, trying to bolster up my courage, trying not to hyperventilate, as I follow the waving valet's instructions and pull up front and center.

Then I grab my carryall sitting in the passenger seat and get out.

"Welcome to The Precedent. Are you visiting a guest today?" asks the valet, holding my car door open.

My stomach clenches with nervousness. I look away, avoiding his direct gaze and manage to say, "No, I'm checking in."

I can see it in his face as he moves toward the trunk to collect my bags. I'm young, but I also look young for my age. He can't figure out why, or how, a kid with a carryall is booking herself into a fancy hotel. Well, he doesn't need to know the details.

"I don't have any luggage," I say. "Could you please, um—take my car?"

"Sure, no problem," he says with an efficient nod. "The reception desk is just inside to your right."

The foyer is a bright with cream marble, metallic accents, and sea foam blue and sunshine yellow fabrics. I walk straight to the check-in desk, staffed by a young slick-haired receptionist, who is busily typing on her keyboard below eye level.

I swallow hard and speak. "Excuse me, sorry. Can I get a room please?"

She looks up at me, eyebrows raised slightly, looking a little surprised and unsure about the 'booking a room' procedure. Well, that makes two of us.

"Yes, of course," she says, brow furrowed with concentration as she looks down at her monitor. "Sorry, this is my first day. Do you a have a reservation?"

I shake my head no. I'm not feeling very well. My skin is clammy, but my body is overly warm. A headache is looming, and my eyes feel like sand paper. I hope I don't look like someone on the verge of a psychotic break. Even though I *am* someone on the verge.

My sister is dating our stalker. Every time I think about it my neurons start backfiring. I half expect gibberish to fall out of my mouth, making this chirpy young woman back away slowly from the reception desk and call the police.

"Okay, do you have any preferences?" she asks. "Single bed? Double?"

"I just need a room. Please. Something . . . secure."

"Oh, this hotel is *very* secure," she says, nodding as she leans closer to her concealed computer screen. "But . . . oh. I'm so sorry. It looks like all of our rooms are booked."

My knees buckle. My mind races. What now? I'll have to summon the valet, stand on the curb, and wait for him to show up with my car. Then I'll have check the backseat again like a lunatic because Dillon could have easily tracked me down and climbed inside. Then I'll have to drive around and hunt for a different hotel, park again, ask again . . .

I can't do it. "Are you *sure*?" I ask. "Can you double check please?"

My right eye starts twitching. I wish so badly, and not for the first time in my life, that I had a call-a-friend feature where I could dial up a human and tell her (him preferably, but that will never happen) about my problem.

Are you kidding me? she'd say.

No. No, I'm not . . .

So the guy who was arrested for stalking you and your sister . . . is now her boyfriend?

I would nod, numb with shock.

There would be a long stunned pause. Then she would say, *Wow. Just wow.*

That would be the long and short of it, and 'wow' would pretty much cover all the bases. I certainly wouldn't have anything else to add besides silent stupefaction. Luckily my handy friend would know what to do.

Pack a bag, she'd say. *You're moving in with me.*

But I don't have any helpful friends. I only have Virginia and hopefully this young receptionist, studying the hotel booking system.

"We do have a suite available," she says to the computer screen. Then she looks up me, grinning. Or is she grimacing? I'm not sure.

I nearly sag with relief. "I'll take it."

She blinks a little rapidly. I can see she's formulating more questions. *Don't you want to know how many thousands that will cost you??*

"Here," I say, digging my credit card out of my phone wallet and sliding it over. "Just put it on my card."

Amy Mathews can pay the bill.

And Virginia can pay her back.

The suite has a nice view of lush property grounds that includes a pool dotted with covered lawn chairs, where Dillon could be relaxing, and a bar cabana, where Dillon could be ordering up a beer (and charging it to my room). I examine all three people down there, enjoying the hotel bar amenities, looking for someone raising their glass to me in thanks. No one does. Good.

That done, I swish the window curtains closed and go to the door to a) hang the Do Not Disturb sign, b) engage the deadbolt, and c) look through the tiny spyglass just to make sure Dillon isn't standing there, grinning at me.

He's not.

Slightly relieved, I draw myself a hot bath in the enormous Jacuzzi bathtub and turn on the rumbling jets. I climb in, lie back, and stare into space in shock and disbelief, my mind running over the past many months, viewing everything differently in this new terrible light.

The *stan* ordeal started with a deluge of social media messages that I dismissed as an exuberant fan with a fondness for the Shatner Comma. I found his musings entertaining at first, and I actually wrote him back a few times. Then I made a joke about his comma usage, which lead to long-winded rants (some of which contained literally only commas), so I blocked the guy.

Then he hunted down my private email address.

"I suppose, I should say, sorry, for reaching out, but I-don't-say-sorry, unless, I've done something, interminably wrong, and being a fan, being your biggest, most devoted fan, isn't wrong. It's glorious. It's, angelic. Can't you hear the heavens, opening up, and singing, about my supine, divine devotion to you?" he wrote.

Followed a few days later with, "I made this tiddly widdly video for you, to show you how innate, our relationship can be, how friendly, how helpful, I can be, if you just, let me. If you just let me, show how sweet, and supportive, I can be. Because that's all, I want to be. I want to be here, for you. To show you, the way. Because, I'm committed to you, but you have to ask yourself . . . ask . . . how, much do you, commit yourself?"

There was a blue hyperlink. I couldn't resist. It was the car accident. I was the rubbernecker. Down went my index finger on the mouse.

Click!

It was a remake of No Doubt's *It's My Life* video. There was a bubble-headed vixen (adorned with a man's head) poisoning his first lover, running the second over with a roadster, and fatally electrocuting a third—all three victim's sporting Virginia's head, the face of Amy Mathews. At the end of the video, the killer then found himself in jail, struggling against some burly wardens. The allusion wasn't lost on me. This bobble-headed character killed Amy three times over.

Virginia went to the police, but they said there wasn't anything they could do about video remakes. They gave her a tip sheet instead, all printed up and ready to go.

"He can send all the videos he wants," she told me later that evening. "He doesn't know where we live."

Suddenly I was grateful that we'd been sparse on details when it came to writing Amy's bio. We'd said she lived in New England, but didn't say exactly where.

The East Coast is home to fourteen million four hundred forty-four thousand and eight hundred people—I looked it up. Even if the stalker wanted to graduate from the digital world and get real, he'd have to investigate six states, sixty-seven counties, one hundred and fifty cities, over three hundred towns, and fourteen million houses. That ought to keep him busy. Very busy indeed, otherwise known as impossible.

He may be a video editing whiz, but he certainly wasn't a one man walking census bureau.

Well, he found us somehow. I'd found the first mangled rose, resting against our front door. We endured the best we could, upgrading the locks and mini blinds in our old rental, while we got 'love bombed' by a complete psycho.

Then we bought our current house. And he found us there too. But finally, thankfully, his rose blitz reign of terror came to an end. I arrived home one evening and heard someone creeping around upstairs. The house was dark. It wasn't Virginia. So I fled, and called the cops.

They swooped in and found Dillon leafing through Virginia's underwear drawer. Then they carted him off to jail, and Virginia took over from there.

After that, we built the perimeter walls and installed the security system because by then I was bone tired of not feeling safe. I wanted to live in a fortified fortress, where nobody could ever touch us again.

Then for some unthinkable reason Virginia turned the stalker into her boyfriend. Her cover story was that she'd met Dillon at a local dive bar, where they'd spent the evening trying to drink one another under the table. Shot for shot they'd gamely matched one another, or so the story goes, until they blacked out in unison and miraculously woke up in the downstairs bathroom.

Dillon is an attractive guy, hitting all the hallmarks with his dusty blonde hair, blue eyes, and gym-honed biceps. But I never did warm to him. He seemed to bring out the unstable part of my sister's personality, the part that scares me. Just thinking about Virginia's personality quirks gives me anxiety. Why did decide to start dating him?

In, one two.

I want my pills so bad.

Out, one two.

I need to get off that shit.

In, one two.

Maybe I can try when I'm not facing a personal crisis.

Out, one two.

Good point. I reach for my jeans, rummage around in the pocket for the vial, crack it open, and swallow a pill. Then I sit there, breathing and waiting for chemical euphoria to envelop me.

That evening, I sit down on the couch in the suite and open up my laptop. I've already accepted that there will be a significant disruption to my daily word count. If Virginia wants to bring an almost convicted stalker into our home, then she'll have to understand the inherent problems I might develop with concentration.

And if she doesn't, our agent, David, surely would. He seems like a reasonable person, even if we've never met. Maybe he'll even have a good solution for me like a group home for writers under existential threat from their relation's poor choice in love interests.

Maybe I could write a book about it, called *So My Sister Is Dating A Psycho Dickhead*. Just for fun I write a few exploratory scenes. That quickly spirals, so I quit, feeling even worse about Dillon's unfettered access to our house over the last many months.

I text Virginia again, trying to determine the extent of our problem, but she doesn't reply.

Later that night, she finally calls me back. She has a call-in appearance with a radio talk show the following morning. She's anxious to get off the phone and get some sleep.

"So what's up?" she says. "I got your text messages."

It's a terrible time to talk about Dillon. If she gets too upset, she could do something unstable, like nip down to a local watering hole and skip the morning talk show. I have to be strategic about bringing up the subject of her dangerous interest in stalkers, but I need some basic facts.

I should wait until she gets home. I should be diplomatic, but the topic is racing up my throat like bile. Bile that I can't keep down. "I moved out," I blurt. "I'm not staying at home anymore."

"What?" she asks, her voice clear and immediate. "What are you talking about?"

"I know about Dillon," I say, heart racing. "I know he was the stalker. I know you dropped the charges. Cody from Quantum Security called and told me. They ran a background check on him."

30

Silence.

"Why would you do something like that?" I ask. Then I can't help myself; I have to say it. "What is *wrong* with you, Jinny! Why would you put us at risk? You, me, Amy—everything. You put it all at risk for that nut job!"

"He's not a nut job," she says, her voice distant and chilly. There, I did it. She's defensive. But it can't be helped. Why should I have to tiptoe around her unstable personality, always trying not to upset her, while she goes on and blithely brings a stalker with a violent past into our house?

"Yes, he *is* a nut job," I press. "Do you not remember the messages? The letters? The video? The *roses*?"

"Roses? Not exactly the stuff of nightmares."

"What sort of *psycho* breaks into someone else's house and leafs around in their intimate belongings?"

"He's not a psycho! He's just . . . I mean, yeah, that was a little weird, but he's really into me. He's really passionate, okay? Is that okay?"

"Virginia, this is serious. He has a past. A *record*. Are you aware of that?"

"No. I mean, yes. Maybe. He got into some trouble a long time ago when he was young and—"

"A long time ago? Virginia, you don't know this guy—"

"Yes, I do know him. I know him because I took the time to get to know him. And you would too, if you had ever bothered to try. But all you ever do is avoid him and call him 'Dillon the Dickhead' or 'shit for brains' behind his back."

"He is a dickhead! And while I can't vouch for the exact type of material found between his ears, it seems to me that he *is* missing a few brain cells!"

Cold, hard silence. "I have to go now."

"Virginia, I just need to know if he has the security code to our house."

No reply.

"Did you give him a set of keys?"

Nothing.

Frustrated, I can't resist. I have to say it. "Is he going to rob us blind? I'm sure he could use the money."

And she hangs up.

CHAPTER 5

During the entire court hearing, which I now realize wasn't a hearing at all; Virginia was always short on details. She was the natural choice to go to court and handle the attorneys. I wasn't able to do it, and besides, I'd never actually seen the guy. I was just happy to see that the ordeal wasn't weighing too heavily on her.

But how had Dillon persuaded Virginia to drop the charges? That is the unanswered question that I plan on asking once Virginia starts speaking to me again.

In the meantime, I stay close to my characters by re-reading passages that I'd written. Then I do some line editing, while I wait for Virginia to come home so we can finally talk, however unpleasant.

The room service dishes are piling up. My suite is a mess, so I do a little house keeping. I make my bed, push the dishes outside the door, and binge on my favorite old movies.

On the third day, I'm sitting on the couch, not writing, getting mightily fed up with living in a hotel, when my phone rings. Virginia.

"Hey."

"How's life?" she asks.

"Could be better. You back home?"

"Landed last night. So . . . where you are staying?"

"At a hotel," I reply.

"Sounds mysterious. Are you ready to move home yet? I'm sure you miss your office."

Aha. The ole pretend it never happened trick—a Virginia special.

I sigh. "I do miss my office, and I miss being at home." And away from the prying eyes of your stalker boyfriend, I want to add but don't.

"Why don't you come home then?" she asks, as if her relationship with Dillon didn't matter.

"I think you know why."

There's a long silence, followed by an offer to meet up for coffee so we can talk about it. Apparently her fatal attraction is not fodder for phone conversations.

I sigh. "Okay, do you want to meet at Beansters in about an hour?"

"Beansters it is. See ya there."

Beansters is Virginia's favorite hangout. It's located in an area close to downtown Glenhaven called the West End, a charming historical part of town nestled against the dense woodlands. It was where Beaver Cleaver would have lived if he hadn't lived at Paramount Studios.

I drive down Chesapeake Street and pull into the parking lot. My tolerance for public places has gone up some since moving out, a nice upside to recent events.

But my stomach still roils with nervousness at the idea of walking into a place where *cool* people hang out, read the scribbly coffee menu, order one, give my name to an inquisitive barista who can neither hear nor spell very well, and find a cozy couch that isn't occupied. That requires some human interaction, which always makes me tense.

Luckily, by the time I arrive, Virginia had already done the heavy lifting. I find her sitting on a corner couch, twirling her straw around in an iced coffee cup, and a steaming mug of tea sitting on the table in front of her.

"Thanks for the tea," I say, sitting down next to her.

"No problem," she replies.

Her curly red locks are chemically straightened. She had some blonde highlights put into her hair that looks like someone with peroxide on their fingers had clawed at her head. She looks sleeker, wearing a fashionable dun-colored trench coat that I've seen online, paired with black ankle booties. She wears heavy kohl eyeliner that accentuates her slanting blue eyes. A bit of blusher on the apples of her cheeks softens her habitual hard looks and makes her look almost pretty. But despite the new upgrades, she's still the same Virginia to me.

"So how was the tour?" I ask, purposely avoiding the unpleasant topic of conversation that lay between us like a decomposing corpse.

"Yeah, it went really well," she says in a lackluster tone of voice. Usually by now, she'd regale me with news from David and recount exuberant fan stories. But her disinterest is cause for concern.

We sit in awkward silence for a few long seconds, while I blow on my tea and she examines the contents of her tall plastic cup. Then I take a bolstering sip of Earl Grey and set the mug down.

"Why did you do it, Jinny? Why didn't you tell me?" My anger bled out over the past few days. I just want to know the whys and the whats now, particularly what are we going to do about it. "I mean, how does something like that even happen?"

"You don't have a right to judge me, Eugenia." She used my full name. That's bad. Full names are only reserved for moments of high alarm or great displeasure.

"I'm not judging you, Jinny. Really, I'm not," I say in my most reassuring voice possible. "I just need to know. Can you tell me?"

She purses her lips and stares into space. Then she pulls in a breath and looks at me. "I really didn't want you to know. I was afraid to tell you. I was afraid that you'd call the cops and have him arrested."

I probably would have, thinking that I ought to do that right now. But I don't have any grounds. Virginia dropped the charges. And he hasn't committed any jailable offenses that I know about. And unfortunately, we live here in reality, where he'll have to actually do something before he can get arrested.

She looks at me with her piercingly blue eyes. "He's not bad, Genie. Really he's not. He's an Amy Mathews fan, that's how it all started. He saw my picture on the back of the book, and he followed me home after he saw me at the grocery store. He was looking for Amy Mathews memorabilia, that's why he broke into the house."

Like Amy's underwear? I want to ask, but I keep my mouth shut. If I interrupt her now I'll never hear the truth, and I need to find out what sort of psycho we're dealing with here.

"Anyway, it was all really innocent, and he didn't think he'd get caught. But he did get caught. And when I heard the police wanted to charge him with stalking in the third degree, a *felony*, I was all for it. I mean that's really creepy, you know? And I was so mad about it, too! Breaking into someone's house? But then . . . you remember I was seeing that shrink?"

I nod, wondering where this is going to take us.

"Well, he suggested that I go see Dillon in prison and try to put my feelings of anger to rest. He said forgiving people is the best therapy because you're actually forgiving yourself. So I went—I went to jail to try and forgive him and we just started talking. And he told me why he did it, and he said that he was really sorry. And he even started crying. And I felt so sorry for him." She takes a sip of coffee. "He's a good guy, Genie. He's a hopeless romantic. And the next time I went to go see him, he'd written this poem about me, and he read it out loud. And you know? That shrink was right. I forgave him and . . . and when he told me that a felony stays on your record *forever*, I just thought, you know, that's not really fair. He's not a felon. He's a nice guy, who needed a break."

"Mmhm." I don't have much else to say. There were so many plot holes in her romantic tale of falling in love with a jailbird that I don't even know where to begin. It's obvious Dillon had manipulated her, but pointing it out is useless. I guess my overwhelming feeling was one of pure astonishment. Is Virginia really that stupid? It's clear she's a victim of that strange phenomenon called 'blinded by love,' but does Dillon feel the same way about her? Enough to curb any violent tendencies?

"How much does he know about Amy Mathews?" I ask, setting aside matters of the heart and getting down to facts.

"Pretty much . . . everything," she says, fiddling with her straw.

"*Shit!*"

Her eyes harden with defiance.

"This could mean the end of Amy Mathews," I tell her. "He could—he could go to the media, he could—"

"But he won't," she replies. "He wouldn't do that."

"But how do you know?"

"I just—"

"Please don't tell me that you *just know*." I look away, infuriated. "Spare me your insight."

"I didn't mean to. I mean, I didn't tell him. I just confirmed what he already knew. It was pretty obvious. We have placards and special edition book covers hanging on the walls. We have piles of autographed books sitting at home. My name obviously isn't *Amy*, and neither is yours. So he'd have to be stupid not to figure it out."

"And let me guess . . . Dillon isn't stupid." I see the defensive linebacker look in her eyes and immediately retreat. "Sorry."

Her shoulders sag, defensive linebacker benched. "Genie, I really *am* on your side here."

I look away, trying to disguise my alarm and deep, resounding disappointment. Everything we'd worked so hard for lay in the palm of that criminal's grimy hand. And what about Virginia? Is he going to hurt her?

"Jinny, Quantum Security ran a background check on him. He's got a rap sheet. Assault and battery and—something about a deadly weapon?"

"But all those things happened when he was *seventeen*. They charged him as an adult. People screw up, Genie. Look at us when we were seventeen. We were train wrecks."

"But we weren't out getting arrested for *assault*."

She looks away, lips twisting. Her patience for this topic is running out. "People make mistakes," she says with finality.

"That's a hell of a mistake, Jinny. And—and what about you? He could do something to you. Doesn't that even register?"

She looks at me with a little sadness in her eyes, and pity, as if I just don't get it. "He *wouldn't* hurt me." And her tone is final, because she *just knows*.

I sigh. "Does he have the code to house?" I ask tiredly, rubbing my eye.

"No," she says, almost proud that she hadn't handed it over.

"Does he have any keys?"

Again comes a proud, definitive *no*. Thank God for small mercies.

"Are you going to move back home?" she asks finally, looking almost hopeful. "It's pretty lonely there without my little hermit."

"I don't now. I don't feel safe there anymore."

"But the house is like Fort Knox. We've got that crazy security system, the perimeter walls—and what about the lion?"

The lion. Virginia's most recent lifelong dream. Rescuing a lion. What does she know about them anyway? It was a childhood infatuation that suddenly became reality as soon as we bought the house with a sprawling backyard. Virginia already had the enclosure built in the back yard and applied for the permits.

And besides, even if we do sell the house and buy another, it's clear Virginia doesn't have any plans on dumping Dillon, which means he'll know where we're moving to before we even arrive, so moving isn't a good solution . . .

"Come on home, Genie," she says softly, hand on mine. "If you're uncomfortable we can just let the lion roam the yard. He can eat trespassers for lunch."

She's joking, of course. I laugh a little. "Yeah, us too, while he's at it. Well, maybe just you. I never leave the house."

She chuckles. "I know you want to move home," she says in a teasing sisterly voice.

I have to admit, I'm more than ready to move home. But first, we have to do some housekeeping.

"OK. But I want the access code and the locks changed, just in case Dillon found a key and copied it," I say, laying out my demands like an attorney. I want him to sign a watertight non-disclosure. I'm sure David has a good one." I pause, for this would be the clincher. "And I don't want him anywhere near me or the house again."

CHAPTER 6

DAN

Virginia swallowed my last term with poor grace. I'm not sure where Dillon lives, but if they can't hang out at our spacious home she'll have to disembark at Dillon's, which I suspect is a considerable step down.

I have a hard copy of the non-disclosure agreement safely stored, and as long as I can keep a healthy distance between him, myself, and my house—I have to accept that Virginia won't dump him.

I worry for her though, but she's the older sister so she knows better, apparently. All I can do is email her articles of stalker relationships gone wrong, hoping to make some impact, but she never replies or mentions them in person.

A few weeks pass. I get the security code and the locks changed. Better yet, I haven't seen a trace of Dillon. Life is becoming normal again, except with new edgy undercurrent.

It's a drizzly gray morning, my favorite type of morning. I'm in my cozy bathrobe, drinking some coffee, looking out at the front yard from my bedroom window. The dogwood trees, lining our half-circle drive, have shed their fuchsia and white blooms. A hickory tree towers over on the right side of the property, where I'd hung a tire swing from one of its thick limbs, harkening back to some fun summertime activity that I'd never enjoyed.

But summer is over now; fall has arrived. Our glorious dogwoods are slipping into wintery stasis. So am I.

But I'm glad to be home, not so glad about Dillon. But that can't be helped. At least we have our dream home, a sprawling ranch style house just outside of Glenhaven, and lots of security.

We're about five miles from town, close enough to suit Virginia, and far enough away to meet my requirements. I wanted a house where I could garden and write in solitude. Here, I had found it.

The house was an estate sale. The owner had passed away peaceably in the home. The house had green shag carpeting with a network of well-worn paths running from room to room. There was a thick odor of cigarette smoke and incontinence that we struggled to alleviate.

The kitchen linoleum was yellowed and peeling. The bathrooms sported soft pink tiles from a bygone era. The concrete walkway was cracked and buckling. The roof looked like it needed some sort of urgent attention.

But we didn't care about any of that. I saw only a sprawling soon-to-be whitewashed ranch home steeped in charming historical details. We put in a generous offer to beat out our competition, complete with a nice as-is clause, and twenty-one days later we closed on our dream home.

Virginia managed the contractors, while I picked out color schemes between popping pills and dodging crumpled roses at our old rental house. Six months later, with a lot of cash and elbow grease, we transformed the property into our own private wonderland.

The previous owner's death in the house could bring goosebumps to anybody's arms. But death is a natural part of life. No, there's nothing about this house that scares me, nothing except the lion that Virginia plans to keep in the backyard.

"*Rescues*," Virginia had told me that day when she and Dillon announced their grand backyard master plan, back when I had no idea he was our stalker. "These animals are going to be *put down* if nobody steps in and saves them."

"It's not like we're going to breed it," he'd said dismissively, opening up the fridge and helping himself to a beer. *Cssh-kink.*

The *cssh-kink* sound of the can opening made my skin crawl. Dillon made my skin crawl, come to think of it. I'd stood in the kitchen that day watching his Adam's apple bob up and down as he packed away yet another beer, mesmerized by my consuming dislike of the guy. Glug, glug, glug.

"It's your money, Virginia," Dickhead had said, shrugging. "You can do what you want."

Technically, it's *our* money, but I let it slide.

He wore loose jeans, a backwards Red Socks ball cap, and a tight t-shirt with a skull and bones on the front that outlined his swelling pectorals. I wasn't sure how long he'd been hitting the steroids, but he certainly hadn't been shy with the dosage.

I had a lovely comment that I wanted to make about spending other people's hard earned cash, but I couldn't muster up the courage to say it. So I just watched as the contractors came and went, building a burgeoning pad of flattened earth in the backyard that would become the lion's own private African savannah.

I watched the work progress from the safety of my office, and pointed out that she'd built the cage in the corner of the perimeter fence where a small escape door had been installed. She helpfully informed me that lions can't open doors.

Ten-foot poles went in every six feet. Then came the wrapping of chain-link fencing and a reinforced gate. Overall it was ugly and imposing. Then it sat empty and silent. Hopefully this is a permanent development.

Despite our conversation at Beansters, Virginia would lose interest in Project Lion, surely, and soon I'll be able to tear the structure down and plant a boxbush labyrinth garden there instead.

While I change into my clothes, I think about drawing up a labyrinth pattern. Then the intercom buzzes. So I walk over to the panel on my wall, next to the door and press the talk button. "Hello?"

A tinny voice crackles over the intercom. "FedEx. Got a delivery for ya."

My heart accelerates. It's *FedEx Man*. I can tell by the quality of his voice. Ever since we moved in, I have admired him from my window vantage point. But I've never actually met him. Virginia always had that pleasure.

"Okay, thanks," I say and press the 'open gate' button. I go to my bedroom window and watch the white truck trundle up the drive and stop in front of the house. I watch him jump out of the driver's seat with a fat envelope in hand. Michael, I'd named him, a handsome sounding name for a handsome looking fellow.

He's wearing his work uniform: dark blue shorts and a dark blue branded jacket. He's in his mid-twenties, I guess, the perfect age for me.

He walks quickly up to the front porch and disappears under the veranda roof. Then he lifts the door knocker and bangs a few times. The sound echoes throughout the house—and my heart.

Virginia will get the door; she always does. I simply admire him from afar and feel sick with disappointment that I can't bring myself to open the door. A few long seconds pass. I don't hear Virginia's faint "I'll get it!" or the quickening of her footsteps.

FedEx Man lifts the knocker and bangs again.

"Virginia!" I call down the hallway, watching the covered front porch. "Get the door!" But I hear only silence. "Where is she," I grumble, feeling the first rushes of panic. If she doesn't open the door, who will?

I rush downstairs, through the kitchen and out onto the backyard patio that overlooks our two acres and the lion enclosure. Not a soul in sight.

He knocks again.

"You can open the door," I mutter to myself, going back inside, trying to slow the precipitous rise of my heartbeat. My palms are clammy. My heart beats in strange little jerks.

Millions of people open the door for delivery guys every single day. They all survive, I tell myself. Common sense should calm me, but nothing stops the rise of irrational fears. No logical course of action, no rational thought, is helping.

My heart beats faster and higher in my throat. I don't have to answer the door, I think to myself. He'll leave the package and go. But I want to meet him. I *want* to open the door.

The distance between the door and myself seems like two long miles. He lifts the knocker and bangs again.

Thunk. Thunk. Thunk.

He knocks, impatiently, unknowing and unsympathetic to my plight.

I'm at the door now, somehow, my hand on the brass knob, working up the courage to twist it. You can do this, I tell myself, pushing away the familiar chorus of childhood voices chanting in my mind. *Pee-ew. Pee-ew. Pee-ew.*

"You can do this . . ." I mutter. If I can Skype with a stranger, check into a hotel, and meet Virginia for coffee, then I can damn well open the front door. But it's *Michael*, a small voice whispers within.

Yes you can! Cries my inner cheerleader. *C-A-N*! With white knuckles, I force myself to turn the knob. The door jumps open a millimeter, and with my heart hammering in my chest, I pull open the door and blink at the outside world. There stands—nobody.

A plume of dust rises from our gravel drive as I watch FedEx Man make his quick getaway, pausing in front of the security gate that lazily swings open. Down by my feet, a thick envelope lays on top of our welcome mat. Bitter disappointment sweeps through me like a blaze.

I pick up the envelope and stare at it. Scared. I can sense the featherweight chains of my fears growing stronger, binding me tighter, and holding me captive.

Standing there, staring at the empty porch, I realize I need to find the strength to break free of my phobias or I will lie in my comfortable coffin of a life and rot six feet under.

The kitchen door slams shut, startling me from my dark reverie.

"Were you calling me? Sorry, I was out in the garage." She walks to the kitchen sink and washes her hands.

"FedEx came," I say, leaning against the counter and holding the thick envelope to my chest.

Virginia dries her hands and walks over to me, cheeks smudged with dust. "Must be the new contract. Did you open the door?"

"Yes."

"Amazing," she says. "And did you encounter a fellow member of the human race?"

"Not exactly. I couldn't get the door open fast enough."

"Oh, poppet," she says in pouty mock sympathy, "better luck next time." And she takes the envelope, laughing.

I want to laugh too, but I can't even smile.

CHAPTER 7

I'm standing by the kitchen window, looking at the marble birdbath in the backyard. A flurry of songbirds splash in the cascading water, happy and free. So unlike me.

I haven't always been like this. So mousy. So unable to open the front door. There was a point in my life where I'd bounded to the front door and opened it with bright enthusiasm. That girl is long gone now. Eaten up first by childhood bullies. Then the loss of Mom, followed by the stalker ordeal and the bright glare of fame.

A blue jay, the Girl Scouts' mascot, douses its bright blue feathers in the sparkling water, reminding me of that terrible day I became Pewgenia, the Piss Drinker, the day all my anxieties began.

As I watch the water glimmer on the bird's long blue tail feathers, the memory comes back to me, wrapping its long wormy arms around me and pulling me back to the day that I had tried so hard to forget. As I watch the bird splash and preen, Monica Schaffer's taunting little voice reaches out from the graveyard of forgiven history, but never forgotten. *Pee-ew. What smells!*

It was Girl Scouts day, and I was late. Mom drove me to the posh gated community where Monica Schaffer, the Girl Scout leader, lived. She had brunette hair with a riot of glossy curls and a pretty dimpled smile that often turned cruel.

In the car, the air conditioner blew gusts of hot air, so I rolled down the window as cars and trucks zoomed past, kicking up dust and exhaust fumes, making the hot day seem sweltering. I dragged my sleeve along my sweating brow, dreading the upcoming Girl Scouts meet.

"Don't do that," Mom said, glancing over at me and catching sight of my shirtsleeve.

"But I'm hot!" I complained.

"We're almost there. And then you can have a nice cool drink. Won't that be nice? I'm sure Monica's mother has some nice refreshments all laid out. But try not to ruin your outfit, okay?"

When we pulled into the driveway my stomach soured. Monica's house was big with imposing colonnades and a bright red door. Monica's perfect mother, a larger version of perfect Monica, cheerily opened the door when Mom knocked.

"Thanks for bringing Eugenia by!" she cried, pulling the door closed as I stepped inside, the sound of girly shrieks and giggles drifting to my ears.

"Oh, okay," Mom called through the closing gap.

My hand tightens around the edge of the counter as I remember back to that cruel narrowing sliver that closed down on my mom's waving hand and enthusiastic smile.

Monica's mother took me over to kitchen table where there were plates piled with orange slices, cheese cubes, and oozy brownie squares. She helpfully loaded up my paper plate, making comments about how I could probably use "an extra snack or two."

"All the girls are upstairs playing," she said, handing me the plate and a cup filled with a bright yellow fizzy drink. "Go on upstairs. We're still waiting for Amanda. I'll call you down when we're ready to start."

I climbed the stairs up to a bright loft area lined with various family portraits of the Schaffer family grinning stupidly at the camera.

The loft had gone suspiciously quiet. I called into the ominous silence. "Hello?"

I heard giggling, vicious giggling. I should have turned back. I should have run.

Lured on by curiosity and buffeted by the Girl Scout law that we dutifully repeated every time the meeting started—*On my honor, I will try to serve God and my country, to help people at all times, and to live by the Girl Scout Law*—I called out again. "Hello?"

Monica had appeared, flanked by Poppy, her usual sidekick. Poppy, with long glistening hair and a smattering of freckles across her button nose, always reminded me of Strawberry Shortcake's meaner sister.

"Hi, Eugenia," Monica said, as the rest of the troop filled in behind her, covering their smiles with their hands, suppressing giggles, shifting from one foot to the other and casting sidelong glances at each other.

"What are you drinking?" she asked, walking toward me.

"Oh." I looked down at my cup. "I dunno. Mountain Dew, I guess. Your mom gave it to me. What are you guys doing?"

"Oh, nothing." Giggles all around. "Do you want to try my lemonade?" In her hand, she held a clear plastic cup half-filled with pale yellow liquid. "We can trade if you want."

To help people at all times.

I wanted to trade. I wanted to trade with the most popular girl in school, who was pretty and cruel and supremely secure of her reining popularity. I wanted to be friends with Monica Schaffer, who commanded a troop of the prettiest girls at school, who never sat alone, who *talked* to boys and boys *talked* to her.

I shrugged. "Sure."

She took my cup and replaced it with her cruel little surprise. I noticed it had a ring of bubbles around the rim and a strange temperature gradient that shifted from warm at the base to cool at the top where some ice cubes jangled.

Monica took a casual sip from my cup. "Go on," she said, watching me.

And somewhere between lifting her cup to my lips, smelling something off, and tasting something weird and salty, I heard someone squeal, "She's drinking it! She's drinking Monica's pee!"

And the girls started chanting, "Pee-ew, Pee-ew, Pee-ew."

I blushed so hard with embarrassment that my face pulsed and hot shameful tears burst from my eyes. Then I dropped the cup and ran from the Schaffer's loft and never stopped running.

The story of me drinking piss passed from one prepubescent ear to the other until the entire school heard about it in collective gruesome rapture. And the story, so despicable and riveting, changed from shock to horror and then into lore. I became known as Pewgenia, the Piss Drinker, who couldn't sit down in a single class without a faceless whisper rising up from behind: *Pee-ew. What smells!*

Always the chorus, cruel and primal, hounded me, chanting: *Pee-ew, Pee-ew, Pee-ew . . .*

Outside, the blue jay flies away. And away I fly upstairs.

I'm tired of thinking about Monica. I'm tired of being Pewgenia, the Piss Drinker. I'm in my bathroom again, pushing back the familiar lump of pain and anger in my throat. That was a long time ago, I tell myself. I made the best of it, I tell myself. Without Monica's evil little trick, maybe *After The End* would have never existed. Maybe Monica had given me a gift.

My eyes sting. I blink a few times and sniff. I pull open my medicine cabinet, like I have so many times before, and look at my vials. There are six in total, filled with uppers, downers and my reliable benzo buddies. The last one is filled with Demerol, a nice upside to getting my wisdom tooth removed. Except now it's empty.

I grab the vial, wrangle off the lid, and peer inside, while that old sinking feeling washes over me; the same one that I felt every time a new mangled rose appeared on our doorstep during Dillon's flower blitz.

I spin around, heart pounding, half-expecting to find him standing there holding a carelessly dethorned rose.

Nobody is there. Of course, nobody is there. He's not a ghost, materializing at will. It's just my mind playing tricks on me. Again.

Dillon's dark presence still hovers around me, conjuring up terrifying memories from the stalker order. But it's over now, I tell myself, pulling in deep breaths. His 'shy courting ritual' worked. Virginia is dating him so there's no need for him to stand in the shadows, watching.

But what about the Demerol pills? Maybe I took more than I remember. No, I don't think so. Maybe Virginia took them. Yes, that's more likely. She asked for a couple a while ago. Maybe she 'borrowed' the rest.

Maybe I should cry, I think suddenly, putting the vial back. Maybe I should let it all out. That might help me break these terrible bonds. I think about religious zealots, arms up in the air, babbling hysterically in Tongues. Maybe I shouldn't let it all out.

I do want to cry, but my soul feels as barren as weeds sprayed with Roundup. Life can't grow when it's buried in chemicals. Life is messy. *Feelings* are messy.

I pick up another vial, filled with pills that promise a better day. But none of them are delivering. I've been taking pills for over a year now, and I can't even open the front door.

I remember back to Dr. Miller flipping through his colorful pamphlet with pictures of happy pretty people, saying, "Why don't we try . . ."

But I don't want to *try*. I want to *do*. I want to get better. I want to open the damn door.

In the back of my mind, I hear Virginia's voice. *Oh poppet . . . better luck next time.*

A swell of anger rises up within me. I sweep the vials from the cabinet and watch them clatter to the floor. I grab one, wrench off the tamper-proof lid, and dump the pills into the toilet.

I imagine screaming gurgles as they sink to the bottom of the porcelain bowl. *But we can help youuuuu!* And Dr. Miller's voice is in my mind too, gasping in horror, all his precious little pills ending up in the sewer. Before courage fails me, I snatch up the next vial and dump its contents down the toilet bowl.

Tears spring to my eyes. A part of me revolts. *My pills! What am I going to do! I need those. I need my pills!* I choke back the chorus of voices, crying out in collective horror. *The pills! The pills!*

With the next vial in hand, good reasoning finally breaks through and stills my hand. *Keep one vial. Just in case. You can't quit cold turkey. Remember last time? Plan it out*, my investor voice of reason is telling me. *Quit, yes. But plan it out . . .*

More tears spring to my eyes, cutting and sharp, and I want them to come. I want them to cut me and make me feel alive again. I sit down on the edge of the bathtub for a good long time, death-gripping that vial, letting the tears come, encouraging them to rise up and wash away my nothingness.

Finally, after my tears die down, I vow, "Next time I'll open the door." I pat my hands together and say it again. "I will open the door."

My stomach flips just thinking about it, followed by an anticipatory swell of nausea. I put my hand on my belly and frown. Even if I do manage to open the door, will I be able to speak? And if I can't quite get any words out of my mouth, will FedEx Man laugh at me?

That might happen, I tell myself.

That could very well happen.

But I have to try.

CHAPTER 8

A few days later, Virginia plumps down on the sofa next to me in the living room, eating a pint of Chocoholic ice cream. "I missed you," she says to the frosty lump settled on her spoon.

I look at her permanently overflowing midsection, her "muffin top," which she takes great pains to complain about but never actually does anything about, and say, "You know you'll need to hit the gym to work that off. That's fifteen minutes of cardio right there."

She slips the spoon into her mouth. "Mmm. Good thing Glenhaven doesn't have a gym."

"You can always borrow my running shoes or get your own pair."

She laughs. "Running is so over-rated. It totally ruins your knees."

"You can always fast-walk around the neighborhood. Get your heart rate . . . swishing," I say with a smirk.

"Hm. Sounds like something the Housewives of Glenhaven would do. Maybe I should change my battery while I'm at it."

I chuckle and flick on the TV. "You're such a dork."

"Not nearly as dorky as checking into a hotel! Genie, *that* was a huge over-reaction. We practically live in Fort Knox."

I shoot her a sharp look. "Except I didn't know if Fort Knox had been *compromised*."

"There's always the safe room," she says without much volume.

"Yeah. That sounds like a lot of fun. Hiding out in my safe room, while Dillon has free reign over *my* house."

"It's mine too."

"Have you dumped him yet?" I tap the face of my watch. "Time's a-wastin'."

I know I'm pushing my luck. Spraying lighter fluid on a smoldering pile of ashes. But the thought of Dillon dating my sister is like living with a malevolent spirit. I want it exorcised. I want it out.

She stares at the TV, chewing on the inside of her cheek. *Not interested*, she's telling me. "Okay," I say to her profile. "I get it. You don't like being told what to do. But just consider it, okay? Give it a good old-fashioned think."

She takes another bite of ice cream and waves her spoon at me. "I really think you misjudged this whole situation. If you think about, if you really give it a good old-fashioned *think*, you'll realize that he didn't really do anything that bad. He just left some flowers, and—"

"What about the video? The bobble-head one, showing three dead Amys?"

"That wasn't him."

I think back to that video. To the guy with the Shatner Comma problem. Was that some other weirdo? Geez.

"Do you really think Dillon is a video editing expert?" she asks. "And do you think he uses colorful phrases and big words? I mean, do you really think someone with quote unquote *shit for brains* would really be that clever?"

I check her expression. She's not angry, even though she just quoted my most flammable insult. She has an even, pragmatic tone of voice. Maybe she has a point. I don't know. All I know that is I'm grateful to be behind the fortress walls.

"He does have a past, Jinny." She opens her mouth to give me a rebuttal, some well-honed excuse, but I'm not interested. I hold up my hand. "Just be careful. That's all I'm saying. I don't want you to get hurt."

"I know you're concerned. But I can look after myself, I promise," she says softly, squeezing my hand. Then she looks away and a hint of concern—guilt?—flickers across her face. Does she feel bad for dating Dillon? Even though she seems so determined to keep doing it? "I'm sorry all that had to happen to us—to you." she says.

"What do you mean?" I ask, a little confused. Is she talking about Dillon's 'courting ritual'? If so, why would she apologize?

She wasn't running that campaign. Or is she saying sorry that she hasn't dumped him yet? That makes more sense, but why say sorry if she has no intention of breaking up with him? But she just shakes her head and says, "I'm just glad it's over. That's all. Hey, before I forget, we need to talk about a few things."

"Oh? Okay."

"Amy Mathews has some new opportunities."

"Mmhm," I say, trying to postpone the inevitable. I suspect the new opportunities have to do with writing more vampire books, a topic I want to retire. "How was the book signing?" I ask instead.

She scoops up another bite of ice cream. "Overall the trip was really amazing. *Miz* Mathews is really taking the world by storm. Well, the young adult world by storm, I should say. All the teeny-boppers and tweenies just *love* Rhenn Larson. Even though he's a vampire that eats blood for breakfast. Ew. Why people think that's sexy, I'll never understand. Anyway, check this out: the last signing was incredible. The bookstore people weren't prepared for the numbers and they had to take out the self-help section to make room for me . . . well, Amy. But anyway, you should have seen the banners. *So* amazing. And there was a *mountain* of books that I had to sign."

She eats another spoonful of ice cream.

"I had to take a break because my hand cramped up," she says, voice muffled, waving the empty spoon in the air. "Then we actually *did* run out of books and I had to sign boilerplates. Who would have thought a story about a stupid vampire boy would cause so much excitement?"

"Maybe because he's not a stupid vampire boy," I say.

"Whatever," Virginia says, scraping up another spoonful of chunky chocolate ice cream. "So then I met with the marketing team. They think we should continue with bookisodes."

"Bookisodes? As in . . . many books?"

Virginia nods. "They think the momentum can only grow from here and everyone is really excited to keep going. So David just sent a new contract. That's what FedEx Man just delivered."

"Oh."

Ever since *After The End* had climbed higher and higher on the charts, I knew Virginia and David would be after to me to replicate its success. But the trouble is, I really don't want to spend more time writing about drinking blood and tearing flesh.

It was an allegory of my own dark soul, buried under my paralytic social phobias and the grief of losing Mom. Now, I want to cast off my fears and live life. I want to buy my own groceries. I want to open the door. I want to finally ditch the pills.

Virginia sticks her spoon in the carton and sets it down on the glass coffee table. "Oh?" she asks, scowling.

"It's just that I hadn't really planned on writing more books. To me, the story is done. As in told. Roger that. Over and out."

Virginia leans back, playing with her adulterated locks of strawberry blonde hair. "Well, tell some more. You know, write about how Rhenn Larson finds out that Madeline Storm is secretly in love with some . . . thing . . . else. Like a werewolf or something."

"My vampires don't fall in love with werewolves, Jinny."

"Why not? It's just a story. Anything is possible."

"It's *my* story. And I'm telling you—it's done."

"Then undo it." She gets up and buses her ice cream carton to the kitchen.

The east facing windows let in bright morning light. Today, it's absolutely blinding. I get up, pull the diaphanous curtains closed, and follow her into the kitchen.

"It's not like that, Jinny. I'm not a machine, where you insert a new idea and after a few months, I spit out a bestseller."

She looks at me with a blank, impatient, and totally uncomprehending stare.

"Writing is about exploring," I continue. "It's about discovering things. It's about working through the minutiae of life and trying to make sense of it all. I think that's why *After The End* resonates with so many people. We're just . . . trying to figure it all out."

Virginia stares at me.

I sigh. "Writing is magic. It's not a formula."

This she understands. "Yes, it is. It's exactly a formula."

And thus begins yet another exasperated conversation about plot layers, beats, character arcs, and subplots. "Why do you think so many movies are remakes?" she continues. "Because they *sell*, Genie. People buy tickets. And it's the same thing with books. People want to read stuff that they've already read before, but in a slightly different way. They want to read stuff that's familiar."

"That may be, but I want to write something different. I want to write under my own name. And why not? If you're so worried about money, consider outliers that have gone on to make big bucks."

"But those are the exceptions," she says, arms folded. "Not the rule."

"Real writing should never be about following the rules. Novelists have a rich history of bucking the norm, questioning, and exploring. That is the *purpose* of writing."

"Then why don't you *buck the norm* in your spare time? In the meantime, we have bills to pay. A lion to support."

I groan. "I thought you changed your mind about that."

Virginia makes a face. "Why would I do that? He's arriving next week."

"What?"

"Yeah, I thought I told you."

"Um. Do you *remember* telling me? That's because you didn't!"

Virginia laughs and looks at me in that certain pinched way that makes me feel a little ridiculous. "Calm down, geez. It's not a big deal."

"Okay if you say so," I say, rolling my eyes.

"It really isn't. He's going to go in the enclosure like we agreed. And then he's going to become fat, shiny and happy."

"Sounds like a real dream. Then what? Is he going to live in our backyard forever?"

"Well, I mean, he can't exactly be released back in the wilds of Rhode Island . . ."

I don't reply. The thought of a *lion* living in our back yard makes me feel both intrigued and edgy. I hadn't really envisioned sharing my peaceable backyard garden with a yowling one-ton cat, but Virginia is right. There's far too many idiots out there who breed lions or ligers or tions or whatever else abomination they can think of, exploit the kittens, then suddenly find themselves with a big growling dangerous problem on their hands. Deep down, I'm glad we can save just one. Even if it does mean carefully avoiding that part of the yard.

"Look, Jinny, we have more money than we ever dreamed possible. If we just spend wisely—"

"Are you going to do all the book signings after you write under your own name? Hop on a plane, meet with the publisher, and negotiate better terms? Attend cocktail dinners and press the flesh? Put on your most dazzling smile and say something witty?"

The very thought makes me queasy.

Her expression softens. "If you turn your back on Amy, you turn your back on *me*. Is that what you really want? To shut me out?"

"No," I mumble.

"Genie, we're a team. Remember?"

I look down at my hands, nails bitten back to stubs. A ring encircles the third finger on my right hand. It's a thin gold band with a cloudy ruby in the center that Mom had given to me a week before she passed away.

Virginia reaches over, covering Mom's ring with her own freckled hand. Tears pool in my eyes, doubling our two hands into four. "That's what Mom would want," she says quietly. "Keep the team together."

Fear and grief had pushed me through *After The End*. Mom had helped me edit book one in the series, before she passed. She said all the manuscript needed was a little teamwork. I can hear Mom's dying words now. *Promise me ... Promise you'll keep the team together.*

"Okay," I say, at last. "All right. I'll try."

CHAPTER 9

Time to spend quality time with Rhenn Larson. A promise is a promise, and I mean to keep my word. I'd killed Rhenn. Hopefully it's not fatal.

Turns out, death isn't eternal, but Rhenn doesn't seem very excited about this interruption of his slumber. He rose, hung a Do Not Disturb sign on the entrance of his crypt, slung his cape over his shoulder, and returned to his coffin.

Funny guy. I'll check up with him later. Right now, I want to work on "Rebecca." Maybe I can parlay some of my enthusiasm for that project over to *Rhenn and Friends*, the working title for book four in the bookisodes adventure.

Can I mix the two projects? Can I insert the second Mrs. de Winter, whom I'd named Amelia, into *Rhenn and Friends*?

Maybe instead of a sequel, I can write a prequel. We can meet Rhenn Larson and Madeline Storm before they met, back when Madeline and Amelia were frenemies.

Or maybe I can tackle book four by rousing Rhenn somehow, maybe thanks to a potion, and he will become a very powerful ringleader, while our heroine Madeline starts to fall for her own version of Maximilian de Winter—a mysterious man who lives in a battered castle up the hill.

No, that won't work. Readers are already attached to Rhenn and Madeline just as they know them to be: a vampire and a human, separated by the species divide, cursed to love one another but never partake of one another.

Virginia's idea niggles in the back of my mind. What if I introduce a new creature into the story, who's also fond of Madeline? Werewolves have been done to death, but what about a minority monster? Cyclops might be just the thing. Could Madeline love both a Cyclops and a vampire?

I'm sitting at my desk, all powered up with tea, brain storming. I came up with a few ideas, but I'm still struggling with Rhenn Larson's storyline. Meanwhile "Rebecca" blooms in my imagination.

So I get to work. And a couple hours later, I'm finishing up a scene where Amelia, my soon to be second Mrs. de Winters arrives at the hotel with her well-to-do group of girlfriends.

Amelia just met Maxim on the hotel terrace in Monte Carlo, overlooking the sparkling blue ocean. She'd had an argument with her on and off-again boyfriend on the phone and had wandered out into the warm evening breeze to clear her mind.

Maxim, dressed handsomely in an ivory linen suit, a light blue collared shirt, and impeccable tan loafers, lent her a sympathetic ear.

He's clean-shaven, smelling of cedar cologne, and has eyes the color of turbid waters. He's an easy character to spend a thousand words on, and his quiet demeanor, good manners, and elusiveness makes my young Amelia fall helplessly in love.

I find myself falling down the rabbit hole with these two. Conversation comes easily, but the quiet mystery surrounding Maxim keeps my eye on the darkening horizon, watching storms clouds gather.

In this modern remake, Maxim and Amelia will eventually head to the bedroom; a scene I know is coming but worry about writing.

I'm pretty sure that would have happened to me at university with a boy whose beer goggles were firmly fastened in place. But my grades were terrible so I'd gone to the local community college, which was more like distance learning center.

I had hopes of transferring over to a real university, maybe experiencing a thing or two, but by then Mom had fallen sick and Amy Mathews happened. So there I was, a twenty-three year old virgin, without even a single kiss to my name.

I was too busy ushering Mom through the poisoned labyrinth of chemotherapy, praying she'd make it out alive. I was too busy to think about boys. That was where, deep in the mystifying folds of loss and pain, a part of myself died along with Mom. The part of me that I want to resurrect.

"Resurrection can wait," I say to myself, turning my attention to my computer monitor. Guilt is starting to burn. I need to keep the team together. I need to honor my mom's dying wishes. I need to write this book.

And so I pull up my Rhenn document and begin filling the blank screen with words, trying to convince Rhenn to talk to me. Sometimes writing is like jump-starting a car. You have to push and push until you get the momentum going. Then you pop the clutch and zoom off into the wild blue yonder. Okay, sputter. But at least you get going.

This is exactly what I plan to do. So I keep typing, waiting for the wave of momentum to sweep me up. I'm filling up the document, unloading about a thousand words on the Cyclops love interest, when the intercom buzzes.

Probably a delivery for Virginia, I think, annoyed with the interruption right when my beater of a car is starting to cough back to life.

I get up and punch the button on the intercom panel in my office.

"Yes?"

"FedEx. Got a delivery for ya."

FedEx Man.

Suddenly, my promise from yesterweek rises to the forefront of my mind. I promised—no I swore—that I'd not give in to my fears. I promised that I would answer the door.

"Come on in!" I cry a touch too cheerily, heart hammering in my chest, and press the 'open gate' button. Through the small CCTV screen, I watch, stomach churning, as FedEx Man shifts his truck into gear and rolls out of sight.

I pace back and forth, listening to the ominous growl of the truck rushing up the driveway. I have approximately one minute to get the front door open.

One whole minute to pat down my flyaway hair and pinch my cheeks. Thank God I put some makeup and took a pill this morning. I feverishly look at myself in the faux-aged decorative mirror hanging on the wall, and see if I look okay.

I pull my hair around the nape of my neck, and let it fall alluringly over my shoulder. Not alluring, I think, pulling it back. Stupid. Then I look down at my outfit. Great. I donned my lucky writing pants today, a pair of pink velour track bottoms with the word 'luscious' heat pressed onto the rear.

The cab door slams shut.

Oh no.

It's not like he's going notice me, I tell myself. He's going to hand over the package, jam the electronic signing thing into my hand, and leave. I feel a little better now. At least I won't have Virginia hanging over my shoulder, offering up caustic words of support. She went over to Beansters to get some work done. It's just FedEx Man and I.

I pull in some calming breaths, big ones, trying not to make myself dizzy.

Do it—don't think about it!

The cheerleader is back. *Yes you can! C-A-N!*

My heart beats high and fast in my throat. But before I lose my courage, I trudge over to the front door—and open it.

There stands FedEx Man. His lips are nicely shaped, his nose small and straight. He's slight of frame, which I like. Then he smiles, revealing a line of straight small teeth which I really like, and hands me the package.

"Sorry about leaving your package last time," he says. "I was running late."

"Oh," I say, heart pounding, surprised he even remembered. I wave my hand dismissively. Stupidly? "It's okay. Nobody stole it or anything."

"That's good," he says. "I'd probably get fired if my deliveries went missing."

"Really?"

"No, just kidding," he says, laughing.

"Oh."

He hands me a small box. I pretend to study the address, anything to distract myself from the fact that I'm talking to a real person, who's talking back, smiling even. A person that I don't want to leave.

"Looks like something for my sister," I report. When I look up, his gaze locks with mine. His eyes are midnight blue with golden prisms that remind me of distant galaxies. Not distant galaxies. Nebulas.

I'd done some research on nebulas when I'd written book two in the *After The End* series. The Crab Nebula had captured my imagination with its spidery filaments of gold stretching across a field of dark blue. Nebulas are remnants of supernovas,

I learned. A catastrophic explosion. A death of an old star in order for there to be the birth of a new one.

"I guess you should sign," he says.

"Oh, right. Yeah, I don't want you to get fired or anything." So I sign, meaning every word.

He takes back his implement. "Well, I'm glad you opened the door this time." He raises his phone-sized tablet that I just electronically signed. "It's always best to get a real signature."

"Yeah, sorry about that." *Sorry for what?* "I was . . . writing. I'm a writer. I was . . . busy writing."

"Oh, are you? I love to read. What kind of books do you write?"

My adrenals are working overtime. I hadn't expected a conversation. I had only prepared myself for an awkward handover of the goods, followed by an obligatory signature, and some generic courtesies. FedEx Man is asking me questions. Questions that I can't believe I'm answering.

"I write about vampires," I say.

"Cool! Bloodsuckers."

I nod, even though I hate to think of Rhenn Larson, my sensitive complex protagonist who slays the Monica Schaffers in his world, as a mere bloodsucker.

"What's the name of your book? Maybe I've heard of it."

Then we stumble into awkward territory. Nobody knows about Amy's true identity. Nobody knows she doesn't exist. Except Dillon, of course. The last thing I want is another interested stranger.

"You probably haven't heard of it," I say, shrugging.

"Oh that's too bad," he says, kicking the toe rail and slipping his hand into his pocket, both of us lost in the moment that we don't want to end. Well, maybe just me.

"Hey," he says, looking up. "There's a Halloween block party in Glenhaven at the end of the month with a 'Dress Up Like The Dead' concert and zombie cocktails and everything."

"Wow," I say, thinking about all that social activity. "Sounds fun." Not.

"Are you going to go?" he asks, nebula eyes searching mine.

"Oh . . . no." I laugh a little, glancing inside my house, my comfortable cushy coffin. "I don't think so."

"We should go," says he, pulling the corner of his mouth into a hopeful smile.

My heart skitters a few beats. My breath catches, while I gaze into his supernova eyes, golden prisms lit up like a galactic event.

"My name is Benjamin, by the way, but people just call me Ben." And before I can reply, he grabs a pen from his pocket, clicks it into action, and scribbles his phone number on the top of the box. "Well, I gotta go. Special deliveries await." His jaw muscles clench ever so slightly. "Call me, okay? I mean—if you want to."

"Yeah. Okay," I mumble, only because I can't think anything else to say. "Okay, I will . . ."

CHAPTER 10

We should go. Did he mean *go out*? As in, a date?

I float back to my office, put the box down on my desk, and carefully copy his phone number onto a pink sticky. Then I place the sticky on the side of my computer monitor and stare at it.

FedEx Man just invited me out on a zombie date. A rising thrill sneaks into my heart. My very first date!

The little flap of pink paper waves in a current of air invitingly. But then disappointment sets in. I'm pretty sure I'll never be able to work up the courage to go. First, I have to call him. Then I have to think of something to say besides: *hello.* And—and a block party? With *how* many people? My heart rate accelerates just thinking about it.

I lie down on Wonder Couch, my studded chesterfield situated in front of the fireplace, and start counting the beams in my coffered ceiling. It calms me. It also takes my mind off of more important things like calling Benjamin.

Maybe tomorrow. Maybe I'll call him tomorrow . . .

Well, tomorrow arrives with a surprise. Two to be precise. It's one of those weird things where you doubt your own sanity, but take your own side.

I find the chair in my office pushed away from my desk. Not far, just enough to give me pause. Distinctive prickles of fear rush over my skin, carrying me back to those anxiety-filled days when the stalker was still at large.

Didn't I push my chair in last night? I usually do. It's one my weird things: a final *sayanara* to my workday.

It's so benign though. A chair put out of place. Do I really need to stand here and think about it?

But this is the kind of wrinkle in my reality that drove me to pills in the first place. Little things put out of place. Lingering questions. I long for the bitter taste of another pill on my tongue now, for the falling away of chains. But I'm trying to give that up. The pills, that is. Deep breaths. Deep breaths.

So I roll my chair back into place and sit down. I'm tapping some papers into order and putting some pens back into my special pen mug, when I accidentally tap my mouse. My computer wakes up. No. No no no.

I never leave my computer on. Every night I close it down because the sleep function doesn't work and I don't want to fry the screen. Thank goodness it's password protected.

But someone has definitely been snooping, and I don't need to be a Mensa member to figure out who.

A shadow outside falls in the corner of my eye. I look up, heart galloping, and examine the bushes just beyond the patio, my mind racing back the good ol' stalker days. Back when we lived in that rental. I'd just taken some sleeping pills and, lying in bed, drugged, I'd heard his footsteps outside my flimsy single pane bedroom window. Between the sedative and the adrenaline, I'd practically had a coronary.

But nobody is there. Nobody is outside.

So, eventually, I calm down and get to work. I make more progress on "Rebecca" and less on *Rhenn and Friends*, while the pink sticky flutters in the corner of my eye. My potential date with Ben stays in the forefront of my mind, alongside panic.

After I finish another scene, I look at Ben's phone number, a sequence of digits that could change my life forever, if I could just worked up the courage to call.

Not today. Maybe tomorrow . . .

Well, tomorrow turns into today. And today turns into tomorrow. A week passes like that, with a promise in my heart and excuses on my lips. Then one bright morning, I hear the telltale beeping of a rig reversing into the backyard.

The lion. He's here.

I stand by my glass-paneled office door and watch. A rig backs directly up to the enclosure gate, which Virginia holds open. The driver climbs out of the cab, yanks up his beleaguered britches, and unchains the trailer door. Then he opens the door and stands behind the metal panel, waiting.

I've only seen videos of these magnificent creatures, roaming the parched Serengeti accompanied by David Attenborough's whisper soft voice describing their hopes and fears as they swipe flies from their noses.

So with great surprise, I see a sorry creature quickly scurrying from one cage another. He's thin and mangy looking with clumps of fur missing from his scraggly brown mane. But even underfed, he's an impressive creature. Once he moves through the gauntlet of gates, his powerful jaw hangs slack, while his glowering yellow eyes roam the enclosure. He moves to the back of the enclosure with a proud, lithe gait. His shoulder blades rise and fall like sharp working knives under his dull yellow coat.

Virginia quickly shuts the gate, and the driver closes up the trailer. She signs some documents before rig pulls away, leaving her standing at the edge of the enclosure, watching the lion. He paces, glaring and snarling, eyes narrowed into furious slits.

She fetches a few frozen chickens from the coffin freezer in the garage that she stockpiled. Then she unwraps some birds and lobs them over to the fence.

The lion gobbles them up, while she watches. And when he's done, she turns and walks inside.

CHAPTER 11

Later that day the lion roars, a loud agonized sound that sends chills through my body. He's hungry. Virginia fed him when he arrived, but she seems to be keeping to a schedule. The lion is skinny and malnourished. He needs to gorge on food. He needs to hurry up and put on a winter layer.

So I research the feeding requirements for one lion. One female can gorge on sixty pounds of meat per day; a male can do ninety. On average, our backyard kitten needs to eat twenty pounds of meat per day, which means that we need to somehow feed him one hundred and forty pounds of meat *per week*. No wonder all the sanctuaries are at capacity.

Moreover, how much is that going to cost? Did Virginia do any of this math before she adopted her lion? I'm fairly sure perennially broke Dillon hadn't bothered to pitch in, so I find myself searching for farm cooperatives that can deliver. Soon enough, I find a wholesale butcher that makes home deliveries. Then I place my order and go outside to the coffin freezer in the garage.

Once there, I pile about fifteen frozen hunks of meat into the wheelbarrow. Then I wobble everything over to the lion enclosure, unwrap the meat and lob each frozen piece over the fence. Two turkeys, three chickens, and umpteen chunks of red meat lay scattered along the fence line. Should be enough to keep his hunger at bay until the real stuff arrives.

I keep my distance though, while he gnaws on a frozen bird, eyeing me. He still scares me even if he's is busy eating.

I wouldn't call him a friend and plunge my hand through the fence, but I wouldn't call him a foe either. He's not snarling viciously or taking deadly swipes at me. His ears, normally pinned back, tilt forward in a friendly sort of way. I think.

An imaginary news reporter clutching a microphone springs to mind. I imagine her standing to my right, talking to the local news cameraman, a gusty breeze tousling her hair as she delivers her lines.

And tonight on Channel 6, we're going to meet Eugenia Ward, who triumphantly overcame her fears . . . to make a new friend. And a very large one at that. Back to you, Jim.

The lion finishes up the turkey, ignoring the reporter and me.

"Enjoy . . . my friend."

A cold wind picks up. And I walk back inside and get to work on *Rhenn and Friends.*

I have the Cyclops complication, but I need something more and quick. So I sit doodling at my desk, leaving Brain to do the storming. Brain never lets me down. So I'm sitting there, pen poised in hand, waiting for inspiration, when Virginia knocks on my office door.

"Genie, can I come in?"

I look up. "Sure."

"Hey," she says, sitting down on a tufted arm chairs opposite my desk. "How's it going?"

"Oh . . . good. Just working out some details. Rhenn's being difficult."

"Uh oh. Defibrillator problems?"

I laugh. "Something like that. I think I've got a monster in here that's pretty taken with Madeline. Vampire versus Cyclops. That ought to make the publisher happy."

Virginia turns her mouth down. "As long as it keeps the fans happy."

"Bram Stoker's *Dracula* was published 1897 and it's still in print. Vampire stories never die. How's that for a pun?"

She shrugs. "Pretty good." Then she runs her fingernail along the upholstery wale. "You think you can hit that deadline? It's pretty tight."

I look up at her. We'd hadn't discussed the new terms of the contract in great detail. She'd mentioned some ridiculous deadline, but then said she'd look into it, and I never heard back.

"That deadline is a joke," I say. "A typo. Clearly. You said you'd talk to David about it."

She puckers her mouth in a great approximation of shame and defeat, brow wrinkled with concern. "Yeah, I did. The publisher won't change it. They want the books rolled out on a schedule so readers won't forget about us and move onto something else."

"So . . ."

"So . . . next book is due in six months."

I shoot out of my chair. "Six months?! Write a full-length novel in six months? That's ninety *thousand* words! Pretty sure my fingers will fall off at that rate!"

"No need to be so dramatic. You just have to hit your word count every day,"—that abashed look comes over her face again—"like, every single day."

I start pacing. "I'm not a dairy cow. It takes time to fix plot holes and find the story. And—and I'm not sure which direction to go with *Rhenn and Friends*. I don't even know if he has any left these days. I killed them all. Remember?"

Virginia crosses her legs and nibbles on her thumbnail. "Can you tell Brain to hurry up? It's kind of important. David says that a slew of copycats came out and the market is starting to get saturated."

"Can't our readers satisfy themselves with some fun fan fiction in the meantime? There's some good stuff out there. Nice . . . colorful stuff." My mouth twists with suppressed humor.

The graphic novelists came out in force after book one was published. Equipped with Photoshop and ripe inflamed imaginations, they created volume after volume of blood-splattered love affairs gone very wrong.

"Yeah, that's the thing. David wants us to ride the wave. He's afraid we're going to miss it."

"Ride the wave," I grumble.

Virginia runs her hand through her badly streaked hair. "Okay, listen. Just go back to basics. Follow the outline. Figure out the plot layers and subplots. Then flesh out the beats and tropes. Make sure you add some high and low moments, you know, dark night of the soul, stuff like that."

She rattles on about various story mechanics, while I chew on my thumb nail. Writing a publishable novel in six months requires military precision. I'm not even a very good trooper.

I'm what's known as a 'pantser,' a type of writer that sits down at the blank screen with only a vague idea of where the story will go, a helpless conduit for happy or unhappy surprises.

With such a tight deadline, my preferred wandering style of writing a book will need some sort of turbo-fueled injection to get me to The End.

Moreover, I have stage fright following the astounding success of the series. As a debut author, whom no one had heard of, failure was a very real possibility. In fact, I'd planned on it. But now that the series climbed to such dizzying heights, I'm expected to send the next installment even higher. And I'm not sure I can.

And there's my deep hope simmering just under the surface: writing under my own name and resurrecting Eugenia Ward.

"Can you wait to sign the contract?" I ask. "I need to get my head around a few things."

"Like improving your words per minute?" she says with a smile.

"Yeah," I agree with a friendly scoff. "That will solve all my problems."

"All right," she says, rising to leave. "But don't wait too long, okay?"

"Sure—hey," I say, just as an afterthought. "I flushed most of my pills. I still have an emergency supply, but I'm getting off the good stuff."

"Really?" She raises her eyebrows in amazement.

"Yeah, it's a brave new world for me now. And you too. No more sneaking my Demerol." I smile.

She looks almost offended. "I didn't steal your pills."

Of course she'd say that. Who wants to be caught with their fingers in the pill jar?

"Of course you did, Jinny. They didn't just walk away. I found the vial empty."

"But you just said you flushed most of your pills. Maybe you flushed them and didn't realize it until afterwards?"

It's the Stay Puft Marshmallow Man conversation again. The same one we'd had all throughout the stalker ordeal, whereby I'd try to tell her that someone lurked in the shadows, and she'd ask if I'd actually seen this person. No, I hadn't *actually seen him*, which only added to the vague uneasy feeling that maybe I was going a little crazy. But I wasn't crazy. The stalker was real. Virginia's dating him now. My pills are gone. And Casper the Friendly Ghost hadn't taken them.

"No," I say. "I didn't realize it after the fact. The pills were gone before."

"I can't believe you're accusing me of theft!"

I drop my head onto my desk. My head hurts. "Jinny, it's not that big of a deal. I was just making a little joke. I don't care if you took them. I'm just saying they're gone now."

"Well, maybe you took them. You certainly don't have a problem popping pills."

I look up at her, surprised and hurt. "I *have* a problem popping pills. Not remembering which ones."

She holds my gaze for one long hostile second.

I break contact and look away. "Okay, you didn't take the pills."

"That's right because I can't take Demerol. Remember?"

My stomach drops. Was that Demerol? I'd forgotten.

Back in California, Virginia's anger and substance abuse issues had landed her in group therapy with three other teenaged miscreants, listening (or not listening) to the counselor drone on about being juvenile.

"I'm not a juvenile," she fumed after yet another bad session. "I'm eighteen years old."

"I think he was talking about your behavior," I told her, much to her disinterest. The therapy lessons fell by the wayside due to the dual reasons of not helping Virginia and the mounting costs.

Then she overdosed. The doctor suggested a blood test just to be thorough, which led to the unwelcome diagnosis of a substance-induced mood disorder. We found out that her Demerol adventure had caused chemical changes in her brain, which triggered her new problem. After that, she swore she'd never take another one.

She shoots me a triumphant glare and leaves the room. I look away, puzzled. Had the pills just walked away?

Then my mind flashes to Dillon. Goosebumps rush over my arms as I think about him standing in my bathroom, emptying my vial. *Of course*, he'd taken them. But when? While I was away at the hotel? Or earlier?

I think back to when I discovered the empty vial. Cody had just delivered his terrible news. I'd been too rattled and scared to take inventory. Was the Demerol bottle empty then? I can't remember. But then I realize it doesn't matter *when* he took them.

It only matters that he did.

CHAPTER 12

Mid-October arrives. The breezes are becoming sharper, the sun setting earlier, and the leaves are turning brighter. There's a lot going on outside of my office window. Unfortunately, not much going on inside.

I meant to talk to Virginia about snooping on my computer, but decided to leave it. I don't have the reserves for another argument.

I sit in front of my computer screen, typing up a snippet of a conversation between Rhenn and Madeline that had popped into my head earlier in the day, something about that Do Not Disturb sign. When the conversation falters, I bring up my guilty pleasure, "Rebecca."

Normally, I work with only one document open, but I keep *Rhenn and Friends* minimized, ready to receive any missives from the land of the undead. After all, the matter is urgent.

But Monte Carlo keeps luring me back to its sun-drenched beaches, warm breezes, and rugged coastline. The story line for Amelia is shaping up quite nicely. Maxim de Winters is almost as alluring as Rhenn, minus the drinking blood part. But Maxim also harbors dark and interesting secrets. Secrets that I can't wait to uncover.

Amelia's sharing a room with her friend Michelle Smiley, who has far too much money than her humble secretary job justifies. Michelle is a little cagey about that particular topic. Amelia suspects "exotic dancing," or a very generous sugar daddy. She's not sure, but she's going to get to the bottom of it tomorrow.

I save and close out the document. Then I move *Rhenn and Friends* front and center, hoping for something good. I need to expand on this snippet of conversation. I need to write this damn book.

I work for about an hour or so, trying to work Cyclops into the conversation. He turns out to be stubborn, not very smart, and very blunt about his aspirations to "get" Madeline.

At one point he held my dear groggy Rhenn by the neck, but that didn't feel right, so I had to delete five hundred words and start over. That hurt. I write until things come to a natural close and turn my attention back to my life. To the pink sticky.

I need to call Ben. At this rate, he'll forget that he ever gave me his number in the first place. And wouldn't that be a great start to the conversation? *I'm the girl you asked out on a zombie date . . . remember?*

So I pick up my cell phone and carefully enter in his phone number. There. Step one complete. But my stomach begins to roil, and cold chills sweep down my arms. I can't do it. So I back out all seven digits and put my phone away.

Tomorrow, I tell myself, feeling a little better. I'll call him tomorrow.

The following day, I get back to work. Rhenn needs to wake up. But how? Maybe Virginia is right. Maybe a werewolf will solve all of my problems . . .

Stellan wasn't the most handsome of creatures. He stood a full two feet taller than his hairier brethren, and when fully transformed into a werewolf, he had pronounced ears that could hear a pin drop in the next county over.

Now, in human form, he stood outside of Bellingham Mall, searching for Madeline Storm. She'd told him that she would meet him there. He checked his watch impatiently and looked up at the bright full moon, which cast an eerie glow across the wet sidewalk. Madeline was never late. Had something happened?

He heard footsteps behind him and turned quickly. There stood . . .

Who? I wonder, fingers poised over the keyboard. But I can't think of a single person or thing. Rhenn in the frenzied throes of vampirism? No. He's still hibernating.

Maybe Madeline herself stands there, agitated and panicky, hoping to stop Stellan from revealing some terrible secret. But what secret? Clandestine kisses? And would that really work?

I drop my head in my hands and sigh. *Oh, Rhenn. Tell me your story. Do you even have one after everything I put you through?*

I stand up and walk over to my glass-paneled door that opens up to the backyard. My garden beds lay in mottled shade. Our water fountain burbles under weak sunlight.

Writing the sequel is damn hard work. A real slog. The words aren't flowing like they had for *After The End*. Is there anything after The End? And what am I supposed to name book four anyway? *After, After The End?* Followed by: *This Really Is The End, I Promise.* I sigh grimly.

Deep down, I know how to solve the problem. I have to go back there. I have to go back to the dark, pitiful place that I had occupied when I'd written the series. I have to relive the cruel chorus of voices, chanting *Pee-ew! Pee-ew!* I have to relive my Piss Drinker years. I have to relive the terrible loss of Mom, followed by the terrifying stalker days. I have to relive it all.

Rising up Rhenn means I have to journey back to that foggy wasteland. I have to rekindle the pain, fear, and terrible isolation, so that Rhenn Larson can finally live again. But I don't want to go back there. I don't want to go there ever again.

I close out my whole two hundred words, not caring if the document gets corrupted and go upstairs.

It's too painful to think about Mom, so I think about Monica Schaffer instead. I hope she's a loser now, working some office job, running off photocopies and taking drunk selfies on the weekend because she doesn't have anything better to do with her life.

She's probably one of the trolls who leaves terrible reviews online, but sits up late at night devouring page after guilty page, not noticing her influence.

Rhenn Larsen, downtrodden and thirsty for the imaginary lifeblood of Monica and friends, had captured the imagination of all readers, not just the 'young adult' crowd that I had in mind originally. The series was a lucrative crossover that inspired our publisher to release bigger and bigger printing runs.

At first I joked that the book's success was due to its sixth grade reading level (Virginia put a sample through an online analyzer). But as it climbed higher and higher in the charts, the heart of its success beat quietly and steadily. People could relate to Rhenn. People could relate to feeling sub-human.

It's true that I want to retire Amy Mathews, but I want to retire her in dignity, not let her perish in the ritual fire of a media witch-hunt. How will I pull that off? I have no idea.

So I change into my running clothes, strap on my shoes, and head out for some fresh air. Maybe that will help.

It's a cool, crisp evening. My anxiety levels are low, but not undetectable. It helps that we live in a rural neighborhood. Our nearest neighbor is situated down at the end of the long road, the house built deep into their plot of land. That doesn't mean I don't feel a prickling rise of nerves as I jog past. I do.

But I just pick up my pace and run a little faster, until I reach the far end of their tall white fence that runs along the road for several hundred feet and slow down.

My heart is pumping at a comfortable pace. My legs burn, but it's an invigorating feeling. So I keep going. I'm out on a run so I can work something out. What was it? Oh yeah. Retiring Amy.

I slow to a nice easy jog, my arms and legs moving efficiently, my ponytail swinging in rhythm. I'm at pace now, so I settle in for a nice ride and let the topic of Amy process in the back of my mind, while I look around at this beautiful pocket of the world.

The evergreens are emerging in dark bunches against the thinning canopy of the deciduous trees, covering the roads and lawns with bright orange and yellow leaves.

It's the color of death, this beautiful marbling of deep red, apricot, and golden yellow. It's the color of Amy. And it's also the color of hibernation and the promise of rebirth. So, is it also the color of me?

This can go two ways, can't it? I don't have to kill Amy just yet, do I? Hope rises up in my heart. Maybe Amy can go into hibernation, while Eugenia takes her first tentative steps out of isolation. Out of fear. Maybe even, out on a date.

That seems like the perfect solution. Don't *kill* Amy. Just put her on ice. And when spring comes around, I'll check back in with her. See if she's ready to be roused, or if she wants to sleep forever.

There's an extra spring in my step. Finally, I found what seems like a workable solution to this Amy problem. What didn't I think of it sooner?

I'm headed home now, propelled by this buoyant new feeling. I'm jogging up a slight incline, looking around at the towering maples and oaks, feeling grateful and slightly amazed that Brain solved yet another problem. Then I crest a hill, heart pumping, and slow down to a fast walk.

A surge of contentment rushes through me. I can't wait to get home and get to work, maybe even, tell Virginia about Amy's new sleeping pattern. That's not going to help the deadline problem, but the contract isn't signed. We can sign it later, maybe next spring when Amy wakes up.

Further down the road, I see our perimeter wall marking the boundary line of our property that sits on the corner of Chesapeake Road and Thornton. The red brick wall is solid and imposing, and I'm almost sorry that it looks like such an eyesore against the soft rolling hills. But it couldn't be helped.

I turn the corner onto Chesapeake Road and stop cold. Stunned. Dillon's truck is parked on the side of the road just shy of our gothic-inspired security gate with spires running along the top.

What the actual fuck? Is Dillon *at my house*?

Then I gather my wits about me and dash behind the thick trunk of a nearby tree.

My heart thumps unevenly, making it hard to catch my breath. I sidle to the edge of the tree truck and crane my neck to see. Virginia is inside the cab. I can see the back of her head. What are they doing?

Seems like Dillon is examining is rear view mirror. Then Virginia reaches over and wrenches his chin toward her. I see his hands fly up, and Virginia grasping at them. Are they fighting? Is he going to *hit her*?

He better not! I fumble for the security gate remote in my zipped pocket, adrenaline pumping through my body making me breathless and lightheaded. I'm going to startle them by opening the gate. Maybe that will give Virginia enough time to slip out of his truck and run. Pray the remote will works at this distance . . .

I extend my arm toward the gate, remote in hand, hoping to see Virginia clock him with her right fist, but I don't see that. I don't see that at all. I see the gap between them closing. I see their figures becoming one. I see . . . kissing.

I drop my arm and press my back against the tree, my mind roiling with disgust and outrage and disappointment. Gawd. They're still together. Better than ever, it appears. Then anger flares. I told her that he's not allowed anywhere near the house!

And my heart sinks because I know exactly what Virginia is going to say. She's going to get me on a technicality. He's not near the house. He's near *the wall*.

Virginia gets out of the truck and closes the door behind her, while Dillon fires up the engine. She reaches inside her purse and pulls out the remote for the gate. As gate swings open, Dillon turns his truck around.

He's headed my way. Oh no. I press so hard against the tree trunk that I can feel the rough knobs of bark pressing into my back. A jittery feeling washes over me. My fingers tingle. My legs feel weak. I know he'll sense that I'm here.

And sure enough, I hear his truck slow down.

Oh no. Oh no. Breathe, Genie. Maybe he won't see me. Maybe—

"Hey," he says, rolling down the window as he slows to a stop. I glance over at him, utterly speechless. "I didn't peg you as the type of person who likes to spy on people."

"What?"

"Spy. I saw you looking at me and Virginia."

Outrage galvanizes me into action. How *dare* he accuse *me* of spying on *him*. Despite my shaky legs, I turn to face him. "I was walking home, you . . ." *Fucking moron*!

Dillon cocks his head, his elbow resting on edge of his rolled down window. "Sorry, I didn't catch that. What did you say?"

My heart is pumping well into the danger zone. I can't believe I'm still standing. But I am standing. And I'm fighting back, too.

"I said I know about you. I know everything about you. I know that you stalked us like a creep!"

Creep? Not exactly the zinger I had hoped for, but it's something. It's not a devastating blow, but it's spunky. And it tells him that I know he's the stalker. Except, he doesn't seem too concerned.

He nods slowly, pressing his lips together, considering. "Everything, huh?" Then one corner of his mouth curls up, followed by the other. And to my horror, his smile turns into laughter. Loud barks, echoing in the still cold air. "I doubt that .I doubt that very much." he says. Then he takes his foot off the brake, and jerks his chin toward me. "See you around."

As he roars off, his words inflate in my mind like a hot air balloon. *Everything, huh? I doubt that very much*. Of course, I was just bluffing. I don't know every detail about him. Thank Goodness. I don't even know where he lives, or what he does for a living. But there was a shadow in his voice and dark irony in his eyes and laughter. It was almost as if *he* knew more than me. About what though? What could he possibly know?

I shiver suddenly, the heat of our confrontation falling away. I kick a bunch of pebbles in frustration and hatred. Maybe he was just screwing with me. He likes to do that. I don't know. All I know is that I'm freezing, and I need to get home. I need to write. I need to relax.

See you around.

And now I need another pill.

CHAPTER 13

I try to find the right moment to confront Virginia about Dillon, even though I know exactly what she's going to say. Yell, rather. It will turn out to be a useless Stay Puft Marshmallow argument, one that we've had so many times before, so I decide to just leave it until a better time.

The following day, Virginia walks into my office and lurks casually behind me, no doubt checking on the progress of the next installment. I kept reminding myself to change the orientation of my desk to face the door instead of the window overlooking the backyard, so I can see if she walks in. But I kept putting it off. Now I'm kicking myself.

In an effort to avoid unwanted lectures on the urgencies of the sequel, Virginia's favorite topic these days, I work on "Rebecca" in secret. To make life copacetic, I renamed an old draft of book one to *Rhenn and Friends* and keep it open in the background. If she stops by for a quick chat, I can easily click over and show her my inspiring progress.

Today, however, I had fallen into the middle of scene in sun-drenched Monte Carlo on the spacious patio of Maxim's suite. Amelia is infatuated. Maxim seems besotted, too. We hope so anyway, Amelia and I. We're on this journey together, exploring the thrilling brush of Maxim's lips against ours, his voice in our ears . . .

Unfortunately for me, lost in the spell, I forgot to minimize the document and bring forth the dummy. It's too late now. So I continue typing, clinging to a thin possibility that she doesn't read the title of the document, while she leans in closer.

"Ben-ja-min," she reads out. "Who's that? A new character that Rhenn slays?"

I glance over at the pink sticky on the side of my monitor, both relieved and annoyed.

"It's a boy," I say.

"A boy?"

I stop typing. "It's FedEx Man, okay?"

"*Mister* FedEx Man?" she cries, snapping up the precious sticky and waltzing away with it.

"Yes, Mister FedEx Man!" I jump up and pluck the sticky note from her grasp. "You know, a fellow member of the human race?"

"And he gave you his number?"

I nod, trying not to smile. "He asked me out on a zombie date."

Virginia breaks out into desperate giggles. I settle back into my chair, smiling, pink sticky safely restored and start typing again.

"Sounds positively deadly," she says. "Are you actually going to go?"

"Yes." Maybe.

"Have you called him yet?"

She got me there. "No," I mumble. "Not yet. I plan on calling this afternoon, after I'm done with this scene."

"Mmhm," she says dubiously, moving behind me and leaning in again. "So how's it going?"

I glance up at the top gray bar of my document that clearly reads, "Balcony Kiss." A discomforting shiver races over my skin. This defining moment can go one of two ways, depending on how I handle it. Mostly terrible if I blurt out the obvious truth, or kind of neutral if I can get her to understand that working on something else will help me with *Rhenn and Friends.* Or maybe now is the time to tell her about Amy's hibernation.

The pink sticky gives me courage. I overcame my fear and opened the front door. Far from the disaster I'd imagined, I'd been rewarded with a date.

Maybe facing my fear of telling her about my work in progress and will result in the happily ever after she always talks about. I hope.

I pull in a big breath, eyes glued to my screen, and say, "I'm working on a modern remake of *Rebecca*."

"Who?"

"*Rebecca*. It's a classic."

She straightens. "Who cares about classics?"

"I care about classics," I say, annoyed. "Besides classics get remade all the time. Jane Eyre is on permanent repeat and non-classics alike. *Freaky Friday* anyone?"

"People want to read about vampires. People want to read about Rhenn Larson."

I sigh. "Lots of people read about lots of different things, Jinny. Can you please leave me alone? I'm trying to work."

But she stands there, steadfastly rooted to the carpet. I minimize the offending document and swivel around on my chair to face her. Fresh from my high of answering the door, I plow on. "Listen, I've been thinking a lot about this. About *After The End*. I did say that it was really meant to be a series of three books. I planned that from the very beginning. And—and I know I said I would continue . . . but it's just not working. I'm really trying, but Amy needs to take a break. She needs to go into hibernation."

"*Hibernation*?" she cries. "Like a bear?"

"Well, kind of like a bear. Other animals hibernate too. But they all wake up when spring rolls around. I'm sure Amy will too. Let's just see how she's feeling then."

Silence.

I'm trying to keep things light, but Virginia's deepening scowl isn't helping matters.

"I want to write for adults, Jinny. I want to explore other things. You can be my publicist if you want, and David will just have to understand. He'll—"

"But he *won't* understand!"

"He'll have to—"

"He won't because we already signed the contract."

"We?!"

"Yes, *we*. As in you and I. As in Amy Mathews. There are financial penalties and little things called *breach of contract.* Things—"

"I told you to wait to sign it!"

"Well, I waited long enough. David called thirteen thousand times asking for the contract back."

"I don't care if he flew to the moon looking for it! We're a team, Virginia. That means you talk to me first before you make major decisions, and I talk to you like I'm trying to do now."

But she doesn't reply because she's secure in the machinations that she cast into play. She stands with her hands defiantly on her hips, exasperation written on her face. We both know she laid a trap—a trap that stole away any choice I had in the matter.

"I want to write under my name," I say. Damn the legal repercussions. "I am *going* to write under my own name."

"Eugenia, you don't get it, do you. You're nothing. No one cares about you and your hopes and dreams of writing under your *own name*. People only care about Rhenn Larson and Madeline Storm. You have this illusion of grandeur that just because you wrote *After The End*, publishers will fall head over heels to buy whatever long-winded stinking pile of crap *classic remake* that you type out. When are you going to get it through your head? You. Are. A. Nobody," she says, enunciating every word with swift jabs of her finger into my shoulder.

"Stop!" I cry, pushing her hand away.

Her eyes gleam ominously. I recognize all the signs of a looming rage: the quickening of her breath, the tightening of her lips, and the rising color in her cheeks.

She has a predatory nature that sniffs out weaknesses. If she chooses, she can be stunningly brutal. Except . . . except she'd never turned that rage on me.

That had changed the day in the hospital right before Mom passed away. I'd gone in early so I could be there right when visiting hours started. Virginia said she'd come in a little later. After talking with mom for a while, I got up to get a cup of coffee, and found Virginia standing behind the curtain separator, looking shocked, angry, and—hurt?

Just ask her what happened, my therapist had advised me. *What harm can it do?*

Short answer? A lot. After the Mom Time episode so long ago, my relationship with Virginia turned volatile. I couldn't figure out why. I'd tried to talk to her about it, but got only sarcastic comments.

After we'd lost Mom, I started going to a therapist to work through the grief, to get my head straight, to try and figure out why Virginia wouldn't talk to me about what had happened that day at the hospital. After four inconclusive sessions and

Virginia's persistent double-talk, I stopped asking. The more I tried to talk to her about it, the worse our relationship spiraled.

"Ever since that day at the hospital, you've been so terrible to me," I say.

"Not this again," she says, keeping her finger holstered.

I want to push back and say—*yes, this again*—but she's already fuming. And I'm nervous about pushing her too far. She may be angry, but she's still talking. I'm scared to journey into the silent, misty lands of estrangement. Because I need her. I need her to love me, to talk to me, to be there for me, even if sometimes she makes me feel like a dog and pony show. Even if she loses her temper and tells me that I'm a nobody.

"I am somebody," I say quietly, heart beating fast. "I'm Eugenia Ward."

She looks at me with bloodshot eyes, a result of her precipitous mood, and says through clenched teeth. "Then be that somebody after you're done being Amy."

And she walks out of my office.

CHAPTER 14

Virginia, never one to let an argument slow her down, kept pressing me about book details. She wanted to know how much progress I was making, and if I'd discovered any new characters or plot points that she could mine for forthcoming interviews.

"I have to keep the fans interested," she tells me one night in the kitchen after I warned her about the dangers of touting a book that hasn't been written yet. So many things can change between 'Once Upon A Time' and 'The End.' Whole characters can get wiped out of the book.

"How about you stick to your job, and I'll stick to mine," she says me after I inquired about her upcoming interview and what she plans on revealing.

"I have a right to know, Jinny," I reply.

"The only thing you need to know is that I'm hustling to keep Amy relevant, while you dink around with your crap classic remake, trying to figure out if you even *feel* like writing the next installment. So you'll have to forgive me if I resort to a little . . . fabrication."

"Fabrication? You mean lies?"

"I mean story telling. You know, the stuff you're supposed to be doing? I can't keep hauling Amy around like an animated corpse. You're going to have to deliver sooner or later." She goes on chopping some onions. "I mean, don't you feel a little self-indulgent? Maybe a little selfish? This isn't about you anymore. It's about our fans. Our publisher. It's about *us*. It's about the *team*."

The team. I don't reply. Guilt wafts over me. I do feel bad. That had been Mom's single dying wish. *Keep the team together.* And Virginia *is* hustling. It helps that she's a born hustler, but I can't discount her willingness to break a sweat.

But this Amy Mathews thing is starting to feel like conjoined twins walking in opposite directions. A while ago, I read an article about two sisters joined at the shoulder, who declined separation and went on to marry two different men. The sleeping arrangement must have been awkward, I remember thinking. Almost as awkward as Amy Mathews. At least Amy makes a decent living. Okay, a really nice living. And I don't have to witness Virginia's intimate moments. I guess things could be worse.

So I get busy. She has a point. What else am I going to do? She signed a legally binding contract. I'm still going to work on my classic remake, but I need to keep pushing Rhenn. So I write, and I write some more. And dumpster loads of drivel spew from my fingertips. I pump out my daily word count, so Virginia will get off my back, but secretly I really am beginning to worry.

My heart isn't in the grave anymore like it had been when I wrote the series. My tone is changing. *I* am changing.

Maybe there's an upside to this whole event. Maybe I'm changing enough to call Ben. I have to call him. If I wait much longer, I'll miss Halloween entirely.

"Carpe diem," I mutter to myself, sitting down at my desk and picking up my phone. I punch in his phone number, pulling in deep breaths, finger hovering over the call button. But my innards turn to water, and my heart thumps so hard my vision jumps.

So I put the phone down, feeling sick with disappointment. My pills will help me. My benzo buddies. But I need to get off the pills. I need to just *do it*. But I can't. Oh God, I just can't. And I drop my head on into my hands and try not to cry.

The lion food arrives the following day in the form of one cow carcass, helpfully cut into big pieces. Virginia had the deliveryman load up the coffin freezer in the garage. She then proceeded to throw a few chunks of meat over the fence, call it good, and head off to Beansters.

I'd done some preliminary math and determined that our stash of meat would last only last about two weeks, three if we're stingy, but one look at the lion makes me rethink my numbers. He's been starving for probably most of his adult life. He's had a few good meals since arriving at Chez Ward, but he's still too skinny. So today, I decide, is Lion Thanksgiving.

Over the next hour or so, I lob half of our stash of meat over to the fence for the lion. Then I stand there, pleased and happy, as the lion gorges himself, and his belly fills out.

I stand a few paces back from the fence, afraid of him, but captivated. He growls and drags a hunk of meat away from the pile toward the back of the enclosure.

"It's okay boy," I say mostly to myself. "You eat as much as you want. Nobody is going to take it away from you. I'll make you fat and shiny if it kills me."

He stops and looks up, his glowing yellow eyes fixing on me. Did he understand that last part? I step back and scan the fence line for any weaknesses, heart beating fast. Will he lunge? He is a killing machine, after all, driven by sheer instinct. I expect that he would kill me, or as least try, if given the opportunity.

But he walks toward me instead, his tawny coat sliding over his sharp shoulder blades. He's beautiful and stunning, even if he is a little skinny.

I step back further though. He arrives at the fence and presses the tip of his black nose against the chain link, his dark mouth hanging open, showing his enormous teeth. He seems to be interested in me, interested in something other than eating me. Maybe he's grateful for Lion Thanksgiving. His golden yellow eyes meet mine, and the deep irrational part of myself that I try not to ignore tells me that he's not going to hurt me. But it's a theory I'd rather not test.

He rubs his face against the fence, his coarse golden fur poking through the holes. Then he turns away and saunters over to his meal. As I walk back inside, a strange feeling of happiness comes over me, a light airy feeling as if I'd just made a new friend.

A few nights later, I hear the TV blaring loudly in the living room. Virginia must be "unwinding." So I decide to warm up a bean burrito and watch a documentary on my computer. I'm spending more time in my office cave than usual, trying to avoid Virginia, trying to get *Rhenn and Friends* sputtering to life.

In the meantime, the hot Monte Carlo sun continues to lure me into the world of Amelia and Maxim. She'd fallen in love with him, and now she's about to embark on a wild, chilling ride into the moorlands of England.

Meanwhile, Rhenn and his friends are in various phases of not so dead, an apt metaphor for how I felt when I had written the series. I was not dead, but I was not alive.

I loved Rhenn, but when I buried him, I never planned on breathing new life into his shriveled appendages. But that is what the reader demands, apparently. That is what David and Virginia demand.

I watch the microwave count down, while my recent 'conversation' with Virginia roils around in my mind like bad gas. Virginia and I are like the tide. We're either in or we're out. Sometimes we're very close. Sometimes we're as distant as galaxies. But we share a common memory bank of horrible childhood experiences, half of which she'd blocked out, the other half I had.

15 ... 14 ... 13 ...

We find common ground in reminiscing about our childhood (Virginia called it our childhell). I'd told Virginia about the piss-drinking episode; she knew that I'd been bullied all through school. But we were sisters. We were bound by blood. And that stuff is pretty messy.

During the few years that we'd attended the same school, she'd stuck up for me. After Monica and friends witnessed Virginia's awesome brutality, they had largely left me alone. But then she graduated, and the Mom Time episode happened.

Suddenly, she wasn't so keen to take my side. Suddenly, I didn't know whose side she was on.

10 ... 9 ... 8 ...

I look at my reflection on the microwave door and watch my chin pucker as my eyes fill with tears, thinking about our big argument. She'd fought for me. Now, she says I'm a nobody.

Ding!

I'm picking out a knife and fork from the silverware drawer, when I hear her hushed voice float in from the living room. I stop and listen.

"She wants to *be* somebody," I hear Virginia say disdainfully. "And I told her, I said we have a contract. We have legally binding *deadlines*."

"But she is somebody," came Dickhead's tinny voice, loud and clear over the loudspeaker. "She's *Pewgenia*, the Piss Drinker."

There's a tussle as she dives for her phone, killing the speakerphone setting. She giggles, talking in a low scandalized voice. "Sssh! Don't say that so loud! You're not supposed to know."

Her voice drops into low inaudible tones. And I stand there, unmoving, while the poison dart of her betrayal soars through the air and pierces me in the heart.

CHAPTER 15

I spend the rest of the night trying to forget Dillon's disdainful voice and Virginia's vicious giggling. It's excruciating to know that she shared my most humiliating secret with *him*. It's a painful reminder of my school days that I had tried so hard to forget, days that had destroyed so much of me.

Lying in bed that night, I stare up at the dark ceiling, while a painful lump forms in my throat, realizing that Virginia had resurrected the very thing I had tried so hard to bury. Why? Why had she done that? Maybe she wants to make herself look better in Dillon's eyes. *She* hadn't been bullied. *She* didn't drink Monica Schaffer's piss.

But as the days pass, the painful lump in my throat crystallizes into hurt anger, which morphs again into cold hard resentment. Resentment that stops me from furtively hiding "Rebecca." Open burning resentment that is going to send Amy Mathews into early retirement.

"What's the matter?" Virginia asks the following day, walking into my office and plumping her wide behind down on the edge of my desk. "You haven't said a word to me in three days."

"Do you mind?" I ask, glancing at her leisurely placed posterior.

She removes herself from my desk and sits down on Wonder Couch. "What's gotten into you?"

"What's gotten into *me*?" I ask, scoffing and looking away. Tears prick my eyes. Her vicious whispering is still so fresh in my mind. "I heard you the other night. Rather, I heard your shit for brains boyfriend." I look at her, blinking back the tears, chin trembling stupidly. "How could you?"

"How could I what?" she asks, but her expression shifts, and she's not outraged with my description of her boyfriend.

"You know," I say with a cold voice, wiping away a tear with my knuckle. My throat aches; I swallow hard against it. "You told him about—about *Pew*genia." My voice cracks. "The *Piss Drinker*."

Resounding silence.

"Oh, Genie!" she cries. "Don't be so sensitive. It was just a joke!"

"Jokes are typically meant to be funny."

She reaches for a book on my coffee table and begins leafing through it. "Only if everyone involved has a sense of humor . . ."

Suddenly, I'm tired. I'm tired of being ridiculed. I'm tired of being told that I need a sense of humor, while others tear me down mercilessly. And I'm tired of being Pewgenia—the Piss Drinker.

"There's nothing left for Rhenn," I say. "You can tell David whatever you want. It's over."

She shoots up from the couch and strides toward me. "What do you mean? There *needs* to be something left for Rhenn. There *needs* to be more books!"

"It's not going to happen."

"Eugenia!" she shouts, sending a precipitous chill across the room. "You'd better think of something to write," she continues after a brief pause, struggling to calm her voice, "and you better think of it quick. This isn't write what like comedy hour. This is serious business. David is counting on you. I'm counting on you. Millions of our stupid little fans are counting on you."

"All those *stupid little fans* pay our bills, Virginia. And if it weren't for them, Amy would be nothing. A nobody." That seems to stop her monologue short. "And they aren't stupid. They're nice. I *like* them."

"Plenty of *professional* authors manage to hit their deadlines. You just need more discipline. That's what it is." She starts pacing my office. "You need to just sit down everyday and—"

"Discipline? I'm the one who produced the entire two hundred and seventy *thousand* word series in the first place!"

"—Type-type-type." She pretends to pound away on an invisible keyboard. "It's not that hard, Genie."

"Oh, isn't it? Why don't you try then? Go on. Go *type-type-type* out a best selling novel. Or three."

She glowers at me, eye hot with anger. "You listen to me, Eugenia, and you listen hard. When that deadline approaches, you better have something *sellable* to give to David."

"Or else what? He'll cry into his soup?" I lean back in my swivel chair, defiantly meeting her gaze. "Rhenn is dead. How's that for a joke?"

"Yeah, real funny, Genie. A fucking hoot."

"I'll tell you what's a hoot. Finding you and your stalker-boyfriend in his truck the other day, sitting outside our *house*."

She freezes.

I lean forward quick, before she can get her tongue back into action. "The next time I see him anywhere near our property, including the street out front, I'm calling the police. You got that? No questions asked."

"Yeah," she deadpans, after a long pause. "Yeah, I got it."

Then she gets up and leaves.

CHAPTER 16

Overnight, our three thousand square foot home seemed to double in size. After my version of a joke, Virginia disappeared, but I can still hear her early in the morning, clattering around in the kitchen. We used to eat breakfast together, but we avoid each other now, an arrangement that suits me just fine.

I listen for the sound of her tires crunching on the gravel as she drives away in the morning, then I come downstairs. This puts my schedule somewhat out of whack, but at least I don't have to face her. I like to be up by seven, coffee'd by eight, and writing by nine. But my avoidance measures mean that I'm sitting down to write by ten or so. And each day the time slips even later.

After a few days, I begin to wonder who will break down first and toss a half-hearted apology over the trench. Not me, I assure myself every morning, locking eyes with my own reflection. She owes me a sincere and heartfelt apology.

Definitely not the other way around.

There is a nice upside, however. I can write whatever I want, whenever I feel like it. But as the days stretch into a whole week, the atmosphere around the house becomes stifling and lonely, and "Rebecca" is starting to lose some luster.

So I drift back to Rhenn and Madeline, my first loves, wondering what they have been up to, if anything, since I'd abandoned them last.

As it turns out, there's a new character in the land of the undead. A shape-shifter named Falco emerges from the shadows, dark and silent, capturing Madeline Storm's attention. Suddenly I have a love entanglement on my hands that enthralls me, too.

I spend about three thousand words on this new development, trying to get a better grasp on how Falco came to be and just exactly what forms he can take. As I progress, I realize that maybe Falco can carry Amy Mathews on to more books.

It's a possibility. It's also a good solution to my sisterly stalemate. Lots of writers work on two different manuscripts at the same time, don't they? I don't know.

As I polish off a Falco chapter, I think about surprising Virginia with the next installment. Falco's rise will disrupt the carefully balanced world that I had created. I smile, thinking of

Rhenn's hollow incisors growing long and thirsty with jealous rage. Maybe Falco could off the Cyclops character that's been bumbling around in my manuscript for fifty pages too.

So he gets to it. By the time Falco finishes off Cyclops, I look up and realize that the sun had set, leaving me working under a single column of light. My office is dark; the house unusually silent for a Friday night. I save and close my document, feeling content and productive. Then I rise from my chair and flick on the ceiling light.

Virginia usually 'pre-parties' with friends at the house, drinking and growing louder by the minute before going out, abruptly abandoning their sweating beer cans and drained tumblers sitting on the kitchen island. But tonight, the lights are off; the house is dark and silent.

I walk down the hallway toward the kitchen, flicking on a few lights and calling out, "Hello?" I hope I won't catch her furtively talking on the phone to Dillion somewhere in the dark depths of the living room.

There's a single shot glass sitting on the kitchen counter next to a mostly empty bottle of Jack Daniels. Bottles of hard liquor are staples in the Ward household, courtesy of Virginia's ever evolving philosophy on self-medication.

"Do you ever watch what you drink?" I had asked her one Sunday afternoon, after she had spent the entire day comatose on the couch, nursing a nasty hangover, one arm slung over her eyes, moaning about the light, the light! "I mean, because of your condition," I clarified.

"Alcohol isn't the problem," she replied. "Doctors are the problem. They're just government sanctioned pill pushers. They don't know half as much as I do about my—about mood disorders, or whatever. They just prescribe whatever pharmaceutical company pays them the most. Besides, I'm not really convinced there's anything wrong with me. I watched this really interesting video on YouTube by a guy in Norway called Dr. Jorgensen or something like that."

"Sounds legit," I said.

"You should watch it. He says that all these so called disorders are just created by big pharma. For example, ADD was miraculously diagnosed right when Eli Lilly developed the *cure* for it." Here she used air quotes. "Adderall, by the way, is just a combination of amphetamines. As in crystal meth? This is your brain on drugs? Now, we have a whole generation of kids that are meth-heads thanks to our advanced medical knowledge."

"Jinny, you have a chemical disorder. I read a bunch of scientific papers that said alcohol was the key factor in—"

"That's old stuff."

"But it was all recently published."

"You really ought to watch that YouTube video," she said, patting around futilely. "Is my tablet over there?"

I abandoned my efforts that day. It was clear that Virginia had acquired some sort of superhuman power of denial that simple logic could not overcome.

"Hello?" I call out again, picking up the bottle of Jack Daniels and looking at the contents. It's two-thirds empty, the generous dent of which Virginia had made last weekend. So she drank only a shot or two, I guess from where the line of tawny liquid hits the label (I keep track). Not great, but not catastrophic.

To save her liver, I dump the rest of the whiskey down the drain. Then I walk over and stomp on the trash can pedal. The lid flies open. There lays another bottle of Jack Daniels—empty.

Slowly, as if handling a snake, I reach down and pick it up. I hold two empty bottles of Jack Daniels now, one in each hand. This means that one is new. One is not. This also means that Virginia somehow finished off an enormous, possibly deadly, amount.

The house is silent. A dark shadow crawls over me, a sinister whisper in my ear as soft as breath saying, *Virginia . . . where's Virginia?*

I hear the driving sound of water running. It's a heavy demanding flow that could quickly fill Virginia's Jacuzzi bathtub.

It's also a sound, I suddenly realize, that has been on for some time as if draining every last drop of water in Glenhaven. There are no telltale sounds of water splashing. It's eerily silent in the house, except for the deep rumbling sound of free flowing water.

I rush up the stairs, two by two. Virginia's bedroom door is ajar. I slam the door open and call out for her. The room is dark. Her furniture shrouded in shadows, the sound of rushing water loud and immediate.

Her bathroom door is closed; a bright sliver of light glows underneath. Water seeps out from under the bathroom door, spreading across the carpet in a dark semicircle.

I push the bathroom door open, heart pumping in my chest like a locomotive, praying that I'll find the bathroom empty, knowing all the while that it won't be.

I find her propped up against the bathtub, wearing a purple bathrobe that gapes open at the waist. Water pools around her, wicking up the sleeves and waist. Handprints mar the foggy bathroom mirror as if insane people had tried to claw their way out from the other side.

"Jinny!"

But she doesn't move. I cough, waving away the pungent smell of metabolized alcohol, slog over to the overflowing faucet, and turn it off. I bend down to her slumped figure and pull long strands of red hair from her pasty moist face, watching her ribcage rise and fall in quick little jolts.

"Jinny," I say again, patting her pale, drawn cheeks. I try to haul her upright and ease the compression kink in her neck, but I can't budge her solid weight.

So I lay her down on the bathroom floor instead, her hair floating around her head like a halo of fire, her expression peaceful.

I pull up her sleeve to check her pulse and freeze. A flat razor lay in her loosely closed hand. Tiny slit marks mar her palm. Frantically, I yank up the sleeve, looking for the telltale gash of a life thrown away, and nearly sag with relief when I find her wrist whole and unharmed. But the sinister whisperings are back, urging me to lift the sleeve higher and see for myself . . .

There, cut deep into the flesh of her forearm lay the bloody homage she'd paid to our fictitious writer. She'd scrawled 'AMY' in large block letters along the length of her forearm, some gouges deeper than others, weeping with dark red and pinkish rivulets of blood.

She rouses, choking and coughing. Gently, I lift her head and encourage her to pull in a deep breath. She looks up at me, eyes red and swimming, and says with a faint voice and pungent breath, "Don't let us die . . . don't let Amy die."

CHAPTER 17

It took us both about a week to collectively recover from Virginia's alcohol poisoning. My stash of pills took a beating. So did her liver. But we're on the mend now. Her and I.

After I found the cuts, she passed out again, coughing up sputum and bile. Somehow I dragged her downstairs, levered her into my car, and rushed her to the nearest hospital, where they pumped her stomach.

She stayed overnight so the doctors could monitor her recovery and take immediate action if she lost consciousness again, which she had on two separate occasions.

That night, I slept on an armchair next to her bed with the emergency buzzer in my hand, listening to the soft reassuring beeps of her heart rate monitor.

I went into medical mode, a mode I know all too well. I felt like I was back in the hospital days with Mom, driving her to the emergency room, answering all the nosy questions that admission secretaries seemed to think they had a right to know: "What kind of infection?", "Has she had a bowel movement lately?"

The following morning, the doctor stood at the foot of Virginia's bed, clipboard in hand, lecturing her about the dangers of hard boozing and how close she'd come to dying. "I haven't pumped that much alcohol out of someone's stomach in a good long time," he told her. "You're lucky you survived."

When he started talking about the effect that alcohol has on brain chemistry, especially for those suffering from mood disorders, she gazed out past window slats, clearly disinterested in the topic at hand.

At least she survived. And I'm grateful for it. Under the hot urgencies of almost losing my sister, our disagreement faded into nothing.

Once back home, she slept mostly. Yesterday, she rose like a zombie dressed in a terrycloth bathrobe, dug around in the pantry for some snacks, and disembarked on the couch, box of Ritz cheese crackers in hand. Just to be sure, I went ahead and emptied every bottle of alcohol we kept in the house.

The following morning dawns bright and warm. Virginia is making good progress with her recovery. Amazingly, she agreed to stop drinking for the foreseeable future, and I can finally turn my thoughts back to writing, and perhaps even, calling Ben.

The end of the month is here, the zombie block party only four days away. If I don't work up the courage to call him, I'll miss the big day entirely.

Well, I'll think about that later today. During Virginia's hospital stay, I had some good plot ideas. I'm anxious flesh them out before I forget. While I get dressed, I go over the more salient points.

Amelia is going to have some trouble with her possessive ex-boyfriend, who will fly out to Monte Carlo on a surprise flight and cause quite a scene, which Maxim will valiantly defuse. Sigh.

Then she'll get an inkling about Maxim's dark and conveniently undisclosed secret. But she'll turn a blind eye to that red flag because love causes lapses in good judgement, apparently.

Then I'll work on *Rhenn and Friends*. Falco, I discovered during a short vibrant dream sequence at the hospital, has white wings, a fitting tribute to his name.

Pink velour sweatsuit donned, I go downstairs to make the coffee. While it percolates, I think about Falco's finer details. It seems that his wings aren't fully formed yet, the development of which will provide some interesting plot points. I imagine Rhenn clashing with Falco in a battle of good versus evil.

Rhenn, my hero clad in black, will fight for good. Falco, who will eventually sport great white wings, will gravitate toward evil. I like the opposing symbolism.

Rhenn and Friends doesn't seem so dire. Maybe I can hit that deadline after all. A little swell of hope rises up in my heart.

Maybe I don't need tragedy to drive me through another installment. Maybe I just need legalese.

I pour coffee into two mugs and splash in some milk. Then I take the mugs up to Virginia's room. Her room is bigger than mine, overlooking the side of the property and the dense forest beyond.

I set the mugs down on her mirrored bedside table, pull the heavy curtains open and slide the sash window up, letting in a gust of fresh autumn air that chases away the musty smell of the infirm.

She groans from within her cocoon of plush bedding.

"You're supposed to take the decorative pillows off while you sleep," I say, sitting down on her cloud of a bed.

She pulls the comforter down and rubs her eyes. She looks like she's been electrocuted. Her eyes are bloodshot and swollen, her chemically straightened locks are starting to grow out, leaving tight curly roots that I sometimes joke look like pubic hair.

But I won't joke today. I reach over for a mug, glancing at a framed cringe-worthy photo of her and Dillon, while a shiver runs over my arms. He's wearing that backwards ball cap and a clingy t-shirt with Virginia tucked under his arm.

Maybe he didn't edit that scary No Doubt video or send me crazy messages online, but his eyes look as hard and menacing as ever, arrogant and challenging like career criminal's. I put the frame face down and hand her a mug of coffee.

"Here you go."

"Thanks, Genie." She eases herself up to sitting and takes the warm mug. "Thanks for everything. I don't know what I would have done without you."

I run my hand over her silver-blue sateen bedding that she'd ordered from an ultra-expensive store in New York City and want to say something along the lines of—*Well, you wouldn't be able to waste any more money*—but all my sarcasm has withered. It's enough to know that she's still with me, warts and all, and she's getting better.

She takes my hand. "I'm serious, Genie. I'm so sorry for everything. For telling Dillon about—about that terrible name. For drinking. I don't know what happened. I just—the thought of losing Amy Mathews made me want to . . ." She doesn't finish her sentence, but I'm well aware of what it made her want to do. My only worry is: will she do it again?

"You started cutting again," I say, squeezing her hand. "You said you wouldn't do that anymore. You said you'd get help, remember?"

"I'm trying," she says, looking down. "I really am."

"I know," I say softly, wishing she'd try a little harder. "Have you seen your arm?" I smile a little. "You look like Amy Mathews's number one deranged fan."

The corner of her mouth turns up. "Who needs a stalker when they have me?"

We laugh a little, but not much. The stalker-induced scars are still raw. Well, at least mine are anyway. She takes another sip of coffee, closes her eyes, and says, "So are you still going to kill Amy?"

I thought a lot about Amy over the past week. Amy Mathews represents a part of me that died with Mom, a part of me that I buried alongside her. I felt as though I'd discovered everything I needed to know about being mostly dead. Writing about the undead was a perfect allegory for how I felt at the time, for who I was when I lost Mom. And it's true that I want to write about life now.

But if rising up means losing Virginia, then it's not worth it in the end. Falco will have to carry us through the next few books on his white wings of evil. Falco would have to rise up for us both.

"Not yet," I say. "Rhenn just made a new friend."

She doesn't reply, but a palpable calm falls over the room. Without opening her eyes, she says softly, "Don't forget about lover boy. He needs a new friend too . . ."

CHAPTER 18

Don't forget about lover boy . . .

Virginia's tired voice stays with me for the rest of the day. I have to call Ben. I've had enough time to work up the courage. I'm about as stocked up as I'll ever be.

But the thought of calling him up gives me so much anxiety that I allow myself one half of one pill, which turned into a whole one as the moment of truth closes down on me like a noose.

The day comes to a close. Eventide falls. And I need to call. Feeling chemically stabilized, but still sick to my stomach, I sit down at my desk and death grip my phone. This is it, I tell myself, dialing in his number. Just *grow some balls*. I think of said balls, bouncing along the lyrics of my life that runs like a ticker tape across my mind to the tune of *Knick Knack Paddy Whack.*

"Grow some balls. Grow some balls," I mutter.

And while I'm tapping my finger on the face of my phone, thinking of something that rhymes with 'balls,' I accidentally push the call button.

The screen changes to 'calling now.' I gape at it, heart thumping in my chest. I have two options: push the red kill button or green to continue. Red—push red!

"Dominos Pizza. You make 'em, we bake 'em," a voice says through the receiver.

"Oh." I put the phone to my ear and clear my throat. "Sorry, I guess I dialed the wrong number." And I hang up.

At first, amazement sweeps through me. I actually called. But then bewilderment sets in. Dominos Pizza? Followed by a sinking feeling. Did I copy down his number wrong?

I'm comparing the number on my sticky to the one I just called, digit by digit, when my phone rings.

"Hello?" I ask, confused.

"Hey, I was just kidding," says the friendly voice on the other end. "This is Ben. Who's this?"

My breath catches. It's *Ben*. "Oh. Hi. Ben. It's—it's Eugenia from . . ."

"Hey hey!" he cries. "I was beginning to think you'd never call."

I can't think of a single thing to say. I'm not used to telephone conversations with boys. But Ben, bless him, steers us toward friendly ground.

"So what have you been up to?" he asks, in an easy breezy tone of voice. "I haven't had a delivery to your house since I dropped off my number. Have you been cheating on me with UPS?" He laughs. I break out in a cold sweat.

"No! Never. I guess my sister hasn't ordered anything lately. But don't worry, I'm sure she's working something up." *Working something up*?

"Oh, that's good. Good. So how have you been?"

"Good."

"Good . . . hey, don't talk my ear off okay?" He laughs again. "How's your book coming along?"

Books. Now that was something I can talk about. "Really great, actually," I say, leaning back in my chair and propping my feet up on my desk. "I'm kind of busy checking out new genres. Urban fantasy. I'll see how it goes."

"Cool. Aren't vampires considered fantasy though?"

I hadn't expected him to be versed in the nuances of genre. "No, not technically. Vampire stories usually fall under paranormal. You know, paranormal romances? That's when vampires or werewolves, kind of known and established monsters, have some romantic moments. Fantasy is when you get to make up your own creatures. And urban—well, that just means the setting."

"Oh right, kind of like Dungeons and Dragons, with elves and warlocks."

"Yeah, kind of like that."

"And zombies? Where do they fit in?"

"Well, they kind of don't. They're just . . . zombies." I try to think of where zombie books might fit in the bookstore. "I guess they would fall under horror, but even that's not quite right because in horror the bad guy is a monster. Though zombies are kind of monsters . . ."

"So they're misfits."

"Yeah," I laugh. "I guess so."

"That must be why I like them so much. Hey, did you hear about that new street drug? It's called spice and turns people who takes it into something pretty close to a zombie."

"Really?"

"Yeah, really! I just read about it the other day. It's crazy."

"That's kind of scary . . ."

"Not as scary as my zombie costume. You ought to see it, seriously. I've been working on it for a good four years now."

"Wow." Wow, indeed. I can't believe we're actually talking.

"I'm sure you have a good costume around there somewhere, don't you?"

"Actually, I don't." I wouldn't have any use for it. I don't go out. Parties especially. And after the stalker episode, we stopped welcoming strangers to our front door.

"Well, you better get one. The zombie block party is this Friday. You're coming, right?"

Coming? As in meet him there? As in get dressed in some stupid costume, drive over to a block party filled with loud drunkards, query all badly dressed zombies—*Excuse me! Do you know Ben? Ben!*—until I find him, standing in a circle with his friends, surprised that I'd managed to find him so quickly.

Not a chance.

Then disappointment sweeps over me. Friends. That's what he wants. He wants to be *friends*. How stupid of me to think that he actually wanted to take me out on a date. Totally stupid! Of course he didn't want to ask me out on a date. Why would anyone—

"I mean," he says, voice quiet. "Can I take you?" My heart beats in big loud thumps. "I'd really like that . . . to take you out."

"I'd like that too," I say, heart thoroughly lodged up my esophagus.

Then he says the resounding words that will echo in my soul for all eternity, the first three words I have ever heard: "It's a date."

"Okay," I manage.

"I'll be there at seven, looking my very worst." He laughs a little.

"Okay . . . me too . . . bye . . ." And slowly, I hang up the phone.

CHAPTER 19

I spend the next few days scouring the internet for a good zombie costume. I'm both surprised and fascinated to discover the world of DIY zombie enthusiasts. I'd initially expected to find a costume in a bag like your standard vampire, fairy, or superhero. But I quickly fell into the multifaceted world of zombie subculture, including origin and subclass.

When I discovered that zombies, like plants and animals, have their own kingdoms, I briefly toyed with the idea of including a rage zombie in the second installment of *After The End*, but decided that I didn't want the book to be a vomit fest of every possible monster.

No, my imagination will have to work on the finer details of my costume, while Rhenn and Falco work out their differences on the page.

So I decide to be a zombie nurse from World War II, which would require some specialty clothing and yards of gauze. A mummy-nurse-zombie, why not? So I go to an online vintage clothing store and order a parcel of bulk clothing, hoping to find some clothes that will work.

Virginia, feeling better, went to go pick it up and stopped by Party Supplies on Decatur Street for fake blood, flesh wound kits, fishnet tights, and some medical props.

The rest of week passes with sickening speed. It's Thursday night, the night before our date. I'm sitting at my desk, composing a 'sorry I can't make it' text message. I intentionally left the 'to' field blank, just in case I get a case of fat fingers and accidentally push the send button.

My stomach churns and roils. In less than twenty-four hours, I will be answering the doorbell, leaving the house with a boy, and going on a date with said boy.

It helps that I'll look like a car crash victim. I'll be able to hide, in a way, under my gory costume, but under it all, it's just plain ole me, Pewgenia the Piss Drinker.

Nobody will recognize me, and the bullies are two thousand miles away, but human nature scares me. The primal nature of bullies that can scent weakness doesn't change regardless of the zip code.

Girls are the worst. Correction: the masters. They're like black widow spiders, sneaky and poisonous. I'm wary of girls.

Boys are easy going. They're simple. Mostly, they're nice. And they seem to be something worth jealously guarding.

I sigh grimly and lean back in my chair. Will there be any girls there tomorrow with a crush on Benjamin? One that will slash me to pieces in front of him just to make herself look better? Maybe I shouldn't go.

"Hey," Virginia says, startling me from my dark reverie. "What are you up to?"

I pull in a long quavering breath. "Oh . . . just thinking about canceling tomorrow night."

"What? Why?" She sits down on the arm hair opposite my antique desk and props up her feet. She's wearing her favorite fuzzy house slippers that look like hairy Frodo feet. "Talk to me. The doctor is in."

I smile. It's an old line from our tumultuous California days, back when she was in therapy and I was getting torn to shreds at school. "I just . . . I don't know. I don't think I'm ready."

"What do you mean?"

"It's just that . . ."—tears prick my eyes—"I'm really afraid he won't like me, you know? Nobody has ever liked me. Except Amy Mathews's fans, but they just like my stories and your face."

"That's not true," she says.

My office is dark. My lamp casts a cone of light over my desk, highlighting the contours of her face.

Virginia is only twenty-six, but life has already brought out hard lines on her face. I can see the hint of a scowl line forming between her eyebrows. Life's challenges had galvanized her into a warrior, while they had shunted me into the shadows.

"Genie, there's so much to like about you. Just go out there and be yourself," she says.

"Easy for you to say. Everyone always likes you."

"That's because they don't have a choice." And we both laugh.

Virginia can be the funniest girl in the room or the most brutal. Nobody dared bully her, and I admire that rough side of her character. The confident, independent side that doesn't care what other people think. I wish I had some of that now.

"You have to stop making this into such a big thing, okay?" she says. "You have to compartmentalize. Just shove whatever's bothering you into a nice little box, put a bow on it, and toss it aside in your mind, never to be thought of again. That's what I do."

"That's your super power," I say. "Compartmentalization."

I, on the other hand, have a mind like a broken record player that goes over things again and again, trying to dissect where I'd gone wrong.

"You just have to embrace your super power," she says.

I scoff. "I don't have any super powers."

"Yes, you do. You have a sixth sense. You can intuit things about other people that I miss entirely. You're *smart* about people, whereas I just go barging into a room like an elephant, not even noticing if I've knocked over a priceless vase with my big fat ass."

"It's not that big . . ." I tease.

She smiles. "You're sensitive, Genie. Too sensitive. And, you know, that's a big part of this phobia problem. You just have to train yourself to be a little less sensitive. Don't care so much about what people think about you. I mean, don't get all rough and tumble on me. We don't need two Thunder Bums in the room, but try to put a little padding around your heart. Okay?"

I think about what we'd both look like if people could see inside of us. Virginia's mind would be a dusty attic filled with thousands of discarded boxes. And my heart would be a giant pulsing ball, haphazardly wrapped in gauze.

She gets up from her chair and walks around to desk to me. "C'mon, I want to show you all the great stuff I got at the costume store. I even got some padding for your heart."

I rise, pushing away my phone. "Thanks, Jinny. You think of everything."

And then, for the first time in a long time, we hug. "I try, little sis. I try."

In her arms, I think about how nice she can be. How sweet. And how cold she'd turned that day at the hospital. That day that had changed everything between us. Unbidden, the question rises in my mind. What had happened? And why won't she talk about it?

I'm afraid to ruin the closeness, but this seems like a little window of opportunity. A window that I don't want to close.

"Jinny," I say, arms still around her, afraid to ask, afraid not to ask. "Are you ever going to tell me what happened that day at the hospital?"

She doesn't move. I brace for her Arctic blast. But when she pulls back, I see that her eyes are misty, soft with what seems like sadness and maybe a little pity. Then she purses her lips, shakes her head a little and says with a shrug, "You already know."

But I don't. I don't have the first clue. And by the time I open my mouth to say something she pulls away. Conversation over.

CHAPTER 20

Virginia must have bought up all the gauze in Glenhaven. We started on my costume four hours before Ben was due to arrive, which turned out to be barely enough time to transform me into a mummy-nurse-zombie. Now we're rushing, dabbing on more fake blood here and there and adjusting my wrappings, when I hear the intercom ring.

"He's here . . ." I say, looking at Virginia, fear and exhilaration rushing through my body.

"He's here!" she cries, dashing over to the intercom and pushing the talk button. "Hellllloooooo? Ward residence. May I help you?" she sings out. I hear his voice in the background, made small by the magic of distance. Then Virginia's chirpy voice, "Come on up! Commencing Operation Zombie Date now . . ." And she pushes the gate release button with a flourish.

She spins around, facing me. "You look awesome. So great. Seriously, I did such a good job." She pats herself on the back and laughs. "Good job, me."

I'm supposed to laugh along, but I'm too nervous.

"Oh geez," I say, looking in the mirror and patting the gauze wrapped around my head. "Do you think he's going to like it?" Jinny stands behind me, peering over my shoulder. I look at her reflection. "I think I'm going to be sick."

"Hey." She turns me around and takes me by the shoulders. "You got this," she says with conviction.

"Really?" I mumble. Her faith in me makes me feel emotional, but strong.

"A hundred percent. You *got* this. Now, let's get you downstairs. I can't wait to see what he looks like!" And off she goes in a rush.

Not so fast for me. I need a pill. That's non-negotiable. And even though I hate myself a little bit more every time I cave in and swallow another one, there's no way I am going on a date to a block party without any help.

In my bedroom, I quickly down a pill, grab my small satchel bag and slip the vial inside. Just in case.

Then I walk downstairs, every footfall ringing out like a death knell. Virginia appears at the base of the stairwell with a glass of chilled wine in hand, working on some sort of superhuman speed. "Here, have a sip. It'll help with your nerves. I'll go get your date."

I'm not a big drinker, but tonight calls for some new rules. "Thanks," I say, taking a big gulp. Then I make my way into the kitchen.

I'm leaning on the marble island, nursing my glass of wine, while Virginia walks through the foyer to collect Ben. I hear the front door open before he even knocks; I hear her voice floating in from the entryway—"Hi, I'm Virginia, the big sis. Wow, you look so scary!"—and I hear the calm tones of his voice in the house, his footsteps on the few steps leading up to the kitchen area. Then he walks into view, and a jolt of panicky exhilaration races through me.

"Come on in," Virginia says to him. And to me, "Doesn't he look great?"

He looks like road kill. The left side of his face looks like it had been scraped off in some terrible accident, leaving behind a bloodied eye socket that droops down his cheek. Half of his scalp is exposed in a talented play with fake blood and latex. His jeans are ripped up to his thighs. But under all the crumpled, bloody clothing and copious hanging fake flesh, I can see that he's the handsome person I've ever seen.

I take another bolstering swig of wine. "Hey, Ben," I say, waving lamely.

He crosses the room towards me. "Are you a mummy-zombie?" he asks, eyes wide with what I hope is pleasant surprise. He stand so close that I can see the bright prisms in his eyes and feel the warmth emanating from his body. He picks up my stethoscope and runs his thumb across the resonator.

I pat the loose bandages on my head, my cheeks pulsing with a hot blush. "Yeah, I guess so. A mummy-nurse-zombie. Hope I don't offend anyone's classifications."

"You look . . ." I swallow hard, bracing myself. What is he going to say? *Please* don't let it be something mortifying. He locks eyes with mine, still holding the resonator, and says, "You look amazing."

Suddenly my world falls silent. I feel like I'm falling, falling into his midnight blue galaxy eyes and drifting out into deep dark space, watching a distant star explosion.

Virginia clears her throat. "So, Ben, do you want anything to drink?"

He takes a glass of water. They talk about stuff, but I'm not listening. My thoughts are racing ahead to the very near future, when I'll be sitting in the car alone with him, trying to think of something to say.

"Well, we better get going," Ben says, leaving his empty glass on the counter. "Are you ready?"

I don't think I'm ever going to be ready, but I'm going to damn well try. I nod. "Yes, I think so."

Virginia follows us out and stands on the patio, while Ben opens up the passenger side door of his vintage Mustang. I get in and wave to Virginia, who sticks two enthusiastic thumbs in the air as Ben walks around to the driver's side. Then she turns and goes inside.

"Nice car," I say when he slides into the driver's seat. I feel like we're sitting in a time capsule that's about to whisk us off to a simpler time. The vinyl dashboard is cracked, showing its yellow foam innards. There are three instrument bezels that sit behind the steering wheel. Everything appears to be original, except for the after-market radio that glows dimly in the shadows.

"Thanks. Yeah, I love it. This is a 1968 K-code. My dad gave it to me as a graduation gift. I'm trying to restore it." He pats the dashboard. "Life goals, life goals," he adds almost wistfully.

"I've heard of a Shelby. Is it the same thing?"

He turns to me, surprised. "Hey, you sure know your stuff!"

I look away, blushing. The internet is a wondrous thing. "Nah. I did some research once. I had a character with a vintage car obsession."

"Oh right, yeah." He jams the key into the ignition and starts the car with a loud satisfying roar, puts the car into gear, and rolls down the driveway. "So the K-code was an added feature that went into both the Shelby GT's and the normal Mustangs. Think of it as an optional package. Back in the day, people could either buy the regular Mustang or the Shelby GT option, which was a special high performance 289 cubic-inch engine."

When we stop at the security gate. I pull the small remote out from my satchel and push the button.

"And from there, you get the extra K-code, with upgraded pistons, cylinder heads, a chrome air cleaner and so on. There's supposed to be a little K-code badge on the front fender that says 'high performance 289,' but I can't seem to find one."

As we turn onto Chesapeake Drive, I listen to him talk about horsepower, carburetors, and high-rise intake manifolds, feeling amazed and grateful that the conversation hasn't slipped in the land of awkward silences.

"Sorry if I'm boring you," he says apologetically after a while, glancing over at me.

"Not at all!" He could be talking about how crayons are made and I would have found every word interesting. "Sorry I don't know more about engines."

"You know a lot of stuff. You know how to write books. I couldn't write a book if my life depended on it."

I laugh. "Sure you could. They say everyone has at least one book in them."

"Yeah, but what kind of book?"

"I don't know. Memoirs?"

"Boring."

"I love autobiographies." He keeps his eyes on the road. *Was that the wrong thing to say*? "So," I venture, "do you think there's such a thing as a zombie Mustang?" I turn away and bite my lip. What a stupid thing to say! But I'm so afraid to let the conversation die.

He laughs out loud. Then he slaps the car on the dashboard. "What do you think, ole gal? Are you a zombie Mustang?" And he looks over at me, eyes bright and glowing under the mask of fake gore. "Maybe that would explain why I can't find very many spare parts."

"I wouldn't know about spare parts. I drive a Honda."

"You know cars say a lot about a person?"

"Oh, I don't believe that." *Stop disagreeing.*

"They say people who drive Hondas are very reliable," Ben replies. Does he mean boring?

"And Volvos?" I ask, thinking of Virginia's SUV.

"Driven mostly by women and bad drivers."

I chuckle under my breath. Virginia is a terrible driver.

"And what about K-code Mustangs?" I ask.

He looks over at me and shrugs. "Driven by people like me."

But who is like him? And is he like anybody else I've ever met? I don't have much knowledge about boys so I can't draw comparisons, but I had a few guy friends in high school. Loners, mostly, computer geeks, and good all-American misfits.

We walked to class together sometimes. They told me about role playing or software programming difficulties. But they were outcasts like me, and the romantic disinterest was mutual. But I didn't need to experience one hundred men to tell me that Ben was special.

When he looks at me, his supernova eyes become soft, almost effervescent. He has goals and parents. Parents. What in the world will he think of me when I tell him about mine?

Soon, we'll reach downtown Glenhaven. Soon, I'll have to laugh and smile even though my bowels are turning into water. As we pass under a street lamp, the interior of the car lights up. I catch a glimpse of myself in the side mirror and almost gasp.

A fake bloodied gash runs from the corner of my eye down to my jaw. Bloodied mummy wrappings hold together my exposed latex brain matter. Fake blood oozes down my forehead. But even though I look like a monster, for once I don't feel like one.

I glance down at my right hand and touch the ruby ring my mom had given me, winking faintly in the dim receding light, and smile when I hear her voice. *EGBOK, honey . . . everything's going to be OK.*

CHAPTER 21

Halloween is my favorite holiday. It's far cooler than Christmas, where everyone sits around a tree and pretends their lives aren't that messed up. They laugh with their family, or argue, trying to put on a happy face and good cheer that the season demands, secretly wishing they were somewhere else—somewhere warm preferably—made worse by the bleak landscape of winter.

On Halloween, everyone is a misfit. You don't have to think about family dynamics, reflect on your past year, and hope the next one will be better. The year isn't quite over yet, so there's still time to revisit all of those flagging resolutions.

Halloween is the holiday of escapism, fun, and play. It's the time of year where you get to be somebody else, look like somebody else, and leave your old persona behind for just a little while.

Downtown Glenhaven had been transformed into a spectacular Halloween wonderland. The crisp autumn air smells of roasting kettle corn, corn dogs, and barbecue drippings on open pit fires.

A few fairground rides whiz people around in bright, blurred light. Intermittent screams drift down from the swinging chair ride, spinning barrel, and Freakout.

A troupe of young zombies hurry past us, limping, growling, and collapsing into gales of laughter. There's a cover band playing *Dead Man's Party* by Oingo Boingo. There's a lot of dancing and hooting. Thank God I took my pill.

Ben and I wander over to a row of craft fair booths with zombie-inspired arts and crafts on display. There are zombie key chains, paintings, and shredded but unbloodied clothes that one can wear on zombie off-days, presumably.

One booth features black rose art with petals encased in little lockets, desiccated flower arrangements complete with fake cobwebs, and potpourri.

"Mmm," I say, lifting a jar to Ben's nose. "Yum."

He takes in a deep welcoming breath and grimaces. "I'll bet that's a top seller," he says, coughing. "What is that smell? Old socks?"

I put the jar down, laughing. "Geriatric blues. It's a very popular scent these days."

"I can see why," he says flatly.

We pass a cotton candy stand and wander over to the silent movie section, where *Dawn of the Dead* is playing to an audience of mostly empty lawn chairs.

"It looks like a graveyard in here," I remark, trying not to smile. It's a terrific pun, made possible by the Xanax coursing through my system. "Where is everybody?"

Ben laughs. "I don't know. Maybe . . . six feet under?"

"Oooh. Good one," I say with a smile. I love that he gets my jokes.

Then we make our way over to the zombie obstacle course. I'm doing my level best to think of things to say, or at least not say the wrong things. The **benz**o has a firm grip on my anxiety levels, but I can feel them bucking just underneath, trying to work free from the chemical confines.

I'm also keeping up with my breathing, in—one two, out—one two, trying to keep my mind on Ben and what he's saying, or not saying. I'm trying to look calm, cool, and casual, not like a panicky goose is taking flight inside of me.

The roped off obstacle area has a blow-up kiddie castle, burlap sack slides two stories high, and ball pits where zombies wallow, trying to get to the other side (so many jokes, so little time). It costs two tickets to run the gauntlet, which Ben hands over to the attendant.

We move through the turnstile, and I stop short. Parallel bars stand in front of me, carrying me back to my piss drinker years, back to my long solitary lunch breaks at school.

Racing kids on the parallel bars was my therapy back then, an avenue to vent my anger, and a place to hide my solitude. No Friend Nigel could have something to do besides stand around, looking like a loser.

The panicky goose inside me flaps harder. I'm struggling to get a hold of myself, while a taunting voice rises up. *Pee-ew. What smells!*

In—one two.

Out—one two.

But the memories are coming for me. Hunting me down. I was the resident champ on the parallel bars, not because I was more athletic than the other kids. But because I had the most anger to vent. Anger pushed me faster and faster as I swung my legs over the bar, and I launched myself an extra foot, until I gained on my opponent, until I was just behind him, barreling down on him like a—

"Are you okay?"

I jump, heart pumping too fast. The pill—it's losing its grasp. Its power is fading. The panicky goose is breaking free, and soon, so very soon, I'm going to be standing out here in public, with Ben, unable to breathe.

"I'm good," I reply, my eye twitching, my voice too loud. I clear my throat. "I'm just . . ." Just what? Falling apart? In public? In front of Ben?

"Do you want to hang out here?" He steps between the parallel bars and lifts himself off his feet. "Not really sure what you're supposed to do . . . but I guess it could be fun."

Ben. So nice. So accommodating. What's he doing out with a girl like me? One who can barely keep her heart rate out of the endurance zone. *Relax. Just relax.*

But I'm not relaxed. I'm losing control. The voices from my past are coming at me quick, a collective howling group of them. *Pee-ew. Pee-ew. She drank Monica's pee!*

And I hear Dillon's voice too, his low cruel laugh mixed with the chorus of voices just under the tones of hysterical schoolgirl glee. *But she already is somebody. She's Pewgenia, the Piss Drinker.*

My heart rate is surging into the no-go zone. My stomach is churning. I'm hot, and I'm cold, and beads of perspiration are popping out on my skin, running down my chest.

No. Not now. Please, *not now.*

People are looking. And Ben is too, his brow creased with concern. He's placing his hand on my arm, asking if I'm okay. *Do you need a glass of water?*

I nod. Yes, I need some water. I need some help. I need to get off this ride called Panic Attack. Please God, not in front of Ben.

And he's gone, rushing between staring groups of people. And when he slips of out of view, I step in a shadow and frantically rummage around in my satchel bag for a pill. I need another pill.

I need to get it down my throat quick before he comes back and sees that I have a pill problem. I need to get that goose under control. I fumble with the vial with shaky hands. The damn tamper proof lid won't come off.

"Come off, *please*," I beg, finally wrenching it off. Two pills tumble into the dirt. I bend down and pick them out of a shoe print, wipe off the dust quickly, toss them into my mouth with shaking hands, and swallow against a zing of alarm. I took too many.

I feel better because I know that my benzo buddies are on the way. They're going to get that goose back under control. Except, there's an undercurrent of dreadful anticipation. What's going to happen now? I've never taken so many at once before. *But I need them.*

I know. I know. But I can't—I can't keep it together. Not with all these people gawking at me on the sly as they walk past. *Nobody recognizes you. Nobody knows who you are.*

I put my hands on my knees and focus on pulling in deep breaths, trying to get my internal matters to calm down some. Bring my heart rate down into the green zone. Get my guts to toughen up a little.

I jump when I feel a hand on my back. It's Ben with a plastic cup filled with water.

"Here you go. The line was too long so I just grabbed some tap water. I hope it's okay. Do you need some ice?"

I shake my head and gulp down a tepid mouthful. The pills will dissolve and encase me in a chemical coffin. I'll feel a little bit like an actual zombie, but at least I won't blow up inside. I hope.

Then I realize I'm exactly where never wanted to be. I'm at the butt-end of an awkward situation, embarrassed, and panicking inside.

"What happened?" asks Ben. "Did you eat something bad?"

"I don't know. I guess so." That's a good cover. Food poisoning. Except I haven't eaten anything. At all. But it's a much better topic than my pill-popping problem that I desperately don't want him to know about. "Can you take me home?"

"Yeah, of course." Ben is saying, his hand under my upper arm. I take my first step, and the world swirls around me. I stumble to the side, trying to win back my balance. "Whoa!" Ben says, catching me mid-pivot. "Geez. Are you sure you're okay?"

No. I'm not. I took too many pills. My stomach sinks. Followed by incongruent laughter. I'm definitely losing my shit.

I want to hurry up and get out of here. I want to break down and cry. If Virginia were here, she'd understand. She'd tell everyone to step back! Make way! And she'd tuck me under her arm and usher me to the safety of our home because that's really where I belong. Not out here in public.

My hands begin to shake uncontrollably. And here it is, folks, the main event. A gorilla climbs on top of my chest. My breath comes up short. I can't breathe. My vision narrows. Nausea races up my throat. My benzos? Nothing in the face of a panic attack tsunami.

And then I'm falling. Distantly, I can hear Ben calling for help. *Help! Someone—call an ambulance!*

Shakes and shivers overcome me, while I fight for wisps of breath, feeling like I'm fighting to stay alive, while inside I'm crumbling apart.

I'm down on my knees now, my heart pounding out of my chest. I'm so far into the red zone. I'm desperate for medical help and industrial strength tranquilizers.

Hang on, I hear Ben's voice, distant and far away. A strange, floaty feeling washes over me, but I also feel weighted down with perspiration and costuming and latex.

I start ripping off the stifling gauze. *Get it off*! I'm fumbling to open the first few buttons of my nurse uniform, trying to get the neck slit in my costume to open up. Trying to get some air. Trying not to die. Not on my first date!

Voices surround me. Sirens. And flashing emergency lights.

Then somehow I'm on my back, looking up into a bright field of blinding light, while the rushing tide of panic shunts me down a rocky gully.

It's a journey I know only too well. As the paramedics load me into the back of the ambulance, I close my eyes and turn away from Ben, who is standing there, stunned, his eyes wide.

I look away as the EMT fits an oxygen mask to my face. I'll never hear from Ben again. And who can blame him?

"I'll see you at the hospital!" I hear Ben say.

The back doors of the ambulance slam shut. I'm cocooned on a stretcher inside the white van surrounded by two fast acting EMTs and beeping medical equipment. Oxygen saturates my body, alongside relief and utter disbelief.

He'll see me at the hospital.

CHAPTER 22

"We'd like to keep you overnight for observations," the doctor is telling me after the nurses had somehow stabilized me, giving me enough tranquilizers to stun the gorilla sitting on my chest, but just enough stimulants to reverse the effects of my overdose.

I'm still groggy from the meds, and I'm glad for it. The hospital-grade good stuff is making my mind a little fuzzy around the details of my disastrous date with Ben that somehow, thankfully, feels like a distant memory now.

In time, I hope I'll forget all about it, but deep down I know I'll never forget the wide startled look in his eyes when the EMTs shunted me into the back of an ambulance.

For now though, I'm feeling floaty and vague and well aware that the rocky terrain of reality waits for me about fifty feet below. But I don't want to go down there. Not now. Not yet.

Virginia, sitting next to me on a beat-up pleather armchair, says, "They might as well name the hospital ward after us," she says. "The Ward Sisters? Get it?"

"Ha ha very funny," I say, while the doctor lifts a quizzical eyebrow.

"She was in admitted to the hospital a couple weeks ago," I explain, motioning to my sister.

"Anxiety as well?" he asks. He's a young doctor with sandy blonde hair pulled into a man bun. His nails are trim and tidy, his face clean-shaven, but I can see a glimpse of his tie-dye shirt underneath his scrubs and white coat.

"Uh . . . no," Virginia replies. "I had a—a big night."

I almost expect him to relate with similar a 'big night' story of his own, probably something that pertains to the recreational use of cannabis, but he looks down at his clipboard and nods solemnly at my chart. "I see."

"I'd really like go home if that's at all possible," I say to him. I need some quiet time, not a constant stream of people knocking on my door, checking on this and checking on that.

"I'm going to have to advise against it," he says. "We gave you Flumazenil—the antidote to benzodiazepene. It's very effective for reversing the central nervous system symptoms of an overdose, possible seizures and the like, but it's not as effective for reversing respiratory depression. That was the gorilla on your chest feeling you were having."

"Right . . ." I say, seeing the wisdom in his logic.

"So we'll need to keep an eye on you over the next twenty four hours. You'll be free to go home tomorrow night." It's the ol' assumptive close, giving me the impression that I have a choice in the matter when really I don't. Then he moves into administration mode, asking Virginia to stop by the front desk and provide insurance information.

"I'm sure they already have everything on file," I add as the doctor leaves, parting the half-drawn privacy curtain behind him. Then I sling my arm over my eyes and sigh. "Talk about a date from hell."

"So what happened?" she asks.

"You know . . . the usual blue screen of death."

"Oh, no. What do you think triggered it?"

"Well, we were having a good time, I think, but then there was some stupid obstacle course that had parallel bars of all things." I groan just thinking about the coincidence. "And I had a flashback . . . Monica and all that. I just spiraled—I couldn't keep it together so I panicked and downed too many pills. . ." My chin puckers; I begin to cry. "Why can't I just be normal?" I ask Virginia rhetorically. "Why can't I just go on date like millions of other people manage to do every day of the year?"

And then she's hovering over me, hushing me, and wiping off my caked on make-up with a dwindling packet of Wet Wipes that she retrieved from her purse.

"It's okay," she's saying. "You'll get better."

"Ben will never want to see me again," I blubber. "He said he'd come to the hospital, but of course he didn't. Why would he?

I'm sure he'll fob off his shifts so he doesn't have to deliver packages to our house anymore."

"Seems unlikely," she says.

"Why do you say that?"

"Because he's here. He's sitting in the waiting room."

I jolt up in bed. "What?"

"Don't get excited. I mean get excited, but not that excited. Try to be calm and relaxed and okay, a little happy." The thought of Ben here in the hospital fills me with dread and nervous happiness. "I told him to wait outside until you were ready to see him," she says.

"Good thinking," I say, glad he didn't have to see the unglamorous side of reversing an overdose.

"Do you think you're okay to talk to him?" she asks.

"Oh, geez. I don't know. I probably look like death warmed over."

She smiles a little. "Zombies never die. How's that for a pun?"

I laugh. "That's terrible, Jinny. Don't quick your day job."

"I'm trying not to," she says, the corner of her mouth curling up. "Here, I brought you some clean clothes." She motions down to the canvas bag slouching down by my feet. "Do you want to change out of that costume?"

"Thanks, Jinny. You—"

"Think of everything . . . I know." But there's sadness in her eyes and wistfulness in her voice. The same sad wistfulness that I'd detected that day when she sat on the couch with me, eating her Chocoholic ice cream. What is it about mentioning her sisterly care and concern that causes her such sadness?

She pulls the privacy curtain closed and helps me change into my favorite velour pink tracksuit. As I ease back onto a couple of flattened hospital pillows, Virginia leaves to get Ben.

Before I know it, he's pushing aside the privacy curtain and cautiously approaching my bedside, followed by Virginia, saying, "Hi, how are you feeling?"

"I'm good," I manage to say. "Feeling better."

"She's stable now," Virginia says. "The doctor gave her medicine to reverse the overdose and—"

I shoot a searing look at Virginia's until she mercifully stops talking, but the after affect of her slip-up reverberates on and on and on.

"Overdose?" Ben asks, bewildered, naturally. "But I thought you had food poisoning..."

"What?" Virginia asks.

My stomach sinks. Oh, gosh. This is going from worse to even worse than that. I break out in a cold sweat, while the room swirls around me in a farce of reality. Am I really lying on a roller bed in the emergency room anti-drugged out of my mind, while Ben catches me in a lie?

Fib, I tell myself. It was just a *fib*. And while I'm debating the fine line that separates a fib from a *lie*, Virginia starts covering my tracks.

"Genie's always had a weak stomach," she says, glancing at me, trying to find and follow the correct party line.

"That's true," I say, catching her gaze in approval. "I mean, maybe it wasn't exactly food poisoning. Maybe I just got sick because I—I hadn't eaten very much..."

"If you're stomach is empty then it couldn't be food poisoning, right?" Ben asks, trying to puzzle through this. "And— anyway, Virginia you said she *overdosed*?"

"She—she has these pills for . . . nausea. They're really strong. I guess you took too many?" Virginia looks over at me, trying to gauge to her progress.

"I'm not feeling very well," I mutter, light-headed and ready to curl up and die. I might as well do that now.

"Should I get a nurse?" Ben asks, thankfully diverted away from topic of my overdose, but the stench of misinformation hangs in the air.

"No," I mutter. If we attract the attention of a nurse, or worse, Dr. Man Bun, they'll rush in here and blow my big fat lie. I look at Virginia, whose eyes are alert and anxious "I think I just need to close my eyes for a second . . ." And pretend this isn't happening to me.

Thankfully, Virginia takes charge. She sits back down the pleather armchair and chats with Ben, making jokes, changing the subject, her hand over mine. She's the brilliant, loving, protective sister once again. Ben stayed for about fifteen minutes, chatting mostly with Virginia, until the nurse came and moved me into a hospital room for the night.

Over the course of the next few days, Ben and I talked a lot over text messages. I loved the distant intimacy. I loved that I could take my time and say what I wanted without having to worry about breathing techniques or my heart rate ratcheting up. And a couple weeks after returning home, I invited him over again.

I asked Virginia to stay home in case I had a repeat episode. She could do all the quick thinking, get him out of the house, and help me calm down, hopefully, without medical intervention.

But I do take a single pill.

I get the door opened without any fanfare, except for my frazzles nerves thrumming inside of me, but I manage to keep control of the bundle as I stand in the kitchen, pouring him a beer in a tall pilsner and a sparkling water for me.

Then he follows me down the hallway to my office.

"Jesus!" Ben cries when we walk outside to my patio, overlooking the backyard lion enclosure. "You have a freaking *lion?*"

"My sister does, technically. He's a rescue."

"Okay . . ." he says, sitting down on the lawn chair stiffly.

I break out laughing. "Don't worry. He's well fed."

"Well, that's good news." Ben tears his gaze away from the enclosure and takes a sip of his beer. "You look good," he says. "You look better."

"Thanks . . ."

"So tell me about your book," he says.

I want to correct him. My *books.* My lumbering giant of a series that gobbled up spots on the New York Times bestseller list and spat out spots on USA Today. But I can't tell him that. Amy Mathews would kill me.

I shrug. "Oh, it's nothing. Just something I wrote." I take a gulp of my water.

"What's the name of it?" Ben asks. "I'm not lying when I tell you I'm a big vampire fan. I read all that stuff. I just finished the *After The End* series by Amy Mathews. Have you heard of it? Actually, it's really funny. Virginia looks a lot like Amy Mathews . . ."

Fizzy water gurgles down the wrong pipe. I cough, trying to breathe.

"You okay?" he asks, helpfully patting my back.

"Fine," I choke out. I blink a few times and press my knuckle into the corner of my watering eyes. "Yeah, I read those books. I thought they were pretty good."

Ben nods in agreement, gazing out at the lion enclosure.

"Actually, I write fan fiction," I say. "I'm working on a book now called *Rhenn and Friends*." Which isn't so far from the truth.

He looks up at me, eyes bright. "About Rhenn Larson?"

That he knew Rhenn's last name makes me want to weep for deceiving him. Ben is a fan. He *knows* Rhenn. And he likes him. Somehow, I feel like we had a common friend.

"He's . . . inspiring," I agree.

I take another sip from my glass, trying to think of something else to talk about—anything, besides *After The End*.

Ben sniffs and swallows. "So, I was wondering. About your food poisoning . . . What do you think you ate?"

My heart sinks. I look down and pretend to pick some lint off my shirt, mulling over my options. I can tell him that ate some leftovers that had clearly gone bad. I can tell him it was probably the stomach flu. Or I can tell him the truth.

"Ben, I didn't have food poisoning," I hear myself saying. "Virginia was right. I—I overdosed. I have a problem with anxiety and . . . yeah. I need to take tranquilizers in order to function, basically. Social situations are really tough for me."

Ben's face drops. "I wish I had known. We could have gone to the beach or—or out to dinner or—"

"I didn't want you to know. I guess I was kind of hoping you'd never find out . . . or that I'd somehow get better instantly. Kind of like on the job training."

Ben laughs sympathetically. "Well, that didn't go according to plan, did it?"

And then we talked. And we ordered pizza. And by the time the cold air drove us inside my office to the Wonder Couch, he knew that I'd had a stalker, but I couldn't bring myself to tell him who.

He knew about my pill popping problem. And I knew that I never wanted him to leave.

CHAPTER 23

Ben and I are seeing each other a lot now. We went out to dinner, and he took me over to his house. Best part? I didn't end up in the hospital. I'm starting to hope that maybe I'm getting better; maybe I'll be able to bury Piss Drinker forever.

An early winter storm blew in. From the comfort of my office, I watch the wind and rain rattle the tree limbs, shaking loose colorful bunches of leaves. Soon the killing frost will arrive, finish off my vegetable garden, and propel us into the dead of winter—my favorite time of year.

I pull my cardigan tight around me, looking out of my glass paneled patio door and watching the lion pace along his fence line. He moves with lithe and powerful movement. He's filling out now. Putting on some weight. His mane is growing back in, thick and dark. That makes me happy.

I run my hands up and down my arms, and turn to face my fireplace. Guess it's time to build my inaugural fire for the season. I'm on my hands and knees, blowing on a wad of newspaper, when my phone rings. Ben.

"Are you keeping cozy?" he asks.

"Trying," I reply, looking at the smoldering ashes in my fireplace. "Not doing such a good job though."

"Uh oh. Is there anything I can do to help?"

"I could use a good fire. Are you an Eagle Scout?"

"As a matter of fact, I am."

I laugh in earnest. "Are you really? Badges and sashes or it never happened."

"Have I ever lied to you?"

"Well, I'm not sure, but I can always fire up my polygraph."

Then it's Ben's turn to laugh. "You actually have one of those things?"

"No," I say, sinking down on my couch and smiling. "I thought about getting one once though, but they're expensive."

"Then you'll just have to take my word for it."

"Okay, I'll make you a deal. You come over, build me nice roaring hearth fire, and I'll beg for your forgiveness."

"Mmm. I like the begging part, but I have a better idea. Have you ever been parking?"

"Parking, as in necking?" Pretty sure, never.

"Well, yeah, that too, if you insist." I blush bright red. "Kidding . . . I wanted to take you up to a special beach. There's a place where you can park and look all the way down the coast. It's really neat."

"That sounds really neat."

"Okay, so I'll be over in about an hour?"

"Oh," I say.

"Is that okay?" he asks gently.

I glance over at my sleeping computer screen. Today turned out to be a bad day. I sat down at nine-thirty and procrastinated by reading the news online, which carried me over to YouTube, where I watched videos of guilty dogs and funny horses and lions tackling antelopes, wishing Virginia's beastie was living free on the Serengeti instead of existing in my backyard.

Then I went outside and paid my yellow friend a visit. After snack time, I went back inside and stockpiled logs next to the fireplace. Then I built a log tepee like the internets told me to do. Then I tried to light the tepee, which took some screwing around with crumpled newspapers, stubborn logs that preferred to smoke, not burn, followed by an untimely squirt of lighter fluid that nearly took off my eyebrow. So here I am.

"No, it's good," I say. "Good timing. I wasn't doing much anyway."

"Okay, great! See you in a bit."

We hang up, and I go upstairs to find an appropriate parking outfit, which consists of some jeans, white sneakers, and a hoodie pullover. Then I take a pill just in case and walk downstairs to eat some cereal, while I wait for my chariot to arrive.

The beach is a two-mile stretch of windswept shoreline that fronts Long Island Sound. We drive down a long two-lane road, flanked with rugged shrubbery leaning and swaying in the wind. Beyond the shrubbery, vast marshlands rush out to the distant roiling sea.

It's a cold windy day that warrants a hot chocolate and a long campout by my fireplace, but Ben has other things on his mind. And so did I.

Rhenn and Friends is starting to flag again. As it turns out, Falco doesn't have the wing power to get Amy Mathews through a few more installments. But there's something heavier weighing on my mind. Virginia started disappearing for days at a time. When she does return home, she seems disconnected in a way that rises above a simple hangover.

I worry about Virginia and the fact that she seems to be growing closer to Dillon, sometimes parroting things he would say, not dumping him cold like I had hoped.

And there's more.

I want to finish book four. I really do. I want to keep Virginia safe. But her pressure is having the opposite effect on me. Every gentle nudge, every innocent question about my progress, pushes me closer and closer to the bleak land of Writer's Block. Brain, my plot hole whisperer, is starting to go on long silent sojourns. And I'm really starting to fret.

The image of the bloody cut on Virginia's forearm is burned bright in my mind. If I can't resurrect Rhenn, if I can't weave together a story for book four and five, I'm scared that something terrible is going to happen.

We drive on further, past bushes and long needle pine trees. The road becomes more desolate. Raindrops fall like shimmering crystals in bright broken sunlight. The pill takes hold, relaxing me.

We pass a network of footpaths that weave through sand dunes and places to pull over and park, but Ben keeps on driving. I watch the choppy seas scamper past my window, thinking about Virginia and why I have such a bad feeling. Is it just an irrational fear?

I remember back to when I ran into Dillon on the road outside of our house. *Everything, huh. I doubt that very much.* He had a knowing derisive look that day, almost as if he knew something that I didn't. But what?

At the very end of the road, Ben slows and parks in an empty parking lot. He switches off the car and turns to me.

"Well, here we are. Let the necking commence." He chuckles and runs the back of his finger along my cheek. Then he drops his hand to my shoulder. "You okay? You're really quiet. Even for you."

I smile and look away, not sure what to say. I feel like telling him everything. I think I should tell him nothing.

"C'mon. Let's go get some fresh air." And he climbs out of the car.

The fresh air is cutting and raw. I follow Ben down a sandy trail, flanked by swelling sand berms covered with coastal grass and false heather that still sports a few valiant blooms.

As Ben walks toward the roiling ocean, the wind whips the sides of his flannel shirt around his tall, thin frame.

We walk down the beach a ways under the leaden sky. Then Ben motions toward two big sand berms. We settle in the trough, me sidling close to Ben for warmth.

"You feeling okay?" Ben asks.

I watch the wind tousle his sandy blonde hair, wondering how much I should tell him about Amy Mathews and her persistent pesterer. I hate to open up any more avenues of blackmail, should things go south between Ben and I, but I need to talk to someone, and he's the only person I know. Besides, I trust him.

I hug my knees to my chest and watch a boat bobbing along the horizon, dipping in and out of view. "You asked me a long time ago about what kind of books I write," I say.

"Mmhm."

"I write about vampires, like I said, but they're . . . very popular."

"Yeah?"

I turn to him. "I mean, really popular."

There's a benign look in his eyes, but his eyebrows are raised in question.

"You know that Amy Mathews series *After The End*?"

"Yes."

"That's me. I mean, I use a pen name, but I wrote those books."

He continues to look at me, blinking, his golden nebula prisms bright against the deep blue field of his eyes. "That's *you*?"

"Well, us technically. I mean, Amy Mathews doesn't actually exist. Virginia and I make up Amy Mathews. She's the face, and I'm the brain. That's why she looks Amy Mathews." This is starting to sound like some freak show, but I've never explained it to anyone before. "Amy is kind of a Franken-author," I conclude with a lame smile.

For once, he doesn't have anything to say.

I grin. "Surprise?"

"Holy *shit*," he mutters, looking away.

"Yeah . . ." Then the conversation well and truly derails. Is he going to dump me? Will he be intimidated by my success? A FedEx delivery guy dating a literary phenomenon?

I watch him, while he stares out at the ocean, desperately hoping that things won't change between us. Then he turns to me. "Dinner is on you next time!"

And we both laugh.

I want to tell him about my modern remake of *Rebecca*, my hopes to retire Amy and write using my real name, without the bolstering guidance of Virginia, but my secrets stick in my throat. That's a conversation for another time, I conclude. Maybe another lifetime.

"Sure," I say. "Where do you want to go?"

"Benihana?" he asks with a hopeful smile.

"Sounds like fun. I've never been there before."

"Genie," he says in a teasing voice. "You really should get out more."

"I get out enough . . ." But the color rises to my cheeks. This sounds like one of those insults couched in a joke.

He wraps his arm around my shoulders, pulling me close, while I try to resist. "Hey," he says softly. "I was just kidding."

"Me and my awful sense of humor," I say, my cheeks burning despite the cold wind.

"I mean I was kidding about Benihana. That place is really expensive."

"Oh, is it?"

He looks at me and laughs in earnest. "Yes it is! Now I *really* think you should get out more!"

"Well I don't know." I laugh, melting with relief that he's not going to eviscerate me with a *joke*. "How much is it anyway?"

"I don't know . . ."

"Look who should get out more," I say, throwing a handful of sand over the toes of his shoes.

He dusts off the pile. "At least fifty dollars per person, I guess. I've only been there once. My parents took me when I graduated college."

"Your parents sound really nice," I say, wondering what it would be like to have two active adult participants in my life. But Virginia and I are proud of each other. We ought to be. There isn't anyone else to provide that service.

"Yeah, my parents are really awesome," Ben says. "They're still married, can you believe it?"

"Wow."

"What about your parents? Are they still together?"

"Not exactly . . ." I say, regretting my benign complement about his parents. I should have known it would be the perfect lead in to ask about mine. Which, so far, I'd studiously avoided.

"Divorced, huh?" Then he adds, as if to make me feel better, "That's pretty common."

I find myself in the trough of another wave now, staring up the steep watery wall of confessions. I'd been able to make it up and over the last topic of Amy Mathews, but I can tell that this rushing wall is going capsize me.

The emotion rises inside me as I think about my beloved Mumsy, lost to me forever.

"My mom—she passed away." I hold my breath as the wave drags me under. "And my dad kind of . . . checked out after the divorce."

There. I revealed my pedigree. I'm a mongrel child, unwanted by one half and loved by the other half in spirit only.

"I'm so sorry," he says with real sympathy. "Can I ask what happened?"

I pull in a quivering breath and shrug. "Cancer. Of the lungs." Tears sting my eyes. My chin puckers. "She didn't even smoke." I'm drowning deep under the churning, breaking waves.

A shaft of sunlight breaks through the gray clouds, washing our small section of the beach in brilliant light that spangles off my ring, making the little ruby sparkle.

I tell him about her illness had started. The first whiff of concern. She developed a cough that she'd dismissed as walking pneumonia. But as the months wore on and winter slipped into spring, her cough worsened. One morning, she coughed up a little blood.

"Just sore lungs," she said to me with a weak smile. Then came the headaches. The shortness of breath. The stints in bed.

The lack of energy. And the final confirmation of what I had feared all along.

Off she went to a specialist after specialist, who all suggested chemotherapy. So I ferried Mom to the 'chemo station' for her chemo cycles. I assembled the bills and organized them in a three-ring binder, working up the courage to call the bill collectors and work out the payment terms. Toward the end, when Mom was too weak to get out of bed, I sat up late at night, reading books to her just as she had read to us.

Ben listens, watching me, his eyes full of sympathy and understanding.

I tell him more stories about Mom, about how she had scrimped and saved to buy me a Girl Scout costume, stopping just short of the Monica Schaffer ordeal, trying not to cry, but doing it anyway. I tell him that Mom was the reason why I started writing in the first place. About how she'd edited the first book in the series, correcting my bad grammar, helping me with plot holes, and explaining the intricacies of the English language that I'd somehow missed in school. I tell him about my pill-popping journey. And my hopes to quit. All the while, Ben plays with the fringe on the hole torn in the knee of my jeans. Listening.

The sun slips behind a cloudbank. The wind blows a little sharper. And then, finally, I run out of things to say. We sit together in silence for a while. And I begin to regret my bad case of motor mouth. What had gotten into me? Geez. I've never talked so much in my entire life. Ben's going to think I'm a blathering idiot. He's going to—

"Hey," Ben says softly, tipping my chin toward him. "I'm here for you. You know that right? You can tell me anything you want, anytime you want to share. I love hearing about you."

"Thank you," I murmur, and look away because I can't take the warm light in his eyes. I put my head on his shoulder instead, my heart swelling with love and fear. I'm falling for this guy. Not falling. I'm rising for this guy. Yes, that's what it is. A strange buoyant feeling overcomes me, a feeling that I never want to end.

We gaze out at the sea and watch mushy waves crash on the beach for a while. Then he pick up a twig and starts drawing lines in the sand. "So world famous author, huh? Wow. Should I ask for your autograph?"

"Hardly!" I say, laughing.

Ben's wind-mussed hair falls over his mirthful eyes. And suddenly, I realize this is someone who might be able to offer me some advice. Someone who might be able to understand, possibly even, help me.

"To be honest, I've really been wanting to give up Amy Mathews. I don't want to write about the undead anymore. I want to write under my own name. I want to write about life."

"Then you should do it," he replies. Simple as that.

"Well, except that it's not really that simple . . ."

"Why not?"

I sigh. "Because there's a lot of money involved. There's a lot of people relying on Amy. Virginia especially."

"What does she have to do with anything?" he asks. "I mean, besides lending her face and to the whole endeavor."

"Well, it's her job. She does the interviews, the tours, handles the agent stuff, contracts, negotiations . . . I just write the books. If I retire Amy, Virginia will be out of a job. *She's* Amy Mathews now, and will forever be." I write a line in the sand with a twig. Then I look up at him. "What do you I should do?"

He looks over at me and shrugs. "I think you should follow your heart."

CHAPTER 24

We walk back to the car in silence, holding hands, as a feeling of peace washes over me. *Follow your heart.* It's so simple, yet so hard.

Once we reach the car, Ben unlocks his door, slides inside, reaches over, and pulls up my door lock, quaintly located on top of the door panel. I jump in, rubbing my hands together. "Let's go put those Eagle Scout skills to use."

"Only if you beg," he says, his mouth curling into a smile, while he puts the key in the ignition.

"You wish!"

"Hey, you offered." Chuckling, he gazes out across the hood of his car and turns the key.

Nothing.

"Bad starter?" I ask, not too worried.

"She's a bit temperamental. Aren't ya, girl?" He gives the car an encouraging rub along the cracked dashboard. Then he tries again, twisting the key in the ignition with more intention than the last casual try.

Nothing again.

"Hm." He bends down, peers into ignition hole, and blows a couple of times. "Sometimes you have to wiggle the key a little bit,"—which he commences to do—"it can be a little tricky."

He tries again, but the car doesn't even reward him with a half-hearted rumble. He flicks on the headlights; a weak beam of light barely touches the wild shrubbery a few feet from the front bumper.

"Is that normal?" I ask, honestly unable to tell. "I mean, for your car?" I don't know much about motorized transport, other than the fact that mine always works, the headlights are always bright, and it requires only a twice-yearly trip to Midas for the usual spurt of pampering and upselling. I've never even looked under the hood.

He smiles, but it's not the usual light-hearted, devil-may-care grin. There's a flicker of concern in his eyes that carries down to his mouth. "Vintage cars have a lot personality," he says with some authority. "That's what makes them so charming."

He must mean the personality trait of unreliability, which I don't find too charming. My mind had already raced home and pictured Ben and I sitting cozily on my chesterfield, faux-fur blankets draped over our laps, gazing at the fire snapping in my fireplace. I planned on showing him my stupendous safe room too, but that delicious version of my future evening is fading against the personality quirk of Ben's Mustang.

"Maybe there's a loose wire or something." He reaches down, chin resting on the steering wheel, and gropes under the dash for the hood release latch. "I'll go check."

"I'm coming too," I say, opening my door and following him out. I want to see what a car engine looks like, and how in the world he's going to find one lone derelict wire.

The sun had set. The wind is cold and sharp. I shiver and tuck my hands into my armpits. Ben opens the trunk, looking for a flashlight. I peer inside, and worry sets in. He is far too prepared for a one-off occurrence.

His trunk is stocked with an emergency kit that contains a flashlight, lots of batteries, a folded piece of foil that serves as an emergency blanket, some jugs of water, and energy bars.

"This isn't your first time getting stranded, is it . . ." I say with mounting dismay as my cozy nightcap slips further out of reach.

"Nope. Don't worry though, she won't let us down."

I want to remind him that *she* has already let us down, but don't want to point out the obvious state of affairs. He fishes out a toolbox and slams the trunk shut with a heavy *thunk*.

We walk to the hood of the car. Ben fishes around for a latch, releases it, and props up the hood with its little metal stick. Then we both lean in like a pair of surgeons.

Ben takes the flashlight from the toolbox and beams the light into the dark workings of the engine, following lines and wires a few inches from his nose. He zeroes in on a few dirty wires and wiggles them.

"Phillips screwdriver, please." I dig around in the toolbox and hand it over. I may be not a mechanical genius, but I know the difference between a flathead and a Phillips.

"Did you find the problem?" I ask, leaning in next to him and peering down at blooms of rust, grime, and a hornet's nest of identical wiring.

"Still looking." He fiddles around for a few minutes, wiggling wires, blowing here and there, and poking around with the screwdriver, until he stops and examines a black circular cap with six good-sized and relatively organized wires snaking out of the top. "Aha. Ok, gotcha. Crescent wrench number thirteen, please."

Over goes the tool. And shortly thereafter, he asks me to try again. Shivering, I rush over to the driver's side and slide inside. With encouraging words on my lips and hope flickering in my heart, I turn the key.

Rrrr. Rrrrrrrrrrrrr. And then nothing.

My heart sinks. I lean out, shivering. "What now?"

Ben sticks his head out from behind the hood. "Try it again!"

I do.

Rrrr. RRRRRRrrrrr.

"Again!"

I try again, this time grumpily cursing under my breath. And then *she* bursts into life like an exuberant puppy.

Scared that the car will die on us again, I stomp on the gas petal. *VROM!*

It's a happy healthy sound that instantly restores my faith in the car and my hopes of a cozy evening spent fireside with Ben.

"Hey take it easy, Jensen Button!" he cries, poking his head out from behind the hood. I climb out of the front seat, while he pushes the hood down. Then he turns, dusts off his hands, and leans against the car, pulling me close. "We need to let her run for a little bit so the alternator can charge."

"Right," I mumble, resting my cheek against the warm folds of his flannel shirt.

A gust of wind blasts over the sand dune, cutting through my thin hoodie. I shiver against the delicious warmth of Ben's body. He's not overly muscular, but his lithe five foot ten frame fits my body perfectly.

I can feel warm runnels of his breath against my cheek. I snuggle closer, grateful that the cold wind gives me a good excuse to press against him.

I don't really know how to do this romance thing. So when he shifts his weight and leans back, signaling something momentous, I miss the cue entirely and lean in with him, clinging to his warm body.

But I don't miss my galloping heart when he runs his hand up my back and holds my cheek. Nor do I miss the dizzy sensation when he presses his chilly cheek against mine, angling his mouth towards mine.

Then he pulls away and looks at me. With one hand, he strokes the back of my neck with his thumb; with the other he tucks a lock of flyaway hair behind my ear, gently, as if handling a spooked horse.

I feel like a spooked horse, nervous and giddy. I'm sure what to do, but I'm yielding to his caresses and holding onto him as a riptide swirls under my feet.

I put my hands on his waist and try to meet his gaze burns as bright as a celestial event, but I look away, afraid of the intensity I see in them.

Instead I focus on his lips, a safer place to rest my gaze. I study the delicious depression in his lower lip middle, while my heart hammers hard in my chest. Then I close my eyes.

He touches his forehead to mine and places both hands on my burning cheeks. Then he kisses me.

And I cling to him as the tide carries me away, so much larger than me or Amy Mathews or Rhenn Larson or "Rebecca."

So much larger than life.

CHAPTER 25

The clouds are back, floating under my feet. But this is different. This is a whole new level of cloud walking. I can feel my eyes bulging with little love hearts every time I think about Ben. I'm exhilarated. I'm nervous. And I'm scared.

Things are going so well for me. I almost want to knock on wood or whatever you're supposed to do to keep the good times rolling. Throw some salt over my shoulder?

But what bad thing could possibly happen? I'm rising up. The lion is filling out. And *Rhenn and Friends* is coming along. Okay, sputtering, but nobody needs to know that.

I try not to think too much about how I'd written *After The End* on a clunky laptop with sticky keys, sitting on uncomfortable hospital chairs as my mom slipped further and further out of reach.

I try not to think about how much I had looked to Rhenn and Madeline to carry me far away from the terrible fear of losing Mom. I try not to think that about that at all. Otherwise, panic will set in.

Writing had been therapy back then, my exorcism, and my savior.

Writing will always be my savior, but I'm journeying out of the dark woods of hopelessness into a mountain meadow bathed in sunlight. A place where I want to stay. With Ben's support, perhaps I can do my own interviews and, maybe even, meet some fans.

That's a wonderful dreamy future, but I need to focus on the now. Right now, I have to figure out what to do about Rhenn. Return him to his eternal slumber and resurrect myself? Or jolly him along for Virginia's sake . . .

Winter came early with a sudden overnight dumping of snow that melted almost as suddenly as it arrived. I get up from my desk and stand by my office patio doors, looking out across the backyard, watching tree limbs shiver in the breeze, thinking about Ben's words. *I think you should follow your heart.*

"Follow my heart," I repeat absentmindedly. He sure makes it sound easy. Maybe it is. I flick off the light and head upstairs for the night.

A mere twenty-four hours later, Virginia starts her innocent questioning about how many words I'm written so far, and how long until I'm done? I don't have the courage to tell her the bad news. I tried. I really tried. But everything I wrote was dead on arrival. The book is over. Amy is done. But—how will she take the news?

Sleep eludes me. Every time I close my eyes and start drifting down to the wonderful watery world of Sleepy Land, worries rise up and stop my journey short. The broken record player is back, spinning around and around, analyzing my every thought. Am I sure the book is over? Can I get a little more mileage out of Falco? No, I conclude every time. I'm just not that person anymore.

And what about Virginia—how do I break the news to her? Should I just blurt it out? Or tell her in public, so she'll be forced to keep a lid on her anger?

There are a lot of other things to consider, lots of stuff that I can't quite remember because it's—let me check.

It's six forty-seven in the morning. I sling my arm over my eyes. Another sleepless night. My brain feels like a congealed mess. I have a low level head buzz. Stress is gnawing hungrily on my innards like a pack of rats. I feel like my eyes are going to fall out of my head if I don't get some decent sleep, and soon.

I peel the covers back and sit up on the edge of my bed, pinching the bridge of my nose. Maybe an early morning run will help clear my mind. Help me find some answers. So I pull on my leggings, shoes, top and hoodie, and head outside.

The wintry sky is lightening from black to midnight blue, which really should be called God Awful Hour of the Morning blue, but nobody asked me. I set off on a brisk pace, pulling in deep breaths of cold, crisp morning air.

Snow crunches under my feet. Dead leaves lay encased in ice like frosty jewel cases. The sun begins to rise, breaking over a misty shrouded furze of trees.

Life is swirling around me, picking up speed. First with the Amy Mathews rocket ship ride up to success, followed by fat advance checks.

Then Ben, kissing him, telling him everything, and now this turmoil brought on by Amy's early retirement. I look up at the sky, a dome of fading stars, where Mom might be looking down on me, watching over me, where I can always find my bearing.

Mom and I used to park at the beach, lay on the hood of the car, and look up at stars in the sky, listening to the ocean crash in the distance. Stargazing always made my problems feel insignificant. I liked feeling like a speck of sand on a giant galactic beach.

I pick up the pace, trying not to think about Mom too much. That will carry me down the long road of anger, despair, and loss—a weary road that I've traveled for far too long. For now, I need to get my blood flowing. I need to raise my body temperature. I need to figure out how to break the bad news to Virginia.

I slow to a fast-paced walk, pumping my arms to help chase away the cold. *You should just tell her*, a little voice says from within. *Just say it.*

That's something Ben would most likely agree with. And it seems simple enough, but my stomach twists with nervous anticipation.

How would we tell the fans? Maybe Virginia can go on a morning talk show and tell the world that Amy needs to take a break. Just a little one. She'll be back!

She's moving to Seattle. She needs a change of pace. She'd lived on the stuffy East Coast for her whole life, and wanted to experience something new, something different, something *vibrant*.

I can hear Virginia now, blabbing on a podcast.

"And I just fell in love with—everything! Did you know the Pacific Northwest is home to the largest temperate rainforest in the world?" Then she'll talk about the *vibe*—that's a word Amy would use—and how Seattle is so *hip*. Seems like another one. She'll tell her audience that Amy feels like so much has happened since she wrote *After The End*, and she needs to some take time to recharge.

The world will go on. Amy's readers will read other books. There will be an initial flurry of half-true articles. David won't be too happy. But Virginia . . . what about her? We still have the house and lots of money. We'll just have to get through it somehow.

On my way home, I resolve to tell her as soon as I can. No more anguish. No more avoiding the topic. No more lies. I hurry up the drive, go inside, and stop cold. Virginia stands in the kitchen, making a cup of coffee.

"Hey," she says, glancing over at me as I walk over. "You're up early."

"Oh, hi. Yeah, I couldn't sleep."

"Everything okay?"

My heart thuds in my chest. I'd expected a few more days of mulling it over, maybe even a change of mind. But here I am, staring down the barrel of *the* opportunity.

"Not really . . ." I say, walking to the bar stool and sitting down at the kitchen bar.

"What's up?" she asks, heaping teaspoons of ground coffee into the filter. She has no idea. None at all. I can make something up. Anything would do. She's pre-coffee. She won't notice my flubbing. Except, I will.

Tell her now. "Um . . ."

"Um?" she asks, glancing toward me. "Sounds terrible."

My mind goes blank. All the fancy words, the easy-peasy conversation that I'd just had with myself, disappear. The Seattle story. It's all gone, except—"Jinny, it's over. The book is done. I can't write it. I'm not that person anymore."

She stops shoveling coffee.

I'm not sure if I should expand on my feelings or what, but Virginia, speaks up. "You sure?" she asks.

That she doesn't attack me, or tell me that I'm a nobody, or strong-arm me makes me want to weep. I nod my head slowly, sadly, kind of in disbelief. "I am."

She presses her lips together and stares at the coffee machine. "Not like I didn't see it coming . . ." She shrugs and looks up at me. "All right. I'll tell David."

And she leaves the kitchen.

CHAPTER 26

Over the following few days, Virginia refrains from blasting me with her fury. For that, I am grateful. But she's professionally distant. That's worries me. She'll come around, I reason. There will be a slew of Amy related events to keep her busy, marking the announcement of Amy's retirement. Maybe she'll find a new direction in life. Maybe even, dump Dillon.

So I try to keep up a normal routine: seeing Ben, making myself available in case Virginia wants to talk (she doesn't), and writing.

About a week later, I find myself working later than usual, polishing up my latest chapter of "Rebecca." Then I yawn, stretch, close the document, and walk into the kitchen for a snack. I'm rounding the corner of the kitchen island, when I catch a snippet of a familiar shoe that instantly stills me.

Dillon.

He's lying on my favorite chaise, one leg splayed to the side, the other stretched out before him, his grimy shoe resting on my Tiffany blue chenille. My heart starts hammering. How could Virginia bring him back here? But my initial anger dims against my rising alarm. Virginia lies on the adjacent couch as still as a corpse.

"Jinny?" I ask, going to her and gently shaking her shoulder. "Are you okay?"

There's a dull reek in the room, smelling like stale food and decomposing plants. Pot. And now they're vegetating in a stoned stupor. She rouses and wipes some drool from the corner of her mouth. "Hey," she says dazedly.

She's conscious. Now onto the next order of business. "What is *he* doing here?" I mouth, pointing at Dillon.

"Oh, that. Yeah, sorry. We just stopped by for a second. He was just leaving. Weren't you, babe?"

No answer.

I look over at the person in question. He doesn't seem to be 'just leaving' anywhere, besides reality.

"He needs to leave, Jinny," I say between clenched teeth. "Now."

"Yep," she says, pushing herself up to a sitting position. "Hey babe, my sister says you need to go."

I gape at her, willing jabs of electricity to fly from my eyes and sizzle Virginia's sleep-creased face. "Why are you blaming this on me?" I whisper fiercely.

Then Dillon stirs. "Tell your sister to fuck off," he says, rolling over on his side, back facing us, both shoes firmly resting on my pretty blue chenille.

I turn back to Virginia, furious. "You get him out of here *now* or I'm calling the cops."

"I'm up! I'm up . . ." replies Dickhead. "I was just kidding. Geez. Your sister is right. You really do have a stick up your butt." Then he slowly stands up. "Can I get a drink before I go?"

Before either Virginia or myself can reply, he walks to the fridge. "You can have some tap water, Dillon," I say, my voice shaking with anger and fear. "Looks like you could use some."

He scratches his head and pulls the fridge door open. "Hey Jinny, are there any beers left?"

Virginia scoots past me and goes to the fridge, eyes glazed over. "Maybe you should get one at the 7-11," she says. She leans in close to his face and mouths, "Anywhere but here."

"Gotcha," Dillon says, closing the door. "I'll take you up on that offer, Eugenia. Tap water it is."

Suddenly, I'm not so glad I offered. I walk to the cupboard and retrieve the smallest glass we stock, one meant for a single shot of espresso, fill it with water and hand it over.

"Thanks," Dillon says, lifting it up and regarding the meager portion. "Cheers." And he sips it. "So how are your books coming along?" he asks in a companionable voice that sends chills down my back.

"Fine."

I never liked Dillon much, even before I found about his red rose fetish. I thought he was rude and arrogant. I could barely bring myself to acknowledge his presence, and he reciprocated with pointed silences. Now that I know *he* was the stalker, I can barely disguise my contempt.

"Virginia says you're done with Amy Mathews?"

"Something like that."

I glance at Virginia. Her eyes look like they've been set on fire. Dillon's eyes, however, are glittering with menace. Virginia half-sits, half-sprawls on the bar stool, oblivious to Dillon's precipitous mood.

He tosses the rest his water down his throat. "Well, that just won't do. Me and Virginia could use the money."

I blink stupidly at him, stunned. Excuse me? Me and Virginia—as in getting married? As in planning a future together? And I'm the cash cow that's supposed to fund this ordeal? While he carefully places the glass on the counter, I mutter, "Why don't you get a job if you need some money?"

"What?" He looks up at me, head cocked to the side as if his hearing suddenly failed. "What was that?"

Virginia speaks up, finally. "Leave her alone, Dillon. She didn't mean it."

"Shut up, Virginia."

I look at my sister, who's suddenly returned from wherever she's been. Her eyes, for the first time I have ever seen, register fear.

Dillon's eyes, however, snap with unspent violence. *"What did you just say to me, Piss Drinker?"* he asks, advancing on me.

But before I can utter a single word, he grabs me by the neck and drives me backwards across the kitchen until the counter catches me painfully and the back of my head slams against a cupboard.

"Let her go!" Virginia cries, rushing over to us and throwing her herself on Dillon's back. Her arms scrabble around his neck, trying to loosen his iron grip. All to no affect. Dillon squeezes his hand tighter around my neck. I sputter, gasping for air, watching contentment wash over his face. He seems fascinated. Relaxed, even.

Dillon easily holds off Virginia with one muscled arm, the same gym-honed arm that she had gushed about on many occasions. She screams and rakes her fingernails across his face. He hisses and tosses her off like a sack of potatoes. She lands with a painful yelp, and in the blurry corner of my eye, I can see that she's disoriented and moving slowly. Far too slow . . .

My vision dims. A tight rasping sound echoes loudly in my ears. In the aperture of my narrowing sight, I can see only Dillon's dilated eyes, cold and black.

He releases me suddenly, laughing that cruel laugh of his. I drop to the counter, gasping and grabbing at my neck, pulling in great gushes of life-sustaining air.

Then I hear his calm voice behind me. "I *said*, me and Virginia could use the money. But apparently you want to follow your heart. Well, I'm here to make sure you follow your heart all the way up to *The End*."

CHAPTER 27

I want to do something brave like I'd seen all my smart-mouthed heroines do in the movies. Punch him in the kisser. Knee him in the balls. But I'm too stupefied with fear to even move.

His eyes are still dilated with pleasure he'd drawn from choking me. Any smart remark will probably send me catapulting down a steep and notoriously short ramp to death. An accident, he would surely claim. Virginia may or may not testify against him, I honestly don't know. Lawyers would pore over their piles of paperwork, thinking about legal strategies, thinking about their conviction rate.

My untimely end would be described to a jury in court proceedings and poster board presentations like a fourth grade science fair. The jury would find him guilty or not guilty; it doesn't matter. I'll be long gone by then.

So I stand rooted to the floor, my legs immovable stumps. I'm scared to run. I'm scared not to run.

"Why don't you leave, Dillon," Virginia says, getting up to her feet. "Just go. We won't say anything. Right, Genie?" She looks at me. I look at her, unable to reply. It wasn't a question anyway. "We won't say anything," she says.

Not now, I think to myself. But I certainly intend to race to the local precinct and press any and all available charges against Dillon, just as soon as I can rid us of his dangerous presence.

"We talked about this, Virginia," Dillon says, leaning against the kitchen counter and folding his arms. "You had your chance to keep her writing. To get her to keep churning out those vampire books. But you couldn't do it. Now I'm going to take over."

So Virginia colluded with Dickhead? I feel like I'm in free fall. Not only had she told him about Amy Mathews and Piss Drinker in full excruciating detail, but she came up with some plan to keep me pumping out books? Is that what drove her to cut herself that terrible night? The two-fold pressure of Dillon pushing her to keep me writing books and my desire to move on?

My hands shake. I tuck them under my armpits. It's one thing to read about scary happenings in novels. But to actually live through a near strangulation and stand across the kitchen from the unrepentant perp suddenly freezes all my faculties.

"Yes, I know that's what we talked about," Virginia replies, "but you can't *force* her to do anything, Dillon. Not here in reality. She has to have *some* volition to keep writing."

"Vol-*what*?"

"Volition. Will power," Virginia says, without a trace of condescension. A smart move, considering his physical advantage.

They're speaking to each other as if I don't exist. I so want to be offended, but there's only one thing that matters. Getting Dillon out of the house. Now. And if I can't get him to leave, I have to get to my cell phone so I can text Ben and tell him to call the police.

"I'll write whatever you want," I say. They both look at me. "I'll write it," I say in what I hope is a believably casual tone of voice. Easy. And carnival sounds ring in my head. A heckler calls out: *Hey hey hey! You want a best seller? I got one right here for ya. Step right up. Step right up!* "I mean, I'm already forty-five thousand words into the next book. I can finish that up and Virginia and I can plan book five. No big deal." The dazzling frenzy of lights in Dillon's eyes begins to fade. "All we need is for you to leave, Dillon. And you have my word."

It's a clumsy trap. But I was the best I could do.

"Forty-five thousand words?" he asks dubiously. He looks at Virginia. "Is that, like, a whole book?"

"Typically ninety-thousand is a whole book," she replies. "But Genie writes to eighty thousand and nobody minds. Obviously."

Dillon is dumb all right, but he's violent and irrational. I don't want to raise suspicions, not sure what he'll find suspicious. But he seems to like my line about writing a bestseller—*hey hey hey!*—so I venture carefully down that path. "I can finish up the book in two months tops. Maybe even sooner. I can start today."

My plan seems to be working. Virginia, thankfully, is also trying to shoehorn him out of the front door. Once he crosses that hallowed threshold, the only place I'm going to put my dedicated effort is making sure he spends as much time as possible behind bars.

My cell phone rests on the counter about three feet from where Dillon stands. There is a clock on the microwave, but I pray he wouldn't notice. "What time is it?" I ask rhetorically, and boldly move toward my cell phone.

There it is, a mere five feet away, sitting on the counter. I focus on my phone like a drowning man reaching for a lifebuoy. Two steps away. One. I reach for it—and Dillon snatches it away.

"It's five-forty," he says, slipping my phone in his front pocket. "Time to get started."

I suppress an urge to demand phone back. Who in the hell does he think he is? But one look in his dilated eyes, feeding off of my fear, tells me exactly who he thinks he is: a real live Teflon Tommy.

A few months ago, I'd read *The Ice Man* by Philip Carlo, a book about a mafia contract killer. I realize suddenly, irrevocably, that Richard Kuklinski, the cold-blooded killer behind John Gotti's long bloody reign bears eerie similarities to Dillon.

I don't know Dillon's past or what sort of violent upbringing mangled his mind, but I'm pretty sure I don't need to know. The similarities are more than enough for me: the murderous gleam in his eyes, the hair trigger temper, and the same enjoyment of cool-blooded violence. It's entirely possible, I realize as my stomach roils with fear, that Dillon could very well have an unsolved murder to his name. Maybe more.

"Dillon," I begin very slowly, very gently, as if speaking to a person on the verge of a psychotic break, eyeing the intercom all the while. "Dillon, I think it's time for you to leave. What you've done is illegal. It's called assault and battery. But I'm not interested in making life difficult for you." I slowly move toward the intercom. There's a red panic button there. One push will summon the police, who will arrive quick smart (because we're high paying customers) and find Dillon standing in my kitchen, with two eyewitnesses to his crime. "We can work out the details of the book when we've all had a chance—"

His gaze flicks to the intercom.

He sees it. I do too.

I bolt. He lunges.

I dash to the little red panic button, stretching out my hand, index finger hungry for the point of impact. So close. Just a few more inches. And then—

I clatter to the ground, Dillon holding tight to my legs. I kick furiously, trying to wriggle out of his grip, while he worms himself on top of me.

I'd done some preliminary research about self-defense for the last book in the *After The End* series. I wanted to find some original ways to choreograph fights. I learned that a well-timed punch to the bridge of the nose could kill instantly. If I can just chop the side of his neck, I can incapacitate him. But that's only if I can get my arms free.

He has me pinned, impervious to my ill-timed kicks and bites and panic-stricken struggling. Virginia launches herself on Dillon, for all the good it will do. I hear her shrill voice, "You said you wouldn't hurt her!" But Dillon shrugs her off, and she clatters to the floor again.

"Get the—Jinny, the—" The button! But I can't get my mouth working against the hot rush of adrenaline and fear. And anyway, she's moving far too slow. It's far too late.

Dillon holds my arms down with his knees, pinning me to the ground, eyes glittering, face flushed. He pulls back his right arm, hand bunched into the fist.

"Jinny!" I scream, pissing my pants. "Jinny! Help me!"

Pain explodes across my temple and radiates down my neck, jarring my vision. Dillon hits me again, a thundering right hook, somewhere on my chin. And then, mercifully, everything goes black.

CHAPTER 28

A door slams shut. I think I can hear drilling; a blurry zooming sound that lulls me back to watery unconsciousness. I'm drifting just below the surface, and I want to stay there. I want to drown.

Sometime later, I hear the sound of doors slamming shut somewhere inside the house. I hear a distant scream. And I feel my my eyes flutter open.

My vision is fuzzy. Above, I can just make out some pink stripes on the ceiling. Exposed fiberglass, I think. Slowly I push myself up to sitting as the room swirls around me. I look around and my heart sinks like a weighted corpse. I've been dumped in the upstairs attic, I realize with a surge of outrage.

Dumped in the attic like a piece of garbage! But cold hard understanding snuffs out my fury. Dillon's voice strikes my mind like sledgehammer: *I'm here to make sure you follow your heart all the way up to The End.*

I've been relocated. Permanently.

I press my hand against my throbbing temple. With the other, I gently touch my lower lip, feeling the contours, trying to gauge the damage. It's swollen and painful all right. Slowly, I draw back my shaking fingertips and dare to look. I see light colored blood, nothing venous, and spittle. I quickly run my tongue along the back of my teeth, feeling for loose ones. All present and accounted for.

Then I look around my new living quarters. Virginia and I called it the Dungeon because it had been partially finished by the previous owner. It's dark and dank despite the one tiny dormer window.

It's also the dumping ground for all of our unwanted crap. Well, one man's trash is a desperate man's treasure. So I pull in a big breath and struggle up to my feet. I'm sure I can find something useful in the boxes of stuff that we'd carelessly tossed aside, something lifesaving. Maybe I'll find a pack of gum and some dental floss so I can rig up a gun like MacGyver. I open the first box and find books, books, and more books. Maybe not.

The rest of the boxes are equally as disappointing. After I find a box of Mom's old clothes that I'd carefully folded and stored, I break down in tears and slowly close the flaps. I don't have the strength to wander down Memory Lane.

So I sit down and look around. Am I really locked up like captive? Just to be sure, I check the door and find it locked of course. The 'window' doesn't matter. I could probably fit my arm through the opening, but nothing more. I can scream, but Dillon will hear me first.

I'll just have to wait until he leaves to go somewhere. So I lay down on a musty single mattress, arm slung over my forehead, and stare up at the half finished ceiling. Then I pull a musty towel over my face and will myself to sleep.

During the first day of my incarceration, I stubbornly bide my time, detailing my every grievance against Dillon and Virginia. Fuck him. And fuck her, too. Her betrayal burns as hot and as painful as a brand, her words seared onto my heart forever: *You said you wouldn't hurt her*!

So my own sister had colluded with that psycho. My mind feels like jelly, unable to comprehend the evil tidings that swirl around in my sister's twisted head.

She's no sister of mine. She's dead to me now.

Soon, I'll find a way to push the panic button and summons the police. Soon, I'll rid myself of these two terrible leeches. I lustily envision the day of their arrest and picture in great detail the defeated hang-dog expressions they'll both wear in court, along with their baggy-ass jailhouse jumpsuits.

Dillon will be skinnier by the time sentencing rolls around, his carefully honed biceps deflated and small, the anvil weight of the justice system weighing him down. He'll look weak and defeated. And he'll cry, oh yes. He will cry.

He'll sob and whimper pathetically, pressing his dirty fingers against his eye sockets, while the judge's voice rings out in the courtroom, sentencing him to maximum security prison where he'll spend the next ten years scrubbing urinals. Virginia too. She can scrub the toilets.

That juicy daydream seduces me wholly, occupying the long hours that stretch before me. It becomes my sustenance, my reason to live, the proverbial fire in my belly that drives me to think of ways to survive this terrible situation, to never give up hope.

They can keep me prisoner, but they cannot make me write. My characters are loyal only to me. Falco had tucked away his wings. Rhenn had retracted his hollow incisors. Amelia and Maxim had retreated to their English countryside manor home, where they remain in respectful stasis, while I go into survival mode.

Soon Dillon and Virginia will relent, and we'll discuss the terms of my release.

I'll agree to whatever Dillon demands. Total silence? Absolutely. Won't go to the police? Never. Forget it ever happened? Already forgotten! Here I'll smile a big shit-eating grin and offer up a few words of sympathy. You didn't know what you were doing, did you? Yes, absolutely, drugs make you do crazy things. I forgive you both. I forgive you so much that it hurts, *you piles of human excrement.*

Across the forefront of my mind, a news ticker runs: *Absolute scum of the earth. Pathetic writhing mealworms. Dumber than a single cell amoeba.*

I'll agree to put something in writing because Dillon will be stupid enough to ask me to do it. The terms of my release, the exact legalese, sends me off on a fresh rant. Of course he'll draft something up himself, written in cramped barely legible handwriting that will make my skin crawl.

He'll pepper his missive with legal terms, which will make his illiteracy stink all the more. I imagine myself suppressing the urge to line out his spelling mistakes. "I (insert name) do, hereby, promice to hold, Dillon Thomas and Virginia Ward, harmless of any and all grievanses . . ."

"Sign here, press hard," I say out loud, envisioning him sliding the document my way. And I'll smile, reassuring them that I'd already forgiven them—water under the bridge, I swear! And I would never, *ever*, go to the police. No way. *You stinking lump of human feces. You pathetic—*

I hear footsteps outside the door. A shadow falls. Locks on the outside of the door rattle. I get up, dread stirring in my guts. And the door swings open.

Virginia stands in the threshold, holding a tray. My knees weaken at the sight of her.

In my earlier days, I'd written clumsy scenes describing "lower mandibles gaping slightly from shock," but I had never experienced the slackening of my own jaw. That is until I watch Virginia slowly cross the room and struggle to place a tray on top of a rickety old desk.

"Jinny?" I ask, afraid to go to her, afraid to touch her. "What happened to you . . ."

CHAPTER 29

Virginia looks like Ben had on our first date, except her bruises aren't fake. Her lower lip is swollen and protruding. There's a bruised graze mark on her right cheek. I bring my trembling fingers up to my own cheekbone as if touching hers. Her left eye is swollen half shut; her unharmed right eye telegraphs fear and dread.

"This is for you," she says, gaze flitting around the room, looking anywhere but at me.

I recover somewhat from my shock, and go to her, placing my hand on her shoulder. She flinches when I touch her and tries to pull away. But I take her by the shoulders, trying to catch her gaze. She stares down at the pea green carpet, while tears slide down her pale cheeks.

"I'm so sorry," she whispers, her chin quivering. She's sorry for betraying me, for conspiring with that dangerous criminal. But now her plans have gone horribly wrong. She shakes her head slowly. "I deserve it. I deserve it all. I'm a stupid jealous simpleton . . ."

"Jinny . . ."

"I should have listened. I should have—" She breaks off and looks at the door, alert to any sound heralding Dillon's arrival. "I should get going," she says in a quiet voice. "I'm not allowed to stay."

I glance at the door, infected with her fear. Dillon could easily overpower us both. And if he arrives in a rage, he'll use Virginia's infraction as a reason to rain blows on us both. I look again at Virginia's face, thinking that she probably can't take much more. Thankfully, the hallway is silent.

"I should have listened to you," she continues in a whisper. "You were always a better judge of character. It's like when your dog doesn't like someone, but you blame your dog for being jealous. You knew there was something wrong with Dillon, but I didn't listen. I didn't want to admit it."

I ignore her unflattering metaphor because we have more important things to discuss. "What does he want with us? Why is he doing this?"

She meets my gaze. I have to look away. A little blood vessel had broken in her 'good' eye, filling the white of her eye with red. "He wants book four and five . . . and more."

He wants it or *you* want it? I want to ask, but one glance at her condition tells me the truth. Maybe she had schemed with

Dillon, but nobody, not even Virginia, would put themselves through this just to keep their day job.

"He's insane," I mutter, thinking back to his flower frenzy. "Totally fucking crazy. Well, I'm not lifting one measly fucking finger for him. You tell him—"

"He wants me to tell you that—that he wants a page a day or . . ."—she clenches her jaw—"or I'll pay for it."

"Oh my God," I whisper, reaching for my sister's cold hands. I squeeze, trying to bolster our collective morale. I don't know if I can produce a page a day under duress. Brain doesn't typically do well with deadlines, let alone threats to our existence. I think about Rhenn, Falco, Madeline, Amelia and Maxim—all lying dormant somewhere out of reach. Perhaps fatally dormant. I'm not sure.

Virginia looks at the tray. "I brought some paper . . . and a pen."

A ray of hope suddenly illuminates an idea. Dillon just wants one page. All I have to do is regurgitate some nursery rhyme. Dillon can peruse my daily offering, none the wiser, and leave my sister alone.

But then Virginia speaks, shattering my clever plan. "A publishable page. He wants book four in the couple of months that you promised."

"What?!" I drop her hands and back away, all the way to the dingy mattress, and sit down. "That's not possible. I was just— that was bullshit to get him out of the house."

"Keep your voice down!" she hisses and slinks over, sitting down on the springy mattress next to me. Nervously, she reaches for my hands like Mom used to do when she was scared. She drops her voice into a whisper so soft I have to lean in to hear. "We need to work together. We need to come up with a plan."

I nod slowly, numbly. Of course we do. But what kind? Mine had just been decapitated. Then another idea comes to me. "You need to push the panic button." I mouth the words, paranoid that Dillon had somehow developed superhuman hearing. "Can you get to it?"

She shakes her head. "He installed metal boxes over all the intercoms. I'd need tools and time. And I'm not allowed out of his sight." Another swift arrow pierces my hope.

"Can you make any calls? Where's your cell phone?" I ask.

"Same place as yours."

In Dillon's pants pocket.

"I'll open the dormer window and start screaming."

"Nobody will hear you," she says. "Except Dillon . . ."

We both fall silent.

Then I have an idea. "Can you get to your email?"

She shakes her head. "He's doing all the 'interneting.' I don't have access to anything. He cut the phone lines too."

"You need to run. You need to escape, climb over the wall, do whatever you can, but you need to run and tell someone. Tell them . . ."

She doesn't even bother to shake her head this time. The sad, forlorn look in her eyes tells me everything I need to know.

"He said he'll kill you if I run."

"Oh," I say, the breath punched out of me.

Cold fear washes over me. There was a short period in my writing life that I had toyed with the idea of writing murder mysteries. I liked the idea of coming up with puzzles and ways to outwit my smarty-pants readers.

So I started some preliminary research on how to actually disappear a body. I looked to nonfiction for information; true stories of how real murderers actually did it.

In addition to reading *The Ice Man*, I'd read books about other contract killers, like *The Butcher* and *Murder Machine*. Then I'd read about the minds of serial killers and watched some interviews. That was an even more depressing topic than vampires. At least vampires valued life, however grotesque, at least they weren't psychopaths, well, not my vampires. Anyway, I gave up on that idea.

But all of my accumulated knowledge rises to the forefront of my mind as I sit next to my sister, looking at her swollen lip and bloodshot eye. I know there are many disturbing ways to kill people and hide their bodies. If Dillon kills me, the chances were pretty damn good he'll get away with it.

"Maybe you shouldn't run," I conclude.

We both fall into morose silence.

"I gotta go," she whispers.

I don't think I can write to save my own life, but maybe I can write to save hers.

"I'll do it, Jinny. I'll finish the book."

CHAPTER 30

After Virginia left, I sat on the edge of the bed for what felt like hours, trying not to panic, but panicking anyway, desperately wishing I could put my arms around Ben's waist and cry. But I can't do that. I can't even contact him. I wonder, in a dull state of alarm, how many messages he sent and how many Dillon had cruelly replied to.

Dillon is in charge of my relationship now. I'm sure he'll take great pleasure in eviscerating Ben with a breakup. Maybe he'll toy with him and make him think I'm cheating—as if.

Oh, Ben. I think back to all magical times that we had shared together. Times that seem like distant memories now. Our first disaster date. How he showed up at the hospital. The walk and talk on the beach. The kiss. The song he wrote for me. I remember that in great detail . . .

He'd invited me over to his house for dinner. *Pizza and beer, no pressure.* He lived alone in a cozy two bedroom cottage in the historical part of town. I sat on a beanbag in his living room under the soft glow of fairy lights. A fish tank burbled on a shelf, a soft pleasant sound that relaxed me, while fish darted hither and yon, their delicate fins trailing behind them like tiny laces.

I remember him sitting on a stool in front of his Randall four-speaker and amplifier setup, cradling a guitar in his lap. Then he started to play a delicate, otherworldly sound.

The guitar was a Paul Reed Smith, he'd explained to me, with mother of pearl birds soaring down the fret board. He'd saved up for four months to buy the guitar, a beautiful instrument that he used to channel sounds.

There was a row of pedals down by his feet that he had fastened onto a homemade chipboard box. There was a loop petal, distortion, one I called 'rock and roll' and a few others that he tapped occasionally, doing what sounded like nothing to my untrained ear.

I watched him in the shadows as he conjured up a driving sound filled with whale song and delicate minor notes. A surreal, dreamy sensation washed over me. That Pewgenia sat in a guy's living room, listening to him play guitar, seemed impossible.

Certainly that was an incredible circumstance for Piss Drinker. Looking back, I realize that was the moment that Pewgenia finally started to die, taking Amy along with her. After that, Amy Mathews was like a foreign correspondent, writing dispatches from the Land of the Dead.

I remember the soundscapes Ben created on his guitar, feeling like flotsam floating under the sea.

Then he sang. "She's my one / my all / my evening twirl / my blue-eyed girl . . ."

A chill raced over my skin. Was he singing about me? No, I thought, chopping that hope off at the knees. Not a chance. Boys write songs about beautiful ethereal women or pneumatic blonds with big fake boobs. Boys did not write songs about Pewgenia, the Piss Drinker.

When the song came to an end, about five minutes later, he flipped a few switches, killing an ambient buzzing sound, and turned to me. "So what did you think?"

"I thought it was amazing," I replied, feeling like I'd been put in a trance.

"I wrote it for you."

Did I hear that correctly? I looked at his shadowed figure. "What?"

I'd heard all those songs on the radio, songs that were so clearly written for special someone who had enchanted (or cursed) the singer into paroxysms of inspired song writing. But those were mythical girls, the Monica Schaffers of the world, not plain girls like me. Nobody sang songs about us.

"Do you know of any other blue-eyed girls?" he asked, putting down his guitar, walking over, and sitting down next to me. My heart thumped unevenly. "Cuz I don't."

"You mean it?" I asked, feeling like the luckiest girl on the planet. "You wrote it for me?"

He laughed. "I promise I wrote it for you."

And then he kissed me, carrying me off into the deep blue sea.

Well, the deep blue sea is vast, dark, and lonely now. And Virginia's words, never far from my mind, came back to me. *I'm a stupid jealous simpleton.* What is jealous about? Had she possibly meant me? I actually scoff.

What did I have to be jealous about? Amy Mathews's success was all hers. I just did all the lonely grunt work. She couldn't possibly be jealous about my relationship with Ben. Clearly, he's not her type.

I watch the light in my room fade to shadows, thinking. Then I shake my head. I don't know. Maybe it was just crazy ramblings. I'd probably think of some real gems too, if I had to spend my every waking hour with Dillon.

I sigh. None of that changes the fact that I need to start writing. Our very survival depends on it.

Night shadows settle in my little garret room. The house falls silent. Brain has probably deserted me along with all my characters, but if either Virginia or I are going to survive this catastrophe, I have to try and find my imaginary friends. I have to coax them back to life.

I flick on a cheap table lamp that I had dumped up here many moons ago. The energy-saving light bulb annoyed me. It gives off a bluish hue of artificial light that seems to cover the room in a faint sheen of plastic. Well, light is light. At least I have some. I pick up the pen and pull a deep, bolstering breath. This isn't going to be easy. But it's my only choice.

I discover that Brain isn't a grumpy gnome in my head, showing up for work whenever he feels like it. Brain is more like an on demand faucet. I just need to prime the pump and out pours some ideas. So I keep writing, hoping for something decent.

Together, Brain and I send out urgent missives to all my long dormant friends. Amelia, my soft-spoken girl, responds almost immediately. She has a lot to share. While she sits in the cockpit of Maxim's sailboat, she fills me in with her latest happenings. She'd romped with Maxim more times than she can count. She thinks she'll probably fall pregnant at this rate.

"If it happens, I won't fear it," she tells me, while the wind jostles her soft curly hair. Then she leans in close. "But you know, there *is* something that's kind of . . . strange. I've been meaning to tell you. I walked up to the village the other day to do some shopping, 'High Street' they call it. Isn't that cute? Anyway, I went down to a local shop to buy some nice new sheets and I ended up meeting the shop owner.

"She was saying stuff about Maxim's . . . ex-wife? I didn't even know he had one. Well, she's gone, apparently. Dead. Maxim forgot to mention that part." She glances furtively over at her lover, who stands at the helm, gazing up at the sails, wind stabbing his steely gray hair. She scoots closer. "Maxim's been acting really strange ever since I asked him about it."

Prior to my personal catastrophe, Amelia was on track to make a very gruesome discovery, but now I have other plans for her. She has absolutely nothing to do with vampires—I don't even know how she feels about them—but she's the only one talking. So I laterally transfer her over to *Rhenn and Friends*.

As I write, I feel bad for hijacking her and taking her away from the cool nights spent in Maxim's arms, but this is an urgent matter. She'll understand. I hope. So I plop her right in the middle of Falco and Rhenn's rivalry, and pray she'll keep on yammering.

Amelia doesn't let me down. Amelia keeps my hand moving. She alone produces my daily word count. She also carries my mind far away from the occasional thumps and screaming matches that rise up from downstairs.

Every morning, like a golden goose pooping out another page, I slip a folded piece of paper under the door with the previous days offering. All this is not made any easier now that my withdrawal symptoms out in full force. I'm sweating and shivering. My head pounds and aches.

And most of the time I'm too nauseas to eat, but Virginia comes once a day with a tray of food, while Dillon stands in the threshold, watching. Virginia's eye is healing, but Dillon's permanent presence is starting to take a toll. She's been a fighter all her life, wresting from life what it wouldn't give freely, always ready for a scuffle.

But as the weeks pass, I begin to feel stronger, while she becomes meek and cowering, an inferior person looking to Dillon for direction. One day, she apologizes for bumping the tray on the edge of the desk and sloshing juice over the rim of a tall glass.

Virginia never apologizes. She bullies and pushes her way through life, with rough words ready on her tongue.

Under Dillon's tutelage, she's becoming vague, like a cartoon slowly getting erased. Long ago, I suspected that Dillon had stolen my Demerol—it was easy and free, perfect for him. Virginia moves a sluggish, uncoordinated speed. I suspect he's keeping her stoned with my stolen medication, but I can't ask, not while he's in earshot. I can only hope and pray that I'm wrong.

But she's like the disappearing girl, cowed and frightened. She's becoming "feminine," Dillon told her one day as she walked docilely out of the Dungeon. It's heartbreaking. It's alarming. And there's absolutely nothing I can do except produce another page and wait for our opportunity to escape.

CHAPTER 31

I keep track of my carbon copy days the same way prisoners have since time immemorial: I scratch lines on the wall. The only variety in my day comes from my characters.

Falco returned. His wings had grown a good two feet since our last meeting. He hadn't lain dormant like I feared. In fact, his quick progression left me running to catch up with him, working in bits of backstory to get the reader to where Amelia found him: lying in a filthy heap, wings battered and bruised, in an inner city gutter.

Amelia has some medical know-how that I wasn't aware of. She cleaned up Falco's wounds and splinted a wing, all the while telling me about her stint as a nurse trainee and how she dropped out of the RN program after a fluid-filled twenty-four hour shift at an emergency room. Things I never knew.

In fact, after all the arguments I'd had with Virginia about finishing the series, I'm starting to enjoy myself. I think if I had some real life distractions, like Ben, then I would still insist on pursuing my writing career as a soloist. But circumstances have changed. I cling to my characters now, desperate for them to get me out of this rapidly deteriorating hellhole.

I'm hungry. I'm cold. And I'm so lonely.

Ben. I think about him almost every minute of the day. I wonder what Dillon has been texting him. I wonder if Ben has forgotten about me. I fill my mind with thoughts of Ben. I live on them. I go over every detail of our time together, every touch, every moment.

I close my eyes and try to remember the feeling of his lips pressed against mine, but I can't feel a thing. The days are cold. The nights are worse. Winter is deepening. And still, nothing has changed. Dillon hasn't left the house once. And I'm beginning to slip into a depression. Will I ever see freedom? If so, how?

This has gotten too out of hand for Dillon to just walk away. He's guilty of kidnapping, holding someone against their will, assault and battery and probably lots more. His only ticket to freedom now is blackmail. Maybe he can somehow intimidate Virginia into silence, but not me. He knows I'll press charges. So what's the answer? Is this my new normal?

The thought of existing up there in the attic for years makes me want to drive that pen into my neck. But I can't do that. If I hurt myself, Dillon will hurt Virginia. If she does anything brave, he'll come after me.

All I know is that I'm going to find a way to get out of here. Someway, somehow. Because where there's a will, there's a way. My inner cheerleader taught me that. Gimme a YAY! Y-A-Y!

In the meantime, I have lives to preserve with my written word.

Dillon had kindly provided me with a folding chair that makes my back hurt and my bum numb. I can only work on the small, uninspiring desk for about an hour before I have to get up and unfreeze my back with a series of awkward stretches and grimaces. I miss my office. I miss my old comfortable coffin of a life. I miss Ben.

I finish a scene whereby Rhenn tries to sink his teeth into Falco's right wing and misses. Falco flies away in a rage, vowing revenge. I stand, stretch, and rub my hands up and down my arms for warmth. At intervals like this, I would normally walk to the kitchen and make myself a cup of tea. But I lost that pleasure long ago.

I'm thinking about Wonder Couch and cozy hearth fires, when I hear the faint buzz of the intercom, followed by clomping footfalls.

I dash to the postage stamp-sized dormer window and look out. My heart rate ratchets up to DEFCON 2. It's Ben. He's here.

He's sitting in his blue mustang, idling just outside the gate. He's leaning out of the car window, arm resting on the doorframe, talking into the intercom. I wave frantically, both arms, but he doesn't see me. He's too focused on the intercom screen to look. I can only hope that his keen sense of perception might detect me. Screw hope. And screw Dillon. I'm going to break the window and start screaming.

I'm rushing to the window, when I hear quick footsteps up the stairs.

I stop cold, listening. The locks outside the door rattle, while a cold sweat breaks out on my skin. The doorknob twists. Hope billows in my heart. Is it Jinny? Coming to say she's found a way to get us out of this mess? Then the door slams open.

Dillon. In a murderous rage. He strides across the room in three long steps, grabs my arm, and shakes me.

"That piece of shit boyfriend of yours is here," he says. "You're gonna tell him it's over. You're going to dump him and tell him you never want to see him again."

And before I can reply, he jerks me across the room, and pushes me down the stairs.

I haven't seen my own house for exactly twenty-seven days. I recognize all the features—the crown molding, the soft wool carpeting, the pale blue tones of paint on the walls—but everything is unfamiliar.

As we move through the house, while Dillon keeps an iron grip on my arm, I notice that the furniture had been rearranged. All of our careful decorating had been obliterated with chaos. There are trails of stains that run along our expensive area rugs. Deep gouges on our wood floors. Newspapers covering our beautiful pieces of furniture, and trash is strewn everywhere.

A distinct malodor hangs in the house, taking me back to the days when we first toured the property, back when the previous owner's corpse had recently been cleared out of a bedroom.

We pass my office, the door mercifully closed. I can't bear to think of the sacrilege. As we enter the kitchen area, I see dirty dishes piled up high in the sink. A puddle of milk lay coagulating on the granite counter top. I looked away, disgusted. Where is Virginia? Why isn't she at least picking up the trash?

Then we turn into the dining room, and I find her tied to a chair, both arms strapped to the arm rests. The sleeve on her right arm is rolled up, exposing the soft white skin on the crook of her arm, marred with tracks. My hands float up to my mouth. So that's how he brings out her "femininity." Drugs.

Upon our five thousand dollar Hermes dining table, I see a film of white powder, hypodermic needles, spoons with folded-over handles, and my stolen pills. My heart sinks down to my feet.

It's confirmed. Demerol. And Virginia is hooked on it.

Then Dillon propels me across the dining room toward the intercom box in the foyer next to the front door.

CHAPTER 32

Dillon smells bad. He reeks of stale cigarette smoke and the pungent odor of someone who hasn't bathed in recent history. I try not to look away when he puts his face in front of mine, his breath washing over me like a noxious tidal wave.

"I'm going to push the button. You're going to talk. And if you say anything like, *Help me! Help me!*"—he throws his hands in the air, mimicking a damsel in distress—"your sister is going to overdose. Fatally. Won't you, Virginia?"

We both look at my sister. Tears fill her eyes. She nods her head in quick little jolts, encouraging me to do the right thing: coldly dump Ben over the intercom like an unwanted piece of trash and save her from her overdose. My heart shatters into a million pieces. But there's a shining ray of hope. The panic button . . . it's there. And it's exposed.

Before my mind whirs out a plan, Dillon pulls out a set of handcuffs from the back of his waistband and roughly cuffs my hands behind my back. "Just in case you decide to do something clever."

Disappointment doesn't crush me. It liquefies me. I can feel my legs nearly give out.

Ben honks his horn. Slowly, I turn to the intercom box in a trance-like state. Dillon stands just off to the side, hypodermic needle in hand. A metal box had been installed over of the intercom, but the lid is propped open.

The screen had already been activated, showing Ben in gray relief. He wears an annoyed expression, verging on the cusp of anger. He's mouthing some words. Dillon pushes the 'talk' button, and Ben's voice breaks through.

"Hello? Hey, listen. I know she's in there. If you don't—"

"Ben?" I ask, voice weak with emotion.

His expression changes instantly. He moves closer to the camera, filling the screen with his beautiful face. I yearn to touch the features that I love so much: his bottom lip, slightly square, his dark blonde mussed hair, his round eyes filled with the magic of the universe.

"Genie," he says softly. His eyes search mine, penetrating my heart. "I've called you so many times. I just—I need to hear it from your own mouth. Did you mean it? Everything you said? Your texts . . . I . . ."

I have no idea what horrible, heartless things Dillon had texted, but I'm sure he took extra special pleasure in torturing Ben.

No! I want to scream. *None of it! I love you so much it hurts. Help me, Ben. Run! Go get help! We're going to die in here...*

I glance at Dillon, standing just off to my right, his hand covering the panel, the panic button specifically, in case I decide to head-butt it probably. I so want to do something as heroic as Madeline and jab my elbow into Dillon's windpipe or sink my fangs into his neck like Rhenn, reveling in his shrieks as I drain his lifeblood in one fortifying gulp.

But this isn't a novel. This is real life bound by hard and fast rules, impervious to imaginative endings. I'm too weak with hunger and heartbreak to do anything clever. And I can't even move my arms. Besides, Dillon holds up a hypodermic needle filled with cloudy fluid, his face impassive, and depresses the plunger. A fat droplet quivers on the tip.

"Yes." I clear my throat, trying to speak through the painful knot. "Yes, it's over."

Ben's hands drop from the screen. He looks away, utterly defeated. I bat my eyelids quickly, trying to stop the rush of stinging tears. He looks back up again, his mouth turned down, his eyes filled with pain. "Can we talk about this? I just—I don't understand what happened. I thought we had something special ... something worth fighting for."

I'd fight the Khmer Rouge for you, Benjamin Walker. And I'd enjoy every minute if your love waited for me on the other side.

"There's nothing to say," I continue in an automatic tone of voice that I don't recognize. I pray that I'm convincing enough for Dillon, but peppered with enough subtle desperation to alert Ben, my ever perceptive Ben.

I focus on sending him a subliminal message—*HELP*! I blink hard, trying to send the message in Morse code. But Ben misses it. He's too shattered to notice.

"I don't understand," he says in a dejected tone of voice, oblivious to my silent pleas. "What did I do wrong?"

Nothing! You're perfect. The most perfect person on this entire planet of eight billion people.

I want to yell, I want to scream, but I see Dillon in my periphery, making the 'wrap it up' signal with his free hand.

"Can I at least come in? See you one last time? I just can't help but think that there's been some sort of misunderstanding. Can we talk in person?"

Dillon runs his finger across his neck. *Cut it off.*

"No, I—I think that would be a bad idea. I'm really busy. I'm just finishing up book four. The deadline is really tight."

"Book four? You mean you're going on with it? *Rhenn and Friends*?"

That he remembered the working title makes me want to weep.

"Yes, four and five." I glance over at Dillon. "Maybe more, I don't know yet."

"But I thought..."

"I really need to go now, Benjamin..." I caress his full name with all the tenderness of a departing lover, memorizing the image of his face before Dillon hits the hang up button. "Please don't call anymore. Or text. I'm sorry that things had to end this way, but it really is for the best."

Ben moves to say something, but Dillon snakes his finger over and hits the kill button. The screen goes black, taking my heart with it. Then he slams the cover shut. I turn to him, numb, waiting for his appraisal of my performance.

"Good job, Piss Drinker." He lowers the hypodermic needle. I dare to breathe. He walks over to our adulterated dining table, sheaths the needle, and tosses it onto the pile of drug paraphernalia. "Looks like *Verge* gets to live, after all."

CHAPTER 33

The short, dark, and very cold days of winter are upon us. I had always loved winter. I looked forward to the sun setting at four, bringing on nightfall and hastening everyone indoors. Winter has so many cozy offerings: evenings by the fire, hot chocolate, warm blankets, and solitude.

But most of all, winter offers relief from the relentless cheerful days of summer that lure people out to parks, festivals, and barbecues. Summer is like the popular girl at school, beaming upon the ones with a social life and casting bright derision on those without. For me, summer always meant watching other people live, laugh, and have fun, while I sat on the periphery, excluded.

Winter is a solitary sport, which suited me great. It's the great leveler, spoiling outdoor fun and chasing everyone inside with bitter winds and rain, where everyone has to sit inside with their miserable selves. Except me. I like my own company.

But not anymore. Looking through the long lens of captivity, I'm dreading the long cold winter nights. Dillon had taken up the job of delivering my once daily meal, making my contact with Virginia virtually impossible.

I have no idea what state she's in, how she's doing, or even what she's doing. And it worries me to distraction. Occasionally, Dillon allows us a few minutes together, always supervised, but those few precious minutes do very little to allay my fears.

Dillon responds to all questions pertaining to Amy Mathews as if he's her new manager. Well, he is. But Virginia could get a message out to David somehow, couldn't she? Occasionally, I get to see her. If I ask casually about Virginia's dealings with the outside universe, Dillon butts into the conversation, reminding us about the 'allowed' topics of conversation. Well, the ones he can understand anyway.

"Elltay eethay esspray. Ideovay allcay. Ooit day!" I say to her in pig latin one day as she turns to go. *Tell the press. Video call. Do it!*

"antcay." *Can't.*

"Yway." *Why.*

"What the fuck?" cries Dillon.

"Yway!" I repeat.

"Ecuzbay ickheadday ancelledkay all eethay omotionspray." *Because Dickhead canceled all the promotions.* She means to say appearances, but you can't dissect words that start with a vowel in pig latin so she picked the next best option. Amy is email only these days. And Dillon is doing all the emailing . . .

"Shut up," says Dillon, propelling Virginia out the door. "That's the last time you'll ever *talk* to Piss Drinker again."

She looks over her shoulder at me, her eyes heavy with sorrow. "I'm osay orrsay." I'm so sorry . . .

"It's okay," I mumble. But it's not. Nothing is okay anymore.

Another day dawns. Another day, another dollar. Except I don't have any. Dollars, that is. Not anymore. I have plenty of days though. I rise from my nest of old towels and pull on the same Hello Kitty sweatpants (found it in a box—one of Virginia's prank Christmas presents) that I've been wearing for thirty-eight days straight, vowing to burn them once this ordeal ends. *If* it ever ends, I remind myself morosely.

Then a depressing wave of futility washes over me. Under what circumstances will this ever end? I think of Victor Frankl's daughter, who lived in the downstairs basement for twenty-five years, bearing children and living her life in a makeshift hovel. Comparatively speaking, the Dungeon is palatial. I even have a tiny window where I can watch life pass me by.

So I do just that. I watch the skeletal tree limbs shake in stiff breezes, shiver in driving rain, and luxuriate under feeble rays of sunshine. I watch a spider spin a web in the corner of the windowpane. I watch snowfall. I watch the stillness when it stops.

Then one day, something happens.

It's about five-thirty in the evening, I guess. The sun had set, draping the front yard in murky shadows. I'm watching a little bird flit from snowy limb to limb, when I hear the front door slam shut downstairs. Someone is leaving the house.

I press my nose against the cold glass, trying to see.

Then Dillon emerges from under the porch roof, walks to Virginia's car, and climbs in. "Please, please, please . . ." I mutter, hope swelling in my heart, bulging painfully against the ventricles. "Please drive away."

He starts up the car and drives down the driveway as the gate swings open. Then he turns onto the main road and drives away, while the gate slowly closes.

This is it! This is it!

I run to the door and scream into the jamb, projecting my voice downstairs and hopefully into Virginia's ears.

"Jinny!" I scream, rattling the door with all the strength I have. Dillon is gone. Now is our chance to escape. "Jinny!"

I hear her quick footsteps up the stairs.

"Genie," she cries from the other side of the door. "I don't have the keys!"

"Go get a pipe or something and bang the doorknob off," I said, pressing my mouth into the crack. "Hurry!"

She runs back downstairs to hunt for a useful implement, and I return to my front yard vigil. I peer into the darkness, searching the shadows with my sharpened animal vision, alive to any movement.

The white landscape, cloaked in shadows, is a paragon of stillness. After what seems like an eternity, Virginia returns, hammering and prying off the locks and stifling sobs.

Finally, the door swings open.

"He's not back yet," I say to her. "But we need to *hurry*."

There's a frightening dazed look in her eyes. "He went to the store. He said he'll be right back. He made me take a Demerol before he left, so I'd be too stoned to move, but I just . . . hid it under my tongue and then I . . . I spit it out when he left."

"Thank God he didn't tie you up," I say, moving past her. "We don't have much time."

Virginia puts her hand on my shoulder. She's sluggish. Too much of the pill must have dissolved on her tongue. "He's a . . . he killed someone, Genie. He—"

I rush of fear sweeps through me. I grab her hand. "We'll be next if we don't hurry." And I pull her down the stairwell.

The house is dark and draped with the same thick stench that I had smelled the day Ben and I broke up. We both run through the kitchen to the back door. The boxes still cover the intercoms, the panic button far out of reach. It will take too much time to pry off the box. We need to escape. Now. I open the door, and together we run across the snow-encrusted lawn. Virginia trips. I look back in just enough time to see her fall.

I run back to her and help her up. "Get up! Hurry!"

She clambers to her feet. She's weak and skinny, as weak and skinny as me. I look around, trying to think.

After the stalker episode, we'd spent considerable time and effort installing an impenetrable perimeter fence that kept all inquisitive Amy Mathews fans securely outside.

I hadn't once considered that my comprehensive security system designed to keep people out, would be equally effective with keeping people *in*. There's an electrical wire than runs along the wall, raised about three inches from the top. I know it's always set at the maximum level, meant to shock any would be visitors out of their sneakers.

Electrocution doesn't discern between friend or foe, and Virginia and I will face the same welcoming jolt as soon as we clamber over the wall. That is, if we can get that high.

Three of the four walls are ten feet high. The wall lining the front of the property is a mere eight, but along with the wire, glass shards are cemented to the top. Virginia and I don't have the luxury of escaping uninjured. We just need to escape with our lives; the rest will heal with time.

"Our best bet is the front perimeter fence," I whisper to Virginia. "We can climb over in that blind spot."

She shakes her head. "The whole fence line is being recorded. He can see everything with my cell phone."

"Does he check the footage?"

"Yes," she says, slipping her hands into her armpits and shivering. Her face is pasty white; there are dark smudges under her eyes. I worry about her ability to get over the wall. "We'll have to try the back fence. He turned the cameras away from there a little while ago. He said he didn't want the lion being filmed."

Dread sinks in my belly like a dead weight. Did he plan on dumping bodies there? I wonder suddenly. If so, he has a far advanced criminal mind than I had ever given him credit for.

Then I immediately feel a surge of relief that he hadn't installed a camera in my room. Maybe he plans to. Maybe he's out buying one now.

"We can climb the lion cage fence to get over the perimeter wall," I tell her.

We won't have to contend with glass shards, but we still have to climb ten feet of chain link, avoid the lion, endure the shock of electricity on the top of the wall and roll off the other side soundlessly, without breaking anything that would hinder our escape into the woods.

"Sure," she says, nodding quickly. "Yeah, okay."

We hurry to the lion enclosure, moving from one puddle of shadows to the next. I blow on my numb fingers and rub my hands together. All the better to climb with. At least I won't feel anything.

We reach the far corner, cloaked in shadows. I peer up at the precipitous wall.

"I'll go first. You follow," I say.

The lion is snoozing at the far end of his enclosure. I pull off my sweatshirt and throw it over my shoulders. Hopefully, it will provide some insulation against the electrical wire when I get up there.

Thick snow had blown in two days previous. It was an idyllic snowstorm with fat fluffy snowflakes that floated around in the atmosphere and settled like dust. Then the wind picked up, swirling and hustling the contented flakes, harrying them into the trees and driving them into the gravel.

For twenty-four hours the world was a horizontal white haze of snow, pummeling down from the white sky. The wind had finally died down, leaving behind two feet of virgin snow and a world as dark and still as death. Our breath freezes in the air. I watch Virginia's blue shivering lips as she speaks. "I'll give you a leg up."

I nod and step onto her clasped fingers, reaching for the highest point on the fence. My fingers, clumsy and stiff with cold, clamp onto the fencing about six feet off the ground. With my other hand, I reach far up further.

Then the lion stirs.

Arms and legs burning, I make it to the top and throw my sweatshirt over the lip of wall, trying to spread the thick fabric wide across the wire, while pinioned against the chain-link fence. My toes dig painfully into the little diagonals. Over the top of the wall, I glimpse the frozen forest just beyond where freedom, glorious freedom can be found.

Headlights flash across the side yard.

"He's back," I whisper. "Hurry, give me your hand."

The lion ambles on over.

She grabs my hand and climbs a few feet off of the ground, her red raw fingers clamped onto the chain-link fencing. She makes alarmingly slow progress, dislodging her right foot, reaching for more height, pulling herself up on shaking limbs.

Tires crunch on the gravel in front of the house.

The lion pulls back his black lips, revealing his huge set of bone-crunching teeth. He nibbles on the toes of Virginia's shoes. Then he rises up on his hind legs, his face even with hers, and rakes his long claws over her fingers on one hand.

She gasps and lets go with the injured hand, dark blood dripping from her fingers.

"Keep going!" I say, reaching down and trying to distract the lion by waving my arm at him. It works for a few seconds. He turns his yellow malignant eyes on me and jumps, his claws narrowly missing me.

I glance up at the house and look for signs of Dillon. Nothing.

The lion sniffs around, a little too interested in Virginia and her bleeding hand. I ball up some snow packed on the top of the wall and chuck it at his giant head.

He shakes the snow from his face, looks up at me, and roars, his deep voice echoing into the still forest. Panic stricken, I look up at the house. And the kitchen light flicks on.

"He's in the kitchen," I whisper, my voice shaking. "Move it!"

Virginia looks up at me, her face strained and white. Then we both hear the ominous creaking of the kitchen door opening and see his dark silhouette.

We freeze. Virginia hangs from the fence like a frozen June bug, while I struggle to keep my toes dug into the fence, my arms resting on the edge of the fence, mere inches from two hundred and twenty volts of arcing electricity.

I hold my breath, watching Virginia, whose hands are shaking, the right one dripping blood where the lion had laid her knuckles bare.

The world is silent, still, and pregnant with terror. Just a few more seconds and he'll turn around and go back inside. Then we'll be home free.

Then the lion lunges at Virginia. She lets out an agonized shriek and falls off the fence, landing on a snow-encrusted bush below and disappearing within.

Dillon breaks and runs toward us.

"Virginia!" I scream. "He's coming!"

Virginia gets up and out of the bush with admirable speed. She's back on the fence, climbing, straining her hand toward me, our fingertips scrabbling for purchase.

I bent down and reached desperately for her. But it's too late. Dillon reaches up and wrenches her off the fence, dragging her, kicking and screaming, away from the enclosure.

He looks like the missing link, hunched over and monstrous, effortlessly dragging Virginia's dead weight across the smooth white terrain. Then he stops and turns back to me.

"You come down off of that wall, Eugenia." I look out toward the dark forest. Just beyond the trees, our neighbors can be found. Help can be found. "You come down now or your sister is lion meat."

"Don't do it!" she cries, hands buried in her red locks of hair that lay bunched in Dillon's fist. He shakes her, while she begs, "Stop . . . don't . . . please . . ." When the shaking stops, she half screams, half sobs, "Run! Save yourself!"

"You come down now and nobody gets hurt," Dillon says. He powers up his fist and lines it up with Virginia's temple. "Or I can keep going until Virginia here learns how to shut her big fat cunt of a mouth."

"You won't hurt us?" I ask, well aware that he could do exactly as he pleases. He has about as much integrity as a suicide bomber, and I have about as much negotiating power as a bug on a windshield.

"Not a hair on your head."

I have no choice. I peer down to the snow-laden ground, ten feet below. The lion paces along the fence, waiting and watching.

And I jump.

CHAPTER 34

As I climb to my feet, Dillon clamps his hand on my upper arm and helpfully jerks me up to standing. He grabs Virginia with his other hand and propels us both inside.

Once there, he maneuvers Virginia over to a dining room chair, sits her down, and starts tying down her arms to the rests. Virginia's eyes grow wide with fear, but she doesn't struggle as if she's used to the procedure and knows what's coming.

I haven't been out of the Dungeon since the day I dumped Ben. But now with some time to look around, I notice that the overall state of the house has slipped into further chaos and filth.

I heard once that a house reflects the interior state of the occupant's mind. It's clear, from the piles of dirty dishes emanating rotten smells, the overflowing trash cans, and a used hypodermic needle lying on the floor, that Dillon is a madman. I had no doubt, but this is madness on a scale I'd never imagined.

I have only a few seconds until Dillon turns his cold penetrating gaze on me. A few seconds to shift the balance of life or death back into our favor. I glance around the kitchen, looking for my dearly beloved.

There it is, resting on a bloodied chopping board. Prankster. Scarily expeditious with rendering down flesh, I stare at the heavy butcher knife, nearly tearing up with relief.

Tired of struggling with my pot roasts, I'd splurged on the heavy rectangular knife at a specialty online store, much to Virginia's amusement. It's a big cleaver that can easily chop through a beef joint. It has a clown red handle made of silicone that gives slightly when squeezed, molding to the compression of my fingers, ready for any demanding task at hand.

After a few practical jokes, whereby Virginia had popped out of the pantry wielding the knife, we started calling it Prankster. I have a thing with good kitchen knives, just like a have a thing with good pens. Thankfully, my thing with knives is about to pay off.

Dillon works diligently to secure Virginia's arms, seemingly unconcerned about my whereabouts. rightfully so. As far as he knows, I'm about as brave as a field mouse.

He assumes I will just watch as docile as a lamb as he tears off a piece of grey duct tape and presses it against my sister's mouth. He assumes I will stand here meekly as she slides into the adjacent chair and rifles through a plastic baggie filled with my stolen Demerol pills. He assumes I will wait with endless patience, while he crushes up a pill on my once gleaming five thousand dollar dining table and mixes the powder with water in the bowl of a bent spoon.

But that's where he's wrong.

He assumed.

Mom's voice breaks into my reverie. *And what happens when you assume things?*

I've spent my time in the Dungeon steeling myself for this very moment. I've listened to agonized screams in my head, and I've hardened myself against them. Over the tenure of my captivity, his animal shrieks have become music to my ears, a special soundtrack that I played over and over again in my mind while I wrote. When I lay on the thin dingy mattress, looking up at the exposed fiberglass, I lustily imagined him *begging* for his life.

While he works on the mound of powder, watching it slowly melt into cloudy liquid, I step to Prankster, grab the handle, and drop my hand down by my side, out of sight, should Dillon trouble himself to look. But he doesn't. Why would he?

Virginia's gaze slides to me. Her eyes, liquid with terror-stricken tears, are begging for help. I lock eyes with her, silently communicating my intent. She blinks a few times rapidly and squeezes her eyes shut.

"You're gonna get a double dose tonight for being so naughty," Dillon says. "You know I don't like naughty girls. Dirty, loudmouthed, trashy girls. That's what you are. You and your sister both."

Prankster comes alive under my quickening pulse. I tighten my hand around the red grippy silicone, pressing against my palm in solidarity. Treading as silent as the lion, I cross the kitchen, driven by a singular animal drive to kill. He continues his monologue, head bent studiously over his handiwork.

"You're both dirty, trashy girls that don't know right from wrong." He inserts the needle into the liquefied mound and siphons up the dome. "That makes me mad. Do you know what happens when I get mad? Hm? Do you?"

Tears stream down Virginia's face. She mumbles something, moving her mouth, the tape pulling her cheeks up and down. Dillon looks up her, expectantly waiting for the answer, even though he'd taped her mouth shut. That's when he catches me in his periphery.

What happens when you assume things?

Dillon turns to me. But it's too late.

I'm standing right over him, looking at the flushed terrain of his face, his eyes wide with surprise.

It makes an ass outta you and me.

And down comes Prankster on his chiseled cheekbone.

There is blood. A great gushing wall opens up on the left side of his face, rimmed with a flap of skin. His cheekbone shines white in the gully of the wound.

He sits there, stunned. Me too. I've never attacked anyone in my whole life, let alone with a meat cleaver. He lifts the flap of skin with shaking fingers and presses it back into place. I grip

Prankster, breathing hard. Blood squishes between my fingers, bringing me back to the task at hand.

I swing again, wildly, aiming for the dead center of his skull.

But he jumps up suddenly, his chair toppling over, one arm raised against my flashing downward swing. With the other, he backhands me, a solid sideswipe that catches me by the temple, sending the Prankster and me clattering to the floor.

While Dillon scurries for the knife, I scramble furiously to release Virginia. She makes frantic muffled sounds and puffs out her cheeks, eyes bulging.

It's a square knot, a knot that can be easily broken I learned in Girl Scouts. I grab a spoon on the dining table and jam the bent handle into the center. It budges.

I jam it in again and wrench the handle upwards, loosening the entire knot. Then I scramble over to her other arm, my heart beating so hard I can hardly see straight. My hands shake. My fingers feel like rubber.

All together, it probably takes about fifteen seconds to loosen both ties, but with Prankster falling into Dillon's frightening grip, it seems like fifteen long years.

I glance up at Dillon, holding a soiled kitchen towel against his gaping cheek. In the other hand, he grips Prankster, watching us, amused almost, none too concerned.

Finally, I free Virginia. She stumbles off of the chair, rips off the tape from her mouth, and together we back away.

"Sit down, Virginia," he says, waving Prankster negligently at the chair she just vacated.

"No. I won't."

Dillon watches her. She watches him.

"You'll have to kill me," Virginia says, gripping my hand. "Me and my sister both."

I don't dare flick a questioning glance her way, thus breaking the sense of solidarity, but I intend to get out of here alive not in a body bag.

Dillon laughs and flips Prankster up in the air, catching it by the handle. Prankster, beholden only to its handler, flashes in the light, the blade sullied by his own blood.

"Frankly, that would solve all of my problems," he says.

"Except the problem of Amy Mathews," I cut in. "Without us, you have nothing."

He peels the bloodstained dishcloth away from his cheek and examines it. "This whole Amy Mathews thing is really starting to piss me off. You've been producing piles of shit, shit that the publisher keeps sending back."

I glance at Virginia for a quick fact check. Her face is blank.

"The royalty checks take ages to finally arrive. Checks that are getting smaller and smaller, I might add. I think Amy Mathews is better off self-publishing. That way I can track all the sales and collect the money. Eliminate the middle man."

"We don't own the rights to any Amy Mathews books," Virginia says. "You can't publish something unless you own the rights. Book four and five are also tied up on contract."

I've never been more grateful for a contract in my entire life.

"I'll make you a deal." He waves Prankster at me. "You're going to write a new book. Virginia is going to slap her ugly mug on it, and I'm going to collect all the money. How's that sound?"

Nobody replies.

I feel like we were back at the very beginning of my upstairs tenure. Back when Dillon revealed his grand master plan of locking me up, while I happily produce book after book, and he kindly helps me reach my 'full potential.'

My mind races, trying to think of something to say, something sufficiently reasonable that will break through his deranged thinking and give me an edge. But I realize, with a sinking heart, that there's nothing I can say to him, not a single word in the known English language that will deter him from this new plan. I have to go back to my standby plan: agree, subsist, and wait for the opportunity to escape.

Except, maybe the opportunity is now.

The syringe that he had so carefully prepared sits on the Hermes kitchen table. Loaded. Dillon holds onto the back of a chair. Weakened? I can only hope. The intercom panels are still locked up tight, the panic button far out of reach. But if I can get to the syringe . . .

Visions of the needle sticking out of his neck rise to the forefront of my mind. I imagine him groping at the emptied syringe with increasing sluggishness, until he sinks onto his knees and slips off to Never-Never Land, where he'd just tried to send Virginia.

I can see it so clearly it hurts. Dillon lying face down on the floor. Unmoving. Virginia and I working the box off the wall. Pushing the panic button. I even feel a surge of relief wash over me, imagining the police breaking down the front door.

"I said," he repeats, resting the blunt edge of Prankster on his shoulder like Paul Bunyan. "How does that sound."

"It sounds really good, Dillon," I reply, trying not to look at the syringe resting so casually on the table, my last bastion of hope. "Sounds great. I'll do it, if it saves my sister and I. And you know what? I have just the book. Virginia never wanted me to write it." A little dash of sibling rivalry, a whiff of treason might be enough to give my 'willingness to write whatever' spiel credibility. *Hey! hey! hey!* "She wanted me to focus on the series. But I've already written another manuscript. It's unagented. I own all the rights . . . I mean, you. You can have the rights. I don't care."

I pause, gauging my progress. Did I go too far with that last line? His eyes are still flashing, but he's easing off his fancy handling of Prankster. Finally, he pulls out a chair and sinks down heavily on the seat.

"You're bleeding," Virginia says, softly. "Here. Let me help you."

CHAPTER 35

I stare at the Prankster resting underneath Dillon's elbow, while Virginia carefully removes the dishrag from his face and assesses the damage. The flap of skin had already sealed into place, leaving a crooked red crescent wound on his cheek.

He'll have a nice scar from my ministrations. But it won't be fatal, sadly.

He jerks his chin at me and says to Virginia, "One move from Piss Drinker over there and I'll sink this blade into her neck. Or maybe yours."

We exchange glances. "She won't move," Virginia says. "Right, Genie?"

"Not a muscle," I reply, eyeing the hypodermic needle. "In fact,"—I raise my hands in the air like a good surrendering soldier—"I'm going to sit down on that chair so you can watch me." I nod toward the chair that Virginia just vacated, one arm-tie dangling from the armrest.

Slowly, I move toward my destination and ease myself down on the chair. Then I scoot closer to the edge of the table within reach of the syringe.

Once I arrive, I lift my hands again, signaling my peaceable intentions, and rest both elbows on the table.

Virginia gently dabs at the wound, then bends down to inspect it. "I need to get a little water to clean it up," she says with admirable calmness. "I'm just going to go into the kitchen and get some. Is that okay?"

Dillon nods sullenly, watching me, elbow still resting on Prankster.

Virginia returns with a bowl of water and a semi-clean rag and sets to work cleaning the pulpy wound. After a few minutes, Dillon's attention to me starts to wane. His gaze drifts away, and he stares morosely at the far curtains. He sucks in a quick breath occasionally. Virginia apologizes.

The doctoring is coming to an end. My window of opportunity is closing. But I have to wait for the exact right nanosecond. Virginia tilts Dillon's head to the side. He closes his eyes for one whole second as Virginia diligently scrubs some dried blood from his cheek. *This is it*! My heart thunders in my chest. *Do it now!*

And I pounce.

I grab the syringe and bring my fist down on Dillon's upper arm, plunging the needle into his shoulder. But he jerks away, the untapped syringe poking out of his bicep. Virginia makes a bold move for the plunger and makes a brief connection, but Dillon jumps up to his feet and tears the syringe out of his arm. Then he chucks it floor.

Virginia snakes her arm around his neck and tries to choke Dillon, but her strength is no match against his. His face grows red for a two whole hope-filled seconds, but then he yanks her arm away, sending Virginia stumbling to the floor.

Meanwhile, I hustle to get to the Prankster, scrabbling across the table for it. Dillon leaps up to his feet, also reaching for the knife, but stumbles suddenly, grabbing hold of the table. The drug—it's working!

I snatch up Prankster and swipe the shining blade in a singular deadly arc. I hope. I make a connection. There's more blood. There's screaming.

Blinded with rage and a single-minded focus to wipe the stain of Dillon off the landscape of our lives, I hack at him, wildly, desperately, flying high on the singular hope that if I keep going—he will stop.

But he doesn't stop. He becomes enraged. He fights against the blade and the precious little Demerol that Virginia managed to dose him up with, fists swinging, until one catches me somewhere on the side of the face, and I stumble backward.

As the floor rushes up behind me, I step back to break my fall, but my ankle pops, and hot searing pain races up my leg. Then Dillon scrambles for the syringe and moves in. I feel a painful jab on my upper thigh. And blessed numbness washes over me, rushing me into a dark, bleak, soft unconsciousness that I want to fall into and never leave.

A soft feminine voice floats around me, buzzing like a bee in the warm months of summer. Virginia's? Then I hear screaming.

But I'm floating far above it all. None of that matters. I lay as helpless as a baby, pathetically happy to be swaddled with numbness, glad to be floating above the hard crushing edges of reality.

It's so much better up here. A wonderful cosseted world of nothingness that shields me from pain and hurt and reality. So I fall into it, tossing away all concerns whatsoever for life or limb. Those things don't matter. They're nothings.

I smile, stifling an inward giggle.

Nothings, dahlinks!

Nothings at all.

CHAPTER 36

Sunlight breaks through my closed eyelids. Am I dead? I wonder distantly, kind of hoping that I am. But the bright, hard rays of daylight bring a crushing singular reminder: *You are not dead. You are very much alive. And if you need any further evidence . . .*

A specter of pain ghosts through the misty landscape of my mind. My left ankle aches dully. Something isn't right down there. But I can't bring myself to investigate. I remember our botched attempt at escaping, and nausea overwhelms me.

Is Virginia okay? Did she survive? She's down there with the beast, while I'm safely tucked up here in the cold drafty attic, still a bit drugged. Thank God.

But that pain—it's going to grow bolder and unmanageable as soon as the Demerol wears off. Pray it never wears off.

What had happened? I want to cry thinking about how close I'd come to killing Dillon, or at least stopping him. First, with Prankster. Then with the Demerol. But I couldn't do it. I could only . . . fall and screw up my ankle.

And now, we're in an even worse position. Is that possible? What will happen to Virginia now? They obviously have some sort of working arrangement, whereby Virginia "gets" to live in the house. That requires some level of trust. Well, that's gone now, surely, after she attacked Dillon, and revealed her hand. She's not loyal to him. She's loyal to me. What will that cost her? Will she be joining me soon up here in my dungeon wonderland? At least I'll have some company . . .

Sometime later, the specters of pain returns, bolder now and multiplying. The underbrush crawls with movement. Marauders of pain assemble in the woods, waiting for the drugs to wear off. The numbing mists slowly fade, revealing the true scale of the attack. I grit my teeth and start sweating as pain rolls over me in successive breaking waves.

I rub my belly, trying to calm the nausea. I moan and dig my fingers into a towel, trying to distract myself from the pain. I hear a dispassionate nurse's voice in my head, one of the many that came to assess Mom during her chemo days.

On a scale of one to ten, how bad would you say the pain is?

Twelve! It's a twelve!

Another pill, another pill. Always another pill. That's what I so desperately want right now, a magical pill that will drive away the marauders and render them impotent against the powerful and great white wizard know as *Pain Pill*.

There were so many wonderful wizards that pharmaceutical companies spend billions conjuring, but none of them will come to my aid without a dreaded visit from Dillon. Slowly, mercifully, after much intentional thinking, the pain ebbs a little. I don't dare move.

But I do dare look. Slowly, I watch the grand reveal as I pull up the leg of my sweatpants. My heart speeds with fear when I see my swollen ankle. It reminds me of the time we had blown up a latex glove in the hospital and drawn a face on it.

My ankle also reminds of Surfer Dude from high school, who twisted his ankle in big surf and spent the next two months on crutches. Praying I'm not completely incapacitated, I adjust my position to get a better look, and accidentally put some weight on my ankle. A jolt of hot pain races up my leg, making me dizzy. Carefully, I lay there and pull in deep breaths, while my sight goes blurry.

As I watch splotchy little stars circulate around the room, I realize that my ankle is definitely as swollen and purple as Surfer Dude's.

Dark times. Dark, terrible times . . .

My whole existence is beyond bleak. I managed to immobilize my ankle with some packing tape and two books that I found in a box. There's enough pressure to encourage the wheels of healing to start turning. However long that will take. I can only hope the tender pieces of my ankle will meld together sooner rather than later.

Not to aid me in my escape, you see. That's physically impossible. I just want relief from the pain. I want the Wizard of Healing to help me.

Healing isn't as great of a wizard as Pain Pill, but he's a diligent little creature. Soon, Healing will put me back together again. Soon, I'll be back to plain old despair.

'Addictive' is the word best used to describe great books, but those reviewers have no idea what they're talking about. Addiction is a deep pining in one's soul, a wholly consuming obsession.

I can feel its questing little tendrils snaking around my ankle, my legs, and making its way up to my mind. I thought I was addicted to Xanax and my benzo buddies, maybe Paxil and Prozac too. But nobody *really* yearns for that bland, drug-induced reality. We just put up with it because we're afraid to face life alone, unaided. We're afraid to face ourselves.

But with opioid use comes true yearning. My life had been comfortable and cosseted. My life *was* the escape. Now, it has become a hard, weary load. Pills give me freedom from the crushing weight of reality. It's the only thing I want now: escape from the sharp pressing edges of what my life has become.

Virginia and I had tried to escape. But we failed. This is my life now. One where Healing and Pain Pill hover and swoop, each battling for the win.

I will not give in. I will stay strong. I will not let Dickhead win. Those were my mantras when I lay prone on the carpet, unmoving, scared to trigger the marauders of pain.

But when I tried to stand and rippling pain seared down my leg, I cried out for relief. For freedom. I cried out for Pain Pill.

It arrives, slipped stealthily under the door. And I drag myself to it with a new mantra on my lips: Next time, I will not give in. Next time, I will stay strong. Next time, I will not let Dickhead win.

The pills kept coming. My ankle starts to heal. And I scribble out my daily page of poop, leg propped up on a box, anxiously waiting for my little white reward. It comes. And I gratefully swallow it. And soon, Falco finds himself bedeviled with addition too.

The topic keeps my pen moving. But I need to fight it. I need to get Falco off the good stuff. But I need help getting out of the trenches of pain and despair. I need help battling the marauders.

Soon, Healing outperformed Pain Pill, and soon I don't need the latter anymore. Okay, maybe I don't need it. I want it.

I told Dickhead where to find the first draft of "Rebecca." It's rough and meandering, the manuscript. I hope he'll put it out for public consumption as-is and try to cash in on Amy Mathews's brand equity. I hope my readers will eviscerate it. I hope my sales would tank. I hope I'll drive myself into financial destitution, because that's the only way to get rid of the parasite.

He seemed excited to release it. I hope he doesn't wait.

So I cling to this new hope. Amy Mathews is about to stun the world again, this time with her awesome flop. I envision a blizzard of one star and angry gif-laden reviews.

My fans won't let me down. They're a passionate tribe, outspoken, and very active online. Some even have followings of their own, who can make or break a writer's career. Some of them are very powerful. I need them all now.

I hate to do it. Disenfranchise my fans. I'd gotten to know so some online. They're such kind, supportive, and interesting people. But if I ever survived this, maybe I can announce the incredible reason behind Amy Mathews's stupendous flop. Maybe they'll forgive me. Maybe, they'll even retract a few bombs.

Until then, I need to extract the parasite.

I need to get out of this alive.

CHAPTER 37

Thoughts of Ben are my only sustenance. My memories of him alone keep me fighting. I'm lying on the mattress, staring up at the ceiling and counting the joists, thinking about our walk on the beach. The night he kissed me. He made good on his promise to take me to Benihana.

Our chef was an enthusiastic young man with a flair for throwing food, cracking eggs in any number of odd ways, and fancy spatula work. Ben was right. It was expensive, but luckily for us Amy Mathews offered to pay.

Seems like another life, almost another person. I wonder what he's doing these days. Is he dating someone else? Has he forgotten all about me?

I hear a faint tapping on the dormer window. Must be a bird, so I ignore it and keep counting. Then the tapping stops, and begins again. Curious, I grab my makeshift crutch and prepare to stand.

The knocking stops.

I sit there, wondering if my bland discovery will be worth the effort. I'll probably find a rat or something gross, trying to eat its way into my room, in which case I'd rather not know.

I think I hear a whisper—"*Hey!*"—a real live human voice, coming from outside of my little window. But that can't be right. It's probably the wind howling, my sole companion these days.

It could also be some bad side effects from Pain Pill, the white wizard, who had graciously visited me earlier in the day. The great wizard had materialized under the door, pushed there by Dillon, I presumed, or Virginia. Maybe Casper the Friendly Ghost himself. I didn't care.

I hobbled over to my little white savior, placed it on my tongue, and closed my eyes, welcoming the bitter taste as I swallowed the pill dry. The pill numbed my mouth, my esophagus, my stomach, my body, and then my mind. I'd laid prone on the carpet there for most of the day, grateful for oblivion.

"Hello?"

I look over at the darkened window. What in the hell? I struggle up to standing, careful to keep my weight off my bad leg. This deserves some investigation and a little dash of irrational hope. I hobble to the window, despite the pain, anxious to close the gap. I have doubts. Am I pushing through the pain only to find Dillon standing there? Is there a cruel surprise waiting for me on the other side? I don't know. But I have to try.

I hobble over to the small dormer window, trying to see past my own reflection in the pane and looking into the blackness on the other side. When I get there, I see a shape moves in the darkness—a shape in the form of a human. I swing the little window open. Then the shape steps out of the shadows.

Ben.

"Genie?" he asks, stepping into the light.

My legs go weak.

I blink a few times, trying to clear the apparition from my vision. But it's him all right, standing in front of my face. He's aged since I saw him last. His cheeks are sunken. He's lost weight. His supernova eyes, which had glowed so brightly in the days we'd spent together, are dark and shadowed.

But there's a half-smile on his mouth, hinting at his old good humor. "I'm sorry about showing up like this. I know it must be creepy, but—"

I plunge both hands through the tiny window opening, desperately grasping for him, despite my jittery leg threatening to give out.

He grabs my hands and steps closer. His touch gives me strength.

"What are you doing up here?" he asks, peering into the Dungeon behind me.

But I can't talk. My throat is so tight with emotion and relief and fear. "*Ben*," I croak and dissolved into tears.

He puts one arm through the tiny window and reaches for me. I feel like a gorilla in a zoo left for years in solitary confinement, reaching for something—anything—that will break this terrible curse of solitude. Only a wall stands between our bodies and a small swinging windowpane between our heads.

"How did you get up here?" I ask.

He blinks. "Well, don't hate me, but I saw you punch in your security code after I took you to Benihana. I've been driving by and this is the only light I always see on. So I just—I dunno. I tried to forget about you . . . like you wanted. But I can't stop thinking about that time I stopped by—the time you dumped me over the intercom. And I—"

Suddenly, my voice returns. "I didn't mean it! I didn't mean a single word of it. Dillon made me say it. He had Virginia strapped to a chair and he said if I didn't make you go away, he'd shoot her up and kill her with an overdose. So I said it, I said whatever he wanted me to."

"What? Are you kidding me?"

"I wish. Ben,"—I glance over my shoulder at the door and lower my voice. "You can't stay here. You have to go. Dillon, he—"

"I'm not going anywhere."

"Ssh. Not so loud," I whisper. "He might hear us . . . Ben, we're hostages. Dillon is holding us both hostages. As long as I keep writing books, Virginia survives. If she continues with the Amy Mathews charade, I survive. But he's got on her uppers and downers and God knows what else, she—she's just a puppet. But we—we tried to escape. We tried to climb over the back fence, but he caught us and ..." I can't tell him the rest.

Ben, for once, is speechless. Then he rallies. "I'm calling the cops. Right now."

He reaches into his pocket and pulls out his cell phone. The screen lights up at the touch of his thumb. Relief so stunningly overwhelming washes over me. He has a cell phone, a glorious cell phone that works! All he has to do is type in the three magical digits—nine, one, one—and cops would come screaming around the corner pronto.

They'll break down the front door and find me in my deplorable state. They'll arrest Dillon on the spot. And soon, so very, very soon, this whole nightmare will be over. Dillon will go to jail. I'll press the charges this time. And Virginia and I can both recover, maybe in enough time to save Amy Mathews.

He dials the three magical numbers and holds the phone up this ear, casting an eerie glow across his face. He steps back into the shadows, cupping the mouthpiece with his hand, and waits.

What is he waiting for?

"*Fuck!*"

"What is it? What's wrong?"

"It's some fucking automated voice system!" And into the phone, he says, "Glenhaven ... Glen-hay-VEN."

My heart skitters around my chest. "A voice system?" I mumble, glancing over at the door.

"Emergency. Operator," he says.

We both wait for what seems like one long millennium. Finally, he looks up at me and nods. My good leg almost gives out. Ben presses his back against the outside weatherboards and starts talking in a low voice, while I watch the door.

"Benjamin Walker. Nine-five-four, sixty-seven forty."

Then I see it. A shadow falls under the door gap.

". . . Nine. Five. Four. Six. Seven. Four. Oh."

The shadow shifts. I hear the telltale rattling of the locks lining the outside of the door.

Too small for me to stick my head out, I put my mouth in the small window opening, heart beating so fast I can hardly breathe. "He's here! He's coming!"

He looks at me, panic bright in his eyes, and returns to the operator. "I've got a hostage situation here. I need the cops to come immediately. My—*what?*"

I duck back inside and see the doorknob rattling.

"I'm twenty-five. Look, this is urgent. We need help. I—no, I'm not the hostage."

I hop over to the desk and grab my folding chair. Then I hurry it over to the door and wedge it underneath the doorknob. It won't save us, but it will buy a few precious seconds for Ben to communicate the vital details of our whereabouts. And perhaps even, save us all.

From without, I hear Ben's voice, thick with frustration. "Yes of course everyone is still breathing!"

The door slams open. The chair goes flying. Dillon stands in the threshold, hair disheveled. His stained t-shirt falls around a lump in his waistband—a lump advertising a handgun. He steps into the room, moving quickly past me like a panther, examining the room for an interloper.

"What are you looking for?" I try to sound brave. I try to look believably casual. I try to calm my shaking voice. "I was just—"

Ben's hushed voice drifts in from the window that I'd forgotten to close. "Dillon. I don't know his last name. What? Yes—a guy!"

Then Dillon spins toward me, naked rage in his eyes. "You practicing ventriloquism, Piss Drinker?"

I try to stop him. But he tosses me aside like a rag doll.

I fall over and cry out—"Ben! Run!"—as a sharp ripping sensation rushes up my left leg. I've re-injured my ankle that had so delicately melded back together. How bad, I don't know. I just hope I'm still mobile.

Dillon pauses as alert as a Doberman. He withdraws the gun from his waistband, fixes on the window and starts toward it. I launch myself at his feet, wrapping my arms around his legs and squeeze my eyes shut, ready for the pain of kicks and punches.

He tumbles to the ground, the weapon skittering away from his hand.

"Bitch!" he roars, and starts wriggling out of my grasp, clamped onto him like a limpet. One leg breaks free. He strikes my with his heel. My vision erupts into jagged white lines at impact. I clench my teeth, hunker down, and tighten my grip with one arm, and with the other, I'm reaching desperately for the gun, my fingertips playing on the gleaming steel barrel, each tremulous touch pushing it further away.

But Dillon overpowers me. With one violent jerk of his body, he upends me. I spill off to the side. He raises his close fist to strike me. I put my arms up like a shield and cower.

"Hey!" Suddenly, a phone clatters against his head and falls to the floor, face up, just a few inches away. We both stop. I glance over at the window and see Ben withdrawing his arm. Chucking the phone is the only thing he can do. It's a distraction to give me one scant second to grab the gun.

So I vault a grasp, and grab it, hand on the cold barrel, but Dillon snatches it away.

"Sir? Sir?" I hear a small voice saying.

"Helllllppp!" I cry. "Help us! He's going to kill us all!"

"... Address. Can you verify ..."

Dillon grabs the phone and presses it against his ear. "We're downtown," he says calmly. "Downtown in the warehouse district. 981 Fifth."

"No—!"

And he hangs up. A dark cloud descends on me, a dark impenetrable cloud of utter hopelessness. Dillon sent the police to the wrong address, all the way to the other side of town!

Hope swills away, hope that had burned so bright in my heart and mind. He stands and looms over me, gun in hand, and I feel as if he'd opened up a jugular and drained out my lifeblood.

The phone rings again, a bright jarring *ding-a-ling, ding-a-ling!* It's the operator calling back, trying to keep someone on the line until the cops arrive. Dillon looks down at the phone and shoots it, instantly severing our only lifeline to the outside world. Then he strides to the window.

As he peers out, I scramble backwards, across the room and away from him. I hear Ben's quick footsteps across the veranda roof. Dillon sticks his arm through the little opening and fires. There was a metallic screech of the rain gutter peeling away from the roofline. He fires again, twice in quick succession.

And before I hear another sound, I frantically half-hop, half-drag myself out of the room, down the stairs and into the dark interior of the house.

CHAPTER 38

I skitter down the narrow stairwell so fast I give myself rug burns. I rush down the hallway straight to Virginia's room, to the closest intercom box, dragging my leg behind me, relieved to find the lights off in the house. Dark shadows have never been so welcoming.

I can lock myself inside her room and somehow yank the box off the wall. I just need to depress the little red panic button. I just need to push it once, brush my finger against its grippy red surface and this nightmare would well and truly be over.

Under Virginia's closed bedroom door shines light, casting a dim rectangular wedge into the dark hallway. I impel myself onwards, gritting my teeth against the pain and the cold dread of

Dillon looming behind me, despite the sweat bursting out on my skin, despite the marauders of pain attacking in collective, brute force.

I glance behind me, expecting to find Dillon, bounding down the hallway like a hound from hell. But I see nothing. I get to Virginia's room and rush inside.

I shut the door quietly behind me and lock the door. It's a true sliding deadbolt that we had installed on all of the inside doors. Virginia liked it because it gave the paneled door a rich look and feel. I liked it because of the solid comforting sound of a slug of metal sliding into the thick wall.

I turn and look around the room, hoping to find Virginia. I find only a bedside lamp toppled over, casting disjointed light around the room, and her expensive chenille bedding strewn across the floor in a stained crumpled mess.

I move to the sliding sash window and latch it shut. Then I pull the curtains closed and rifle through the mirrored bedside tables, trying to find an implement so I can pry the box off of the wall and trigger the panic button.

The drawers are filled with junk: old photos, scrap paper, toenail clippers, and the cast off crescents of old nails. There are pens, used batteries, dirty loose pills, and a remote control for the air conditioning unit.

But there at the bottom of the drawer, gleaming under a dirty pile of rubble, I spot the back of my bejeweled cell phone case, its small blue crystals winking at me. I grab it, eyes misting up with amazement.

Frantically, I push all the buttons praying for a response, feeling like a necromancer trying to raise the dead. Nothing. I press all the buttons simultaneously and wait for what feels like seven long years before the screen shifts from dead black to dark grey—a sign of hope!

I wait, heart thundering so loud I can hear the blood pulsing in my ears. And then it winks alive—life!—before the screen settles back into the black abyss, leaving behind its lasting legacy: a digital image of a battery, hopelessly drained.

I cram the phone into the front pocket of my sweatpants and quickly dig around in the drawers for a charging cable. Nothing. I limp to the bathroom and look through the drawers, the cabinets, and even Virginia's closet, searching for either the charging cable or a tool that I can use to rip off the box.

Nothing.

Then something occurs to me. The sink stopper has a long metal rod, fixed with a screw done up finger tight. So I rush to the bathroom, open the cabinets under the seat, clear the contents out with one swipe of my arm, reach back under the sink and grope around for the rod.

I nearly cry with relief when I find it. I follow the length of the rod down until I found the screw. After I unscrew it, the rod comes loose.

Rod in hand and breathless with hope, I hop over to the metal box. I start digging into the wall with the blunt, rounded end, burrowing the metal into the drywall and forcing a tunnel underneath the rim. I press the end of the rod deeper and deeper into the wall, twisting, watching paint and drywall fall way.

Then the rod slips and gouges me in the palm. I hiss in pain, gather up the edge of my sweatshirt sleeve and stuff it between my palm and the rod. "Almost there," I mutter to myself. "Keep going."

Then the rod suddenly gives way. I wiggle it, trying to burrow out a finger-sized hole.

"Hold on, Ben," I mutter, working the hole a little larger. But it still needs more excavation. Damn. I hack away at the top edge, bringing the rod down again and again in roughly the same spot. Wondering the whole time, while panic closes down on me: Where's Ben? Where's Virginia? And where's Dillon?

Drywall powder breaks loose and rains down on my feet. I wiggle my finger into the small hole and start yanking, but the box still won't budge. I can feel the edge of the hard plastic intercom box just inside. I know the red panic button is located on the bottom right of the panel. If I could snake my finger inside the box, maybe I could reach the panic button. Then I could—

Gunshots ring out from somewhere downstairs. The sharp report startles me into paroxysms of panic. I hear footsteps pounding up the stairs. Someone is running down the hallway—Dillon?—pummeling into the bedroom door and rattling it so hard it nearly jumps off the hinges. Dillon! Dear God. What will I do? I'll have to jump out of the window. I'll have to—

"Open up!" Virginia shrieks. "*Please—open up!*"

CHAPTER 39

Quickly I open the door, and Virginia tumbles inside, scrambling away from the frightening figure advancing down the hallway. Dillon moves with the quick tread of a prey animal. In his right hand, he grips the raised pistol. Then he breaks into a run as he bares his teeth.

I slam the door shut right when he makes impact.

Virginia presses her full weight against the door.

"Hold it shut!" I cry, pushing my own shoulder against the jumping door, grabbing for the deadbolt leaver, twisting it until my knuckles turn white. The door jumps and bucks, but settles for one narrow second. I shoot the lock into position.

Dillon bangs on the door. "Virginia!" he roars. "You open up this door right now!"

I collapse next to my sister, panting, my left leg screaming so loudly with pain I can hardly hear.

"If I have to break down this door, you and Piss Drinker aren't going to live long enough to enjoy my company!" He fires a few times. Virginia and I dive for the floor until we hear the merciful *click-click-click* of his empty magazine. Tiny holes pepper the solid wood door. One bullet had struck close to the doorknob—right where I'd stood just two seconds ago. "Do you hear me?"

Virginia drops her pale face to her hands and sobs. Her body shakes as she cries. Her rib cage rises and falls, visible through her thin t-shirt.

She lifts her pleading blue eyes to mine. "Maybe we should open the door," she whispers. "He'll break it down anyway. It's only a matter of time. It's better if we don't piss him off..."

Deafening blows rain down on the door. I look up and see the hinges lurching incrementally against the screws. She's right. It will only be a matter of minutes before he breaks down the door and comes thundering through the threshold, so enraged he'll probably snap our necks with his bare hands.

"I think he's already pissed off," I say.

"I'm sorry," she mumbles, dropping her heads in her hands. "I'm so sorry for everything."

"We don't have time to be sorry. We only have time to save ourselves. That's it." I place my hand on the ridge of her spine rising up like a chain of mountain peaks along her back. "Ben is here. He's outside somewhere. Dillon tried to shoot him, but I think he survived."

She looks up at me, astonished, eyes wide with hope. "Ben? As in Boyfriend Ben?"

I nod. "I told him that Dillon's holding us captive. And he tried to call the police, but . . ." I can't quite share the bad news, but she looks away. She already knows.

"We can go out the window," Virginia says instead. "And try the wall again. With Ben—"

I shake my head and motion down to my swelling ankle. She hisses in sympathetic pain. "I won't be able to make it over the wall."

She looks away, eyes searching for answers. Suddenly I realize that Dillon had fallen quiet. We both look at the door, eyes filled with dread, when Virginia whispers, "He's going around. He's going to break through the window."

"Help me get the box off of the wall!" Virginia pulls me up to standing, a little too roughly and apologizes when I yelp in pain. Sweat breaks out on my body despite the freezing temperature inside the house. I hop over to the box as quick as I can.

Virginia is right next to me, digging her fingers into the top divot, while I pull on the lower right corner. To no avail. She picks up the thin metal rod and starts hacking away at the wall. Still, the box won't budge.

She pauses, winded, her hands bleeding. "Can you get your fingers in there?"

I try to burrow my finger under the rim, but can't get a good grip. She pauses, breathing hard, and looks around the room, searching for a better tool. "It's no use," I say. "I've looked everywhere for a screwdriver."

She grabs the chair sitting in front of her vanity. "We don't need a screwdriver,"—she raises the chair over her head and aims one of its metal legs at the top of the box—"we just need a hammer."

And she brings the leg of the chair down with terrific finality. There's a satisfying *clunk* of metal striking metal. She pauses and puts the chair down. We both lean in to assess the damage. There's a sizable dent in the top of the box. More importantly, it hangs on the wall slightly askew.

"Do it again!" I cry. "It's working!"

With shaking arms, she lifts the chair over her head and brings it down again and again, whipping her back on each downward stroke, trying to get the most out of each swing.

There are various sounds of *clink-clunk-clonk*, depending on how good of a connection she'd made. I watch the metal box jolting on each downward swing, jouncing the screws loose.

"You're almost there, Jinny!"

She pauses, breathing hard, and smiles weakly. "It's working . . ."

"Yes! Keep going! Keep—"

The window shatters. A great gust of cold wind blows in, cutting us to the bone. Dillon clears the glass shards with one efficient swipe of his arm and throws his leg over the sill. He stoops and leans inside, grinning, as cold flurries of snow blow in around him.

"Did you miss me?"

CHAPTER 40

"Get out!" Virginia screams.

We have one narrow second to escape her bedroom, before Dillon squeezes his bulk through the window frame.

I frantically limp to the door, unlock it in a hurry, and hobble down the hallway, totally impervious to the hot, searing pain blasting up my leg. Virginia, right behind me, slings her arm around my waist and propels me faster.

We clatter down the stairwell. I stifle a cry of pain at the bottom and hurry us down the hallway toward my office.

"Hey you little Piss Drinker!" Dillon calls, supremely comfortable with his odds of finding us. As he makes his way down the hallway, I can hear the heavy thuds of his gun whacking against the walls.

I wipe fat beads of sweat from my brow and nod toward the safe room. It's not Kevlar reinforced. The President, for example, wouldn't be safe there, but the door is solid metal. And it features three deadbolts that are virtually impenetrable to any crazed psychotic wielding a gun. What foresight.

From a short distance away, I can see from the dark contours inside my office that Dillon had kindly rearranged my furniture. My beloved mahogany desk lay on its side like a carcass, legs sticking out in rigor mortis. My couch is pushed up against the far wall. Books are gone from my shelves, like missing teeth.

We rush inside. Virginia turns back to lock the door with fumbling fingers.

"Hurry up," I hiss.

But the door bangs open and bounces off Virginia's shoulder before she can get the deadbolt shot into place. Dillon stands there, lowering his leg, eyes flickering with exhilaration.

Virginia dashes to the safe room door, pulling me along by the hand. I follow in a shambolic run. I can feel Dillon's feet landing on the carpet behind me, his looming presence closing down on me like a giant hungry maw. Virginia rushes to the safe room and reaches out for me.

Just as I reach the promised land, my leg gives out. I stumble to the ground, groping for Virginia's outstretched arms, despite Dillon's hand around my good ankle, pulling me back. I lurch myself forward, grasping desperately her forearms, and land a good grip.

With one superhuman heave, she pulls me almost inside the safe room, while Dillon scrabbles for a better handhold. Then he gives a hard tug, wrenching half of my body out. I beg Virginia, even in her reduced state, to pull—pull harder!

But despite my struggling, despite Virginia's desperate tugs, I'm losing ground. I can feel the carpet burns on my hip bones as Dillon yanks me further and further away from my sister's grasp. My ankle screams with pain. I scream with fear.

I vault one last grip onto the threshold, hooking my hand around the reinforced frame. Virginia pinions her feet on both sides of the doorframe, her hands encircling mine, pulling. Her face is as white as a snowstorm, her cracked lips pulled back in a grimace. Her frail arms shake. Her weakening stamina is giving way to the more powerful and unrelenting force of Dillon.

Panic shakes me to the core as I realize this is a losing fight. I'm about to face Dillon again, and this time, no amount of smooth talking is going to save me from the full blast of his fury.

A gust of wind, cold and incongruent, suddenly blows across the room. Dillon looks over his shoulder for the source. I can't afford to look. I jerk one leg free, my good one, and cock back my heel, aiming for the twisted red scar on his cheek. And I fire, knocking his hair askew, cracking the wound clean open.

Dillon yowls, his hands flying up to his face. Virginia makes one last heroic yank, sweeping me cleanly inside of the room. Then she moves quickly to sweep the door closed.

In the narrowing gap of the closing door, I catch a dark shape moving behind Dillon. It's Ben, stepping into a wisp of light, his face contorted with rage, one hand wrapped around his abdomen, the other holding a narrow log. And I see Dillon reaching for his gun.

"Ben!" I cry. "Watch out!"

And the door slams shut.

CHAPTER 41

"Open the door!" I cry, scrabbling behind Virginia and trying to undo the row of locks as she quickly and methodically slides the bolts into final, locked position.

"What are you doing!" she cries, pulling my hands away from the door. "Dillon is out there!"

"So is Ben!"

Virginia stops and presses her back against the door, eyes wide. "He'll kill us if we go out there. He will. He,"—her voice shakes, her eyes fills with tears—"he's a fucking maniac."

I look at her. "You don't say."

"I was trying to tell you before," she continues. "He killed someone . . . or he was involved in it."

"How do you know?" I asks, not really sure I want to know.

Virginia looks away. "I found some Polaroids."

A chill sweeps over my body. This is bad. Real bad. This guy has a tried and true method of offing people. He's been busy laying the groundwork for Virginia's eventual overdose. Then there's the lion, ready and willing to eat all the damning evidence. He has a narrative; he's putting all the pieces into place now. Virginia, Ben, and I are sauntering into his closing act.

I want to cry. I want to retch. I want to somehow save us all, but the sheer impossibility of that particular happy ending dawns on me. We won't make it out of here alive. But we sure can try.

"I need to get out. I need to help Ben." I move towards the door, but hiss when a bright flame of pain races up my leg. I pull up the leg of my sweatpants and look down at my swelling ankle, visible through my thin sock.

"Are you okay?" Virginia asks.

"No, I'm not." I reach down and gingerly touch my tight, hot skin. "Payback for trying to hack off Dillon's face."

Then it's Virginia's turn to fall silent. The air is redolent with her unspoken apologies, burning regrets, and deep sorrows. I'm sure if she could, she'd willingly sign up for crucifixion if it would improve matters any. But it won't.

Nothing will improve matters now, except for a miraculous, but unlikely show of police force. Police, who are currently sniffing around the warehouse area downtown, searching for a hostage situation that they'll never find.

"You're going to get yourself killed if you go out there," Virginia says. "You can hardly walk."

When we had the intercoms installed, it set me at ease knowing that my little red panic button friend waited patiently within reach. I press my palms into my eye sockets. I can't bring myself to look at the wires poking out the wall, waiting for an emergency intercom panel. The safe room had been wired up when we did the rest of the house, but due to contractor delays, we decided to have the panel installed at a later date.

Procrastination dug in its long talons, and soon the outstanding panel dropped down into the murky minutiae of my loathed to-do list. I'd thought of that particular item many times, always riding somewhere at the bottom of my list, but I'd inevitably put it off for tomorrow.

Little orphan Annie with her red curly hair and freckled cheeks had always sang cheerily in my mind when I looked over my list. *Tomorrow! Tomorrow!*

Then I groan and put my hands down. Little orphan Annie stopped singing because tomorrow had turned into today, and she didn't have any catchy tunes about dying at the hands of a raging psycho.

"We can try to find a cell phone," Virginia offers.

"I already found mine," I say.

"You did?" she asks, eyes wide with hope.

I pull it out of my pocket and toss it aside. "It's dead."

Both Virginia and I sit there, staring down at the unhelpful cell phone in mutual, crushing disappointment. It's incredible to think that the only thing standing between us life-saving help and us is a single wire cable. The location of which lay buried somewhere deep inside of Dillon's disturbed head.

"It's all my fault," Virginia says, picking at a hangnail. The tips of her fingers are red and angry. They're like round balls of flesh, torn and pecked over, her nails chewed back into swollen stumps. "If I hadn't—"

"Jinny, what's done is done," I say.

Fists thunder on the door. "*Virginia!*" roars Dillon. Eye meets terrified eye. "Virginia you better open this door!" And the door shakes so savagely that the locks rattle in the reinforced metal frame.

Silence.

Then he changes tacks. "Hey you little Piss Drinker. Your pathetic boyfriend here has something to say to you."

I put my hands to the door. "Ben?" I cry. "Ben, are you okay?"

"If you open the door, I'll let you see him," Dillon says.

A long moment follows whereby I think I hear muffled groans, maybe dull thuds of smacking flesh but I can't quite tell. Then Ben's voice broke though: "Stay in there! Don't you dare—"

I hear cursing, followed by the sound of a table scraping across my now trashed hardwood floors.

"I'm going out!" I cry and start unlocking the deadbolts.

"Wait!" Virginia cries, pushing my hands away.

"No!" And I push her back with all my strength, which isn't much. "He's going to kill Ben if I don't do something!"

"He won't! Just think about it! Think—"

"Ben's the only thing I have," I say, my voice going wobbly. "And now he's gonna—he's gonna DIE! Because—"

"He won't! He won't! Ben is the only tool Dillon has to pry us out of here. If he something happens to Ben, Dillon will never get us out of here. We can live in here for weeks if we need to."

"But I don't *want* to live in here for weeks! I want to get out this *hellhole*. I want to get that intercom box and press that *fucking button*!"

Tears of pain and rage and helplessness rise up inside like a fast rising tide. All the tears that had crystallized in my heart over the past two months thaw suddenly under the unrelenting onslaught of continual sharp disappointments and the hot, searing very real possibility of losing Ben forever.

"Why did you do this to me!" I yell. "Why did you do this to us! To Ben! To Amy! You knew he was dangerous! You knew he was going to do something. You knew!"

Virginia's face crumples. "Yes, I knew, but I didn't—I didn't mean for it to be like this. Dillon said he was just going to scare you a little. Put some pressure on you. I didn't . . . I didn't think it would turn out like this." Her lower lip wobbles. Her chin puckers. "I should have told you," she mutters. "I was just—just so angry. And hurt."

Hurt and angry? Well, that makes two of us. She connived with a criminal to betray me. She shouldn't have done it, but she's paid a hefty price, and I don't have the bandwidth for a therapy session. Not now. We're both hurt. She feels terrible. Making her feel worse won't help matters any.

"Doesn't matter," I say, sniffing, trying to buck up and be strong for us both, afraid that she'll fall into pieces, and I don't have the strength to put her back together. "The only thing that matters is getting out of this mess somehow. Alive, preferably."

"Let me say it. Let me tell you. You asked so many times about that day in the hospital. About Mom Time. The day that everything changed between us." Her eyes are hard, bloodshot, and glassy. "Well, you were right. Everything did change."

I look at her, aghast. I'd been asking her to talk to me about that ever since we'd lost Mom. Never a single clarifying word spewed from her lips. Now—now!—with a psychopath beating down the door, holding Ben hostage, she wants to illuminate me.

Tears spill down her cheeks. "You were always Mom's favorite."

"What?"

"You were. I heard you. I heard *her*."

I blink, taken back with the savagery in her voice.

"You got Mom. I deserved Amy. I *wanted* Amy . . . I needed Amy. Finally, I was someone's favorite."

I think back to that day at the hospital, trying to figure out what had possibly happened that could make her feel that way. I can't think of a single thing. Then a chill races down my back. Dillon had pumped her full of Demerol and God knows what else.

The doctors warned her that more drug use could cause permanent damage. Is she losing her mind? Is she delusional? My stomach twists with fear. If we were going to survive this, I need Virginia by my side with all her faculties intact. Not making up stories in her head.

"Virginia, Mom loved us *both* just exactly the same."

She shakes her head. "No. No, she didn't. I heard you two talking. You didn't know I was there. But I heard. I'd arrived early at the hospital that day, and saw you sitting on the edge of her bed, holding her hand. I stood behind the curtain. And I heard Mom say, 'You know I love you more than anything in this material world. More than the sun rising over the horizon, more than the ocean drawing to the moon. You're the only one that I could ever love. You mean more to me than my own life.'" Her voice breaks. "And then—and then you put the lines in *After The End* for the whole world to see!"

I want to laugh. I want to cry. But I can only shake my head in sheer and utter disbelief. "Virginia, those lines did go into the book. Do you want to know why? Because Mom was helping me flesh a scene between Rhenn and Madeline, where he confesses his love for her. Mom was quoting *Rhenn*!"

Virginia's face falls.

I sit there, utterly speechless. I can't believe how a single misconception became so ruinous, how something unspoken could turn so monstrous. If she had only talked to me, if she had only opened up to me!

"The stalker . . . everything. It's all my fault," she says quietly.

"The stalker?" I ask slowly as my blood runs cold. She nods her head quickly, hands covering her face. I reach down and pull her hands away from her flushed, tear-stained face. "What do you mean the stalker!"

"It—it wasn't meant to be like this. We already had the pen name, but when it came to the interviews and promos and book signings . . . Remember how you were on the fence about it? You were thinking about doing it yourself. And—and so that's when the stalker ordeal started . . ."

"Oh my God," I mutter, understanding dawning. And Dillon's words fall into place.

Everything, huh? I doubt that very much, Eugenia. He was right. I knew nothing.

"Just a flower here and there," Virginia says. "Nothing crazy or dangerous. Just enough to make you edgy . . . and unable to be the face of Amy. It was his idea to poke around the house. But then you come home and caught him and called the cops."

"And then you dropped the charges."

She nods.

"The Shatner comma guy? The crazy video?"

"Me," she breaths, breaking down into sobs.

The floor seems to fall out from under me. "And so when I told you I wanted to stop writing as Amy Mathews . . ."

"Dillon, he—he said he could push you a little bit. Get you to keep writing. To save Amy. So I went along with it. Because Amy was all I had. I needed Amy. But I—I had no idea he'd do this, Genie. I had no idea this is what he had planned . . ."

Numb shock washes over me as everything that I thought I knew about my sister completely breaks apart.

"So you didn't meet him at jail. He didn't write you a cheesy love poem from behind bars." I knew that story stank. "It was all a big fat lie . . ."

While Virginia weeps about her own stupidity and how sorry she is, I notice with a sick feeling, Dillon had become suspiciously quiet. And my office, I also notice with creeping dread, is as silent as a mausoleum.

It's so stealthy; I pass it off as a figment of my imagination. In the corner of my eye, I see a gray finger of something— smoke?—reach under the door gap and quickly retreat. I look down at the gap, but see nothing.

Again comes more trickery of the senses. A singular, but fleeting fume wafts to my nostrils. It's the smell of gas. Correction, it's the smell of mercaptan, the smelly gas additive that signals imminent danger.

"Can you smell that?" I ask, huffing in more air. But the smell disappears.

Virginia looks around, sniffing. "No, what is it?"

"I think it's a gas leak," I say, cramming my nose into the crack of the door. Then I look down and see smoke billowing in from under the door.

Fire.

And we both spring for the locks.

CHAPTER 42

I had ended book three in the *After The End* doomed series with a big fiery finale. So I'd researched house fires. Lacking the courage to interview firemen personally, I'd read *Fire* by Sebastian Junger.

Just like he'd spent three hundred pages describing the howling sound of wind at high speeds in *The Perfect Storm*, so he took care to describe the ferocious elemental nature of fire.

But I'd never experienced an inferno first hand. It's one thing to be separated from the flesh-melting temperatures by the pages of a book. It's quite another to step in a dark room, shrouded with sinister smoke and an eerie glow.

Virginia slips out first and immediately disappears in a dense bank of thick black smoke. Through the shifting smoke, wafting over us in sheets, I can see bright leaping flames scurrying up my curtains.

Smoke. That is something a book can't quite convey. The thick smell that reaches down your throat like fists, pummeling both lungs mercilessly.

Coughing doesn't help. The spasms just leave an open invitation for more smoke to batter your lungs into pulpy pieces of flesh.

I rip off my sweatshirt, press it against my face, and look around for the patio door. Virginia emerges from the wall of smoke, a cloth pressed against her nose. "This way!" she says, hitching her arm around my ribcage.

Hungry flames engulf the room, nibbling at my beloved Wonder Couch and my antique desk. All of it will be just charred remains come tomorrow. I just hope we won't be part of the ashes.

Thick grey smoke outlines a doorframe. I desperately hope it's the door that leads outside, where endless gulps of soothing fresh air could be found. But as we make our way closer, I see smoke billowing out and filling the dark hallway of the house.

I call out for Jinny to turn around and go back, gesturing behind me, toward the patio, but swaths of my heavy brocade curtains fall in one fiery swoosh, blocking the path.

We drop to our hands and knees to escape the suffocating smoke. The flames hadn't quite reached this part of the house, but that's only a matter of time. Dillon had clearly started the fire in my office, then vacated elsewhere. But where's Ben?

Ben. I feel sick. I want to go to him and try to help him, but that's pure folly. I will most likely perish in my journey, and what will I do if I finally find them? Stun Dillon with some strong words? I keep my eyes firmly glued to Virginia's bottom.

We could rush outside, but that will only lead to Failed Escape 2.0, which I don't think we could survive again.

The only way to save Ben is to save ourselves. We have to get up to the battered box hanging on Virginia's wall. We have to press that button. Thankfully, Virginia has the same idea.

We reach the top rung of the stairwell. Sweat pours down my face in great sheets. My shirt sticks to my sweating body. The smoke seems denser up here, making it harder to breath. The air is thick and hot. Around us, orange and blue flames worm up the walls.

Virginia picks up the pace, pausing every now again to hack and cough. The walls are fully aflame by the time we reach her room, the heat bearing down on us like iron anvils.

We scurry past the chunks of drywall that rain down from the charred ceiling, close in on Virginia's room, and hurry inside.

Murky glow cloaks her room from firelight reflecting off of the snow outside. Though smoky, the air is breathable. But not for long. A treasure trove of consumables fill Virginia's room.

She runs over to the metal chair that had made so much progress before, picks it up, and starts pounding away at the box. Again I hear the encouraging sounds of looming defeat: *clonk-clonk-clonk.*

The box jounces more readily. I heave myself up, gritting my teeth against the pain, and watch, riveted, encouraging Virginia to: "Keep going! Keep going! Keep—"

All downward swinging stops. I look at Virginia, who holds the chair motionless above her head, and follow her gaze to the threshold of the bedroom door.

There, with bright splinters raining down on his shoulders, stands Dillon.

CHAPTER 43

Virginia had always been a fighter. She'd taken on girls bigger and meaner than her during our high school days. She was also equal opportunity, confronting any man, woman, or surly teenager that rubbed her the wrong way.

She'd taken on an entire group of vicious girls who had cornered me after physical education class one dismal afternoon, offering to rearrange my facial features for free.

Virginia had fought them all. Her heroic effort had landed her in detention for a month, but she'd been promoted to heroine of my heart, where she stayed until she brought Dillon upon us.

Over the course of Dillon's tenure, I watched broken-hearted, as he systematically broke her down and turned my wild flamed-haired flawed vixen of a sister into a reduced nervous wreck, constantly muttering apologies and looking to him for direction.

But as the flames lick up the walls and curl over our heads, I watch as that rattled shell of a person falls away and becomes the beloved fighter that I once knew.

She advances on Dillon without hesitation and cracks the chair over his head, sending him sprawling to the floor. When Dillon slowly climbs up to his hands and knees in a daze, she cracks the chair over him again. Sensing blood in the water, her killing instincts take over, and she pummels Dillon with the chair, its legs bouncing off his muscled shoulders and back.

Suddenly the room erupted in bright flames. The fire roars. The house is a crackling inferno now, the drywall burning and sagging. Noxious fumes of melting plastic and the sharp acrid smell of an electrical fire gag me.

While Virginia works on Dillon, I frantically turn to the box—our last bastion of help—and try to rip it off the wall.

But the heat . . . it feels like the Devil himself is standing directly behind me, breathing his hell-fire breath on my back and shoulders, pushing me into higher flights of panic. Sweat pours down my face. My hands are slick with it.

Hurry.

Dillon is down, but our temporary victory won't last long. Virginia's rage and adrenaline will eventually bleed away. Her physical strength is nothing against Dillon's. Once Dillon gets that chair out of her hands, we will both lose. And fast.

I dig my fingers into the wall divots and wiggle them underneath the metal rim of the box. Virginia had loosened the box on the wall, but there's still precious little space for my fingers to slide underneath the rim. I can get the tips of my fingers wedged under the lip, but I can't hook the rim and yank it off.

Something crashes behind me, Dillon rousing from Virginia's admirable attack, I'll bet. I glance over, sweat streaming down my face, and glimpse Virginia next to her bed, reaching for a lamp on her bedside table.

Where's Dillon? I turn back to the box, stifling sobs, trying to get the box to budge, but my fingers keep slipping out of their tremulous handholds.

I look around in a frenzy and find the chair lying on its side. I grab it with sore bleeding hands, raise it high above my head, and bludgeon that box with every last bit of strength I have inside of me.

Screaming pain races up my leg. Sweat pours into my eyes. Hot fingers of fire creep over my body, ever closer to the hallowed spot of second and third degree burns.

Suddenly the box jounces crookedly. I throw the chair down, jam all of my fingers into the small gaping hole, grit my teeth, and drop onto my knees, putting all of my weight on the box.

When the box budges more, I cram in more fingers and drop to my knees again. The box rips even further off the wall, and I jam in both hands, frantically ripping it off the wall.

I scarcely believe my eyes when I see the exposed intercom panel ready for action. I lift the little protective flap, jam my thumb onto the red distress button—once, twice, threefourfive times—praying that the LED will turn green, signaling a successful message sent to law enforcement.

Dear God. Please turn green.

Nothing.

Did fire damage the wiring? I keep pushing the button, staring down at the lifeless LED light, frantic and desperate. What if the fire had damaged just one small section, one mere inch of critical wiring that—

Green.

My knees go weak with a sudden rush of euphoria. Tears pool in my eyes, doubling the panel in front of me. I stare down at the steady beautiful green light. It's no bigger than a ladybug carapace, but it's as momentous as spotting land after months adrift at sea.

"Jinny!" I cry, turning around to find her, voice breaking with acrid smoke and tears. "We did it . . . it's done."

But she's nowhere to be found.

CHAPTER 44

Suddenly a section of the ceiling buckles. Splinters and flames pour down. A great wall of smoke closes in on me. My eyes water in painful gushes. I drop to my knees where a thin layer of breathable air can be found, grab my sweatshirt that I dropped over by the security panel, and cram it against my face. I have to find Virginia. I have to get out of this inferno!

But I can't see more than two feet in front of my face. I can't see Virginia. I scurry over in the direction of her bed, mindful of the narrowing opportunity to escape the burning house before a charred ceiling joist falls and pins me fatally to the ground.

My hard won mayday will be for nothing if I don't get out of here, if I don't find her window and climb out of it. But I have to find Virginia first.

Sweat pours down my body. The raging flames dance ever closer, wicked and hot. I keep moving, wiping the sweat away from my stinging eyes, keeping my sweatshirt pressed against my nose and mouth, until suddenly the foot of the bed materializes in front me.

The sash window is to my left, but I saw Virginia grabbing the lamp on the right side of the bed, where her closet is located. I cast a longing glance at the window where smoke is billowing out of the broken pane. That is where I need to go, right now, but that is not where I'll find my sister.

A loud swooshing sound followed by a deep guttural growl, sends me into a panic. The fire is becoming something monstrous. Another section of the ceiling falls onto the carpeted floor, sending sparks across the room.

I grab the foot of the bed and marshal my strength, tamping down my biological drive to survive. *Get out of here*! My head screams. *Not without my sister*. My heart says.

I grit my teeth and turn into the depths of the bedroom.

"Not without my sister!" I scream to the wicked flames that seem so much like a fiery demon rising merrily from hell.

And I press on. On my hands and knees, I cover as much ground as I can, stopping frequently to press my face against the carpet and gulp for air. Soon I bump into a wall.

I look up, expecting to find the steady green savior light of the intercom panel, but instead found a charred poster of Paris that Virginia had bought some time ago. Panic settles into my bones. I'd traveled to the wrong side of her room. She'd hung the poster next to her bedroom door.

I follow the perimeter of her room like a good sniffer dog, making a mental map of the area I had covered. My lungs burn. My eyes feel like they'd been clawed out of my sockets. They might as well: between the sheets of sweat and suffocating smoke, I can't see a thing. My senses have been reduced down to that of a blind man, touch and hearing only.

As for the hearing part, I focus on mewling sounds that Virginia might make, weakly calling for help. But I hear only the roar of fire, the crackling sound of consumption, and the deep guttural groans of a house slowly dying.

Soon the bones of our house will weaken and collapse. Soon, we will die in this inferno.

I keep my arm stretched out in front of me, sweeping it side to side like a windshield wiper. I don't feel anything unusual; I don't catch Virginia or Dillon in my survey.

But I sense something all right. Something hideous.

I roll onto my back and scurry backwards, impelled by looming terror. The glowing smoke swirls like an opening portal, and Dillon steps through.

His dirty mop of hair had been singed off in oozing patches that glisten in the dancing flame light. A cut on his temple is bleeding heavily where maybe Virginia whacked him with the chair. And the crescent wound on his face weeps. But despite his injuries, he's alive. He's worse than alive. He seems to be relishing the pain and drawing invigorating strength from it.

He grins down at me with a mirthless smile, his red crescent wound looking downright sinister. Then reaches behind his back and withdraws Prankster from his waistband.

I start screaming. I flip onto my hands and knees and race toward the window, but his hand clamps down on my injured ankle as final as an iron manacle. He pulls be backward. I can feel the carpet burning my cheek and protruding hip bones as he drags me deeper into the house, deeper into the belly of the fire, where nobody would survive. Including me.

I kick frantically at his clamped hand, his arm, and his legs. But I have so little strength. The smoke is as insidious as an army of ants, penetrating my eyes and lungs, unrelenting and forever advancing. The marauders launch another attack, making me sick from pain. Dillon's hard grasp loosed them all.

I roll to the side and retch, gasping for air and reaching out for something, anything, to stop my terrible inexorable final journey into the belly of the fire.

Virginia rises up behind him, holding Amy Mathews's prized trophy firmly in hand. It's an engraved crystal Waterford vase, commemorating one million in sales. When it arrived, we'd poured in a bottle of champagne and drank triumphantly to Mom, to Froggy, to Tenzing Norgay, even to Monica Schaffer, to everything and everyone we could think of that had brought us to that incredible point of success.

Then, very proudly and with much to-do, we placed it on the mantle, where it stayed, until Virginia brought it up to her room after she came home from the hospital.

She holds the heavy Waterford above her head, glittering in the firelight. Then she brings it down, hard, slamming the vase against the base of Dillon's neck. Crystal shards skitter down his shoulders, dancing in the dull orange light. He crashes to his knees, losing his grip on my leg, losing his grip on Prankster.

"Run!" Virginia cries, reaching for the cleaver. "Get out of here!"

I choke and gag for breath. "Not without you!" I cry, tears streaming down my face.

She takes my hand and says in my ear, "I'll be right behind you. I promise."

And the smoke swallows them both up whole.

CHAPTER 45

I need to find my sister. I need to drag her out with me. There's no way I'm going to leave her behind, not with Prankster at large. Together, we will make our way over to the sash window and get out of this blazing onslaught.

I struggle to my feet and stagger toward the approximate location of where I'd seen her last. Then I bark my toes on something and fall.

"Jinny!" I scream out in pain and fear. I'm going to hit the bottom of my endurance soon. I'm going to reach of point of complete exhaustion. *You can do it*, I tell myself, gasping for air. *You can do it.* I try to get up. I try to stand and keep going, but my strength is swilling away. "Help me . . ." I beg something—anything. *Help . . .*

Get up, girl! It's the cheerleader, whose cheering season is about to come to an abrupt end. *Get up! Keep goin'*!

I struggle up to standing again, but my bad leg wobbles so badly with fatigue and pain that I crash back onto my knees. The pain is competing with the hot burning flames. On my hands and knees, I keep going, crawling like a baby with big baby tears spilling from my eyes.

"Jinny!" I choke out. "Where are you?"

The smoke reaches down my esophagus and scrapes my lungs raw. I'd never thought much about lungs before, certainly I had never given them much credit. They were always just there, quietly pulling in air. In. Out. In. Out. Without any input from me.

But as I drag in one breath after another and wince with burning pain, I realize that I am slowly suffocating to death. Burning hot cinders pummel my throat and lungs, blocking the life-supporting exchange of oxygen.

My vision starts to dim. If I want to save Virginia, I need to get one fortifying breath of fresh air. Just one. If I want to help Virginia, I need to help myself. Then I can gather some strength and return for her. I turn toward the window, toward the cold oasis that awaits me on the other side of the pane.

But I have to get there first. The marauders breach my defenses. My legs are heavy and leaden. I keep going, fighting the urge to lay my weary head down on the plush carpeting and watch, transfixed, as the raging blaze roars over my head in an awe-inspiring arc, carrying me towards the soft, bright land of nothingness.

Get on your feet!

The cheerleader. She's back. She's a good Southern girl with a slight country twang, her long blonde hair pulled back into a sleek ponytail. She has a big future ahead of her. She has hopes and dreams. She wants to go to college. She wants to *cheer* all those hardworking boys onto a G-O-A-L! She doesn't want to die. And the nice girl doesn't want me to die either.

Just a little bit farther!

I can see her so clearly. She wears a tiny pleated royal blue skirt that flashes caution-orange briefs every time she lifts a leg in glee. Her tight sweater has a few varsity letters sewn across her ample bosom. I can even smell her. She smells of perfumed lotion and melting plastic. No, not melting plastic. Burning hair. And that's not her. That's me. I am her, and she is me. And we're both about to die if I don't hurry over to the window.

You can do it!

I drag in another breath and another, wincing with each painful effort, fumbling and forging on through the wall of smoke, praying for divine intervention.

Go left! cries the cheerleader.

Is that it? Divine intervention? Angels don't have to have wings, do they? Who says angels can't be well-fed cheerleaders, wearing scandalously short skirts? I turn left, following instructions, and suddenly, momentously, the smoke clears and a finger of fresh air rushes down my throat.

I've never felt so invigorated. It's as if someone popped me with a shot of adrenaline that rushes through my veins, propelling me faster and faster towards the window, despite my leaden legs and my trashed ankle.

There it is! Just a few feet away! Plumes of smoke billow out of the broken sash window, rushing out in great swaths as if impelled by the same animal drive of survival as me.

Heedless to the sheets of stabbing pain, I grab the window ledge, pull myself up to standing, and wrench open the window frame that's lined with broken shards of glass.

You did it! Cries the cheerleader, who pumps her arms and executes perfect air splits.

While she finishes up her battle cry of *Gimme a Y! Gimme an E!* . . . I fold myself over the ledge, stick my head into a clear patch, and suck in great gulps of sweet air. "Yes, we did it," I mumble to the cheerleader. "We did it . . ."

"Genie," Virginia chokes. I turn and look over my shoulder. Virginia crawls out from under a blanket of smoke, dragging in a long breath, coughing and choking, reaching for me.

"Jinny!" I cry, struggling to get myself out of the window so I can pinion myself against the wall and pull her out. I make it. I reach for her. She reaches for me. Our fingers brush against each other. "Grab my hand!" I cry, straining to reach her, to touch her, to save her.

Finally, we lock hands. I pull her to the wall, up to standing, trying to shimmy her out of the window, but suddenly my leg collapses. And we lose our grip. I skitter down the icy slanted roof, far away from my sister.

"No!" I scream, trying to catch the gutter on my way down, but miss, and tumble straight off the roof into the bushes down below.

CHAPTER 46

I lay on the ground for a few stunned seconds, gaping up at the clear, starry night sky just visible through the spindly branches of the dogwood tree. As I watch glowing embers drift across the sky, I can think only about the vast sea of fresh clean air, paying grateful homage to the planet for providing such a bounty.

Slowly, my lungs stop burning and breathing becomes easier. I feel the molecular exchange of oxygen and carbon dioxide deep inside of my lungs. It's miraculous. It's life enhancing. And it's something my sister is missing.

I claw my way out of the bush, struggle up to standing on one foot, and look up at the window. Great flames lick the window casement like the lashing of a giant reptile tongue. There are dark char marks along the white paint. Flashes of fire break out along the roofline. Flames, eating their way through the ceiling, are closing in like a predator going for the jugular.

"Jinny!" I cry. Why doesn't she fling herself out of the window? "I'll catch you!" I yell. "Just jump!" And then I'm the plump cheerleader with hopes and dreams and terror gnawing at my belly. "You can do it! Keep going!"

But she doesn't do it. I watch, fingers helplessly pressed against my mouth. What is happening? I don't know. All I know is that she's still in there with Dillon and Prankster.

Quickly, I limp over to a trellis that we'd strapped to the downspout long ago. I can climb it, crawl over to the window, and drag her out. I step on the first flimsy rung, and it collapses under my weight. I accidentally catch myself with my bad leg.

A jolt of hot pain stops my breath cold. I groan and fall down as my eyes well up with tears. When the initial wave of nausea passes, I reach down and gingerly pack some snow against my hot throbbing ankle, trying to numb the pain. Then I look up the trellis, my only hope of saving her.

When my ankle seems good and numbed, I get up to standing and reach up high for a sturdy rung, one that hadn't rotted from sprinkler spray, and test it. It holds. I hang on my arms. It holds. Then I lift my right leg to the highest possible rung. I ease my weight onto my foot. It holds.

I'm climbing yet higher, about half way up to the roofline, a good five feet off the ground, when the trellis rung cracks under my weight and suddenly collapses, sending me plummeting to the ground.

The hard strike knocks the breath out of me. I gape like a fish and screw my eyes shut, panic-stricken as my lungs freeze, unable to pull in a single wisp of air. The marauders are back in brute force, but what does it matter if I die?

So I lie on a cold hard crust of snow, my focus brought back again to the simple matter of air and how to get some. Slowly, ever so slowly, my lungs open up again and let in minuscule amounts of air. It's enough to stave off death, but not enough to get going.

My chest relaxes a little; the air comes more easily. I will not die. Not like this. Not without my sister. I'm stirring again, thinking about how I can help my sister, when the cold sets in.

At first, the sharp, crisp winter air had been a welcome antidote the fiery innards of the house. But now, as I lay in a heap of snow in wet sweatpants and a t-shirt sodden with sweat and melting snow, I feel my first shiver.

How nice. I pack some more snow onto my ankle and climb back up to my feet, somewhat woozily, looking up at the empty window.

"Jinny!" I call, cupping my hands around my mouth. But then I stop as the cold hand of reason steals over me. Dillon can also hear me. And if he knows I'm alive, he'll come after me. Far stronger than me, he could drag me back into that flesh-melting inferno, where the witness to his crimes will burn to the ground, silent forever. How convenient.

My hand burns. I plunge it into a mound of snow and scan all the windows, upstairs and down, searching for signs of Virginia. Maybe she somehow made it downstairs. But I see only flames.

I stifle a sob. Jinny. My hard-fighting, sweet dummy of a sister is still inside, fighting for her life. But what can I do? The trellis lay in a shattered heap. Ben had used a more strenuous route, but I can't up a tree in my state.

I withdraw my freezing hand from the snow and clamp them both under my armpits.

Think!

The shivering starts in earnest. The cold, fresh air had restored me. But now it's turning sinister. The insidious cold is creeping into my body and settling into my bones.

As I watch the sea of raging orange flames, I realize that it's warm inside, hot even. I shiver again, a teeth chattering one that knocks my reasoning out of whack.

I could go back in, warm up a little, run really fast. Okay, limp. I could limp as fast as I can. I could find Virginia. I could find Ben. Where had he gone? Don't think about that now.

My sister—I could save her. And I could warm up a little in the process. Then I could find Ben and maybe save him too. I look again at the raging wall of heat. Yes, I could save them both.

And I start toward the front door.

CHAPTER 47

Whoof!

The roof collapses, sending a great arc of glowing cinders into the dark night sky. My heart feels like it seizes mid-beat in my chest.

I collapse to my knees and scream, "*Virginia!*"

But then a wisp of hope washes over me. She's still in there, somewhere. Maybe she wasn't buried in fire and flames. Maybe I can still save her. Maybe there's still a chance.

I hurry toward the house. She will not die in there alone in a coffin of fire. Onwards I stumble, holding my arm up against the heat, trying to see past the wall of flames. There's a pleasant warm zone between the bone chilling temperatures outside, and the flesh melting temperatures inside that gives me pause. I push past the comfort zone and blunder toward the front door.

We will take this final step together. We will—

In the corner of my eye, I see movement up by Virginia's bedroom window. I step back to get a better view and see a figure fall from her window, tumble down the slanted roof, and drop off into the snow. Virginia!

I hurry toward the thick shadows that entomb her, praying that she's okay, that her burns aren't life threatening. I'm thinking about how we're going to get out of the yard, but I stop cold.

Dillon lies there, gaping up at the sky, his face dark with soot, his shoulder flayed, blood seeping into the pristine white snow. Dead? Oh, please let him be dead. Then he gasps for breath.

Oh, no.

Flames roar out of the windows. I put up a futile arm against the heat. A deafening crackling sound booms, and a whole section of the house collapses, sending a great wall of heat toward me, sending me stumbling backwards.

Virginia.

Grief swamps me, thick and foul. My sister lay deep in the roaring funeral pyre of our once beloved home. Hot tears pool in my eyes, turning the blaze into a giant orange and red furze.

I drop my head into my hands and cry, welcoming the tears, wanting them to come and wash this horror away. My throat aches as memories of my sister rush to me, so many sweet and salty memories, a lifetime of them, carrying me back.

I remember her parading around in her prom getup: a hot pink tuxedo. Her young date had loved it. She'd asked a freshman to go with her to the senior prom with her. The poor guy's parents nearly had an aneurism.

I could see their twin mohawks now, finning down the driveway as they hopped in her car and zoomed off to the hotel ballroom. Then there was Froggy. Library beanbags. Tenzing Norgay. Books. So many books. Sharp boogers. Jinx! Horse bite. What is *wrong* with you? Ha! Ha! Ha! Her laugh echoes in mind, ricocheting around in the hollow shell of my blown-out heart.

The flames roar.

Dillon. He's still alive. So am I. And he's not going to stop until I'm charred lion meat. For now though, he just lies there, his face battered and bruised. The flayed gash on his shoulder looks awful. At least Virginia had gotten some good mileage out of Prankster before she died. At least—

His gaze slides to me, his face a hard mask.

He sees it. I see it, too. I'm a live witness to his crimes. I'm a dead woman walking.

If I survive, Dillon will spend the rest of his life behind bars. If I don't, he'll saunter out of this nightmare and claim that a house fire sadly killed the Ward sisters.

He'll probably come up with some sickly sweet story about how we were all roasting a chicken—so cozy and cute—and then the oven erupted in flames that he'd tried so hard to put it out—so hard!—but it just got out of hand.

He stirs, holding onto his right shoulder. He's moving wincingly slow, but my heart booms in my chest nonetheless, adrenaline firing up my shattered body and galvanizing me back into action.

"She's *dead*," Dillon says, pushing himself up to standing. "She's gone, Piss—"

"Shut up!" I scream. "Just shut the fuck up for once!"

Then he cocks his head, listening.

I hear it too. Distant sirens. The long plaintive wail of help coming. They're coming to arrest Dillon, maybe shoot him on sight like a garbage eating bear.

He should be running scared. But he's not running at all. He looks at me, his eyes narrow, a deadly still smirk on face. He knows. I know it, too.

He intends for me to be lion meat by the time the cops finally break down my fortified front gate. Well, he's not going to have it his way.

If I can get the cops to see me, I'm safe from Dillon. He can't attack me in front of law enforcement. Well, he *can*, but they have deadly force. Dillon just has his insanity.

They'll slap handcuffs on him, and I'll be free to search for Ben. My heart aches dully thinking about him. About what probably happened to him. I steel myself up for that ghastly blow.

I start hurrying toward the gate, but something catches my eye. A mound lay propped against the perimeter wall next to the lion enclosure. Ben.

I hear screams. Desperate shrieks. Mine, I realize, followed by laughter. Hoots, even. Dillon's of course.

Anguish twists my heart. My Ben, my sweet Ben. Dillon did this.

I want to run over and kick Dillon in the shoulder, grind my heel into his flesh, make him scream, but I can't. I'm too slow. I'm too reduced. If he gets one finger on me, if I give him just one narrow opportunity, I'll be leaving this earthly plane, right behind Virginia.

"Only one left to go," he says, turning his dark gaze to me.

So I start running, limping, really, getting to Ben the fastest way I can.

He laughs instead, while I hurry toward the lion cage, dragging my bum leg behind me, using it to propel me forward. The lion is hunched in the shadows, watching, making me nervous.

I trip and pummel forward, catching myself on the fence, rousing the interest of the lion. I glance over my shoulder. Dillon stands there, grimacing, his arm still clamped onto his shoulder.

"Ben? Are you all right?" I ask, taking Ben's chilled hands in mine. There's a welt rising up on his forehead. One eye is swollen shut. "How did you get out here?"

Ben groans and shifts in the snow, wincing. "Dillon pistol whipped me in your office. I passed out, I guess, and woke up when I smelled smoke. So I crawled out here. But I'm—I'm hurt. .."

Despite the frigid temperatures, sweat breaks out his brow. I open his coat and lift his shirt, stiff with blood, and find a gunshot wound. Dillon had clearly aimed for his chest, but missed. The bullet grazed the side of his abdomen, how deep I don't know. Ben has lost so much blood though. His shirt looks like a butcher's apron. Nausea overwhelms me. That's about all the looking I can do for now.

"I think you'll be okay," I say, reporting back, desperately hoping so anyway. "But we need to get out of here. Can you stand?" I glance over at Dillon, marshaling his strength.

Beside the bullet wound, there could be internal injuries, possibly a bleed that would silently whisk away his life if he moves. We have to try. We're dead if we sit here. We have to get away from Dillon. We can't go through the gate, not with Dillon blocking the way. And we can't sit here and wait for help to come blowing through the gates either.

I can hear the long plaintive wail of sirens out front, but they seem to be waiting for a battering ram, or a reinforced vehicle to open the gate or maybe the Second Coming. I don't know. All I know is that if we sit here, we'll be dead by the time those gates get blown off their hinges.

We have to go through escape door located in the far corner of the lion cage. The one that Virginia said the lion couldn't open. Pray it's unlocked. Pray I can open it.

Ben struggles to his feet. I try support him, but nearly sink to my knees when he leans his full weight on me. Dickhead is on the move, watching, enjoying his spectator sport, surely.

He knows the only way forward is through the lion cage. And he's supremely confident that my backyard kitten is going to take care of his dirty business before. It's Dillon or the lion.

I'll take my chances with the lion.

So we hurry to the gate, work the wire loose that holds the gate shut (thanking God that Virginia hadn't used a padlock like a responsible owner), carefully open it and slink inside. I hope the lion will sense freedom and bolt, maybe take Dillon down while he's at it.

But the lion doesn't move. He sits in the shadows, watching, while Dillon walks up the lion cage and helpfully swings the gate shut behind us.

I look at the lion, my heart thumping so hard I can barely catch my breath.

"Hey kitty, kitty," I say in a nice friendly sing-song voice, hoping to lull him into complacency. "It's me . . . food lady."

CHAPTER 48

Dillon understands my predicament. That's why he closed the gate. The lion will provide the perfect ending, a far cleaner ending than what Dillon had envisioned in his twisted, violent mind.

He won't be held liable for a lion eating Ben and I or a house fire consuming my sister. Why should he be held responsible for a couple of idiots who got eaten by their pet lion? He'll walk away from this, free to terrorize another hapless victim, free to find his next Amy Mathews.

Police lights strobe red and blue across the yard. The silent intermittent bi-color strobe announces the presence of help, real help, who are stronger than Dillon, who can take him down. But they're not looking for him. The roaring house fire distracts them.

Dillon's reign of terror is about to end anyway, if I can just survive long enough to provide my damning testimony. Distantly, I hear the approaching fire trucks urgently honk their horns. They're coming. Help is coming. But not for us.

As we hobble to the back of the enclosure, the lion closes in behind us. He chuffs, blowing his hot putrid breath on me. This is a game of chess, and Ben and I are in check.

Slow incremental movements might get us out of it. We have to be boring. We have to stupefy the lion with our painfully slow movements. We have to be like a zombie, without the strange lurching.

"We have to hurry," I say to Ben. "But don't startle the lion."

"I'm at maximum speed right now," he whispers, wincing as he inches forward.

Suddenly the front gate crashes open. A fire trucks races up the driveway. Startled, the lion jumps back, snarling. A surge of relief washes over me, but that quickly sours. Nobody is going to come to our rescue in the backyard. Everyone is too busy with the house fire to think to check the backyard for a lion enclosure, where people were about to die.

Then the lion pounces.

"Move it!" I cry.

Galvanized by his snarling mass, we scramble to the far door of the enclosure, well and truly triggering the lion's prey drive.

I can feel his heavy paws landing behind me, hunting us, closing down on us.

He nips, catching the leg of my baggy sweatpants. I trip, but I manage to keep going, arms pin wheeling to gain back my balance. We're closing in on the small back door.

And by God, I'm going to open it. This isn't going to be another intercom saga. I'm going to grip the gleaming doorknob and if it doesn't turn, somehow I'm going to rip that door clear off its hinges.

The lion turns his attention to Ben, lagging behind. He's closing in, playing with us. He knows were his for the taking. This is just a fun game for him, the first in a long time called 'chase the desperately shrieking items of prey.'

Then the lion swipes at my legs and trips me. During my inexorable fall to the ground, I vault a grip for the doorknob . . . and grab it.

My body sags, but my hands hold firm. I twist. It turns. The door does not open. Ben catches up to me, panting heavily. "Open the door!" he cries.

The lion roars. I glance behind me and see the smooth practiced arc of the lion's muscled body, teeth bared, thick lips pulled back malignantly, eyes pulled into angry slits. I heave myself up to my knees and, together with Ben, slam my shoulder against the door so hard my teeth rattle.

But the door jolts open. And the lion soars past us into dark depths of the open forest beyond. Quickly, I shut the door, locking him outside the enclosure, where he belongs.

I cling to the doorknob long after he'd escaped, in shock, watching the red and blue light strobe against the wall, listening to the firemen yelling in the front yard, trying to put out the fire, listening to the squawk of police radios. They're all in the front of house, battling the blaze, trying to get inside the house and find the survivors before it's too late.

But the survivors are out back.

My body shakes. My hands ache. My left leg feels like its on fire, pain ripping my ankle apart. But we were free. We were free. And we're safe, at last.

I listen to the plaintive wail of more sirens. Ambulances. They're coming to our rescue, too. I cling to the doorknob, bow my head, and weep, my body shaking with silent sobs and cold.

Ben slides down the wall next to me and fumbles for my hand. "It's all over, babe," he says. "It's all over . . ."

Dillon doesn't matter anymore. He'll probably try to slink off to save himself and escape his fate like a coward. He is a coward. He's a depraved, sickening, craven piece of—

The chain-link fence rattles. The gate slams open. I look up and see Dillon, lips pulled back, starting toward us.

"Help us! We're back here!" I scream, but my voice is swallowed up by the blasting inferno, the sounds of the dying house, the blaring horns, and shouts of firemen. Once again, we need to save ourselves. "Get up, Ben. Hurry. He's coming." I'm shivering and shaking, but somehow I help him to his feet.

We both fumble for the knob and push the door open. And then we're hurrying, tripping with weakness, helping each other up, limping and dragging ourselves away from Dillon; all the while I keep my eye on the still dark forest beyond.

We desperately head down the five-foot clearing toward the road. The blue and red police strobes blink intermittently, making the landscape jump. The dark forest looms just a few feet away. But before I can scuttle down the length of the perimeter wall, I feel the heavy weight of Dillon taking me down.

I fall face first into a hard crust of dirty snow. Gravel scrapes against my cheek, a hot burning sensation across my face. He flips me over and sits on top of me, straddling me, pinning my flailing arms down with his knees, taking me right back to the very beginning when he installed me upstairs in the Dungeon.

I flail, and I fight. And I try to breathe. But I'm too weak, and he is too strong, even with one arm out of commission. He's too heavy; I'm far too exhausted.

Ben crawls toward us, one arm in front of the other. But he's too slow, and far too weak.

Cold snow melts down my neck, stealing the last vestige of warmth from my bones. I shiver uncontrollably, watching the police lights strobe against Dillon face—red, blue, red, blue—making his face jump to the left and right. Making his face look gruesome, then surreal. Gruesome. Surreal.

His exposed scalp, covered with weeping patches of singed hair, flashes in the strobe lights. The half-crescent scar on his cheek had reopened. A sheet of blood had dried on his face. The meat of his cheek lay exposed.

His eyes are reptilian and cold, the glinting orbs as dark and emotionless as obsidian. Pockets of flesh on one side of his face had melted; the weeping pustules glisten in the intermittent flashes. There are char marks along his jaw. And of course, there's his flayed shoulder.

"Help!" Ben cries weakly. But nobody will be able to hear him.

Virginia had lost in the end, but she'd put up an impressive fight. A swell of admiration rises up in my heart, thinking about how hard Virginia had fought, how much damage she'd caused. But she lost in the end. Just as I will lose, too.

Dillon wraps his good hand around my neck as careful as a surgeon, the cold methodical look in his eyes returning. The naked rage has bled away, replaced by cool analytics. He's going to choke me to death and study my reaction to the very last bitter breath. Then he's going to move onto Ben. He'll get caught. The police will probably walk in on him mid-strangulation, but he's not going to go down without a fight. He's not going to give up. Not now. Not ever.

I wrap my hands around his wrist and try to break his hold. My lungs start to burn, my eyesight dims. I turn my gaze up to a smattering of bright stars in the sky, to beautiful infinity where Dillon wants me to go.

"Goodbye Piss Drinker," he says.

I look at him. "It's Eugenia," I mutter between clenched teeth. "Eugenia Ward."

CHAPTER 49

I tighten my hands around his. I gulp and struggle. Ben's calling again for help. I can hear him distantly as if he's slipping down time tunnel. *Help us*! But the crackling fire, water hissing out of hoses, and shouts, swallow up his calls.

There's an urgent burning sensation in my chest. I try again to pry his hand off my neck, but it's like an iron manacle. My lungs burn and demand air. Just a few wisps of it, I tell myself, just enough to stay alive.

"Genie . . ." I hear Ben croak from some distant faraway place. "Look."

Something about the revived tone of his voice gives me pause. I slide my gaze to the side and see the lion crouched in the darkness a few feet away, tail switching, ears pinned, eyes glowing from the darkened edge of the forest. He draws back his lips and reveals his frighteningly long teeth.

Dillon glances his way.

I see a flick of his tongue, followed by a blur of yellow. And then I squeeze my eyes shut, bracing myself. I can't watch. This is it. This is the end. I think of my sister, waiting for me on the other side . . .

The weight lifts from my chest. Terrible pain will surely follow. I roll over and cover the base of my neck with my arms, waiting for sharp tearing pain to shoot down my back. I squeeze my eyes shut and wait for his hungry fangs to sink into my skinny body, waiting for the lion to devour me like a little Thanksgiving morsel.

But pain doesn't come. Is it just a matter of time?

Then I hear it: soft guttural growling tempered by Dillon's gurgling shrieks. I lift my head and peer into the darkness, shifting with each flashing strobe, and see Dillon climbing to his feet, stumbling along the barren borderland, his right arm swinging limp. He's trying to get away. He's trying to escape.

He makes it a few feet, but the lion leaps. His heavy front paws extended, long savage claws flashing red, blue, red, blue.

The lion catches Dillon by the shoulders, sending him pummeling face first to the ground. Then he sinks his long teeth into the fleshy nape Dillon's neck. Dillon screams and reaches for the lion's big yellow head, swiping and punching uselessly. One fist grazes the lion's eye. The lion snarls and shakes him like a rag doll.

I scoot toward Ben and put my arms around him. He's cold, so very cold. And so am I.

Dillon, on his back now, frantically scurries away from the lion. His legs scrabble in the dirty snow as he tries to escape. But the lion bites down on his ankle and starts yanking him into the cold, dark depths of the forest.

Dillon flops over and digs his good hand into the snow. But he's no match for the lion. As he gets pulled to the edge of the forest, he leaves behind long bloody scrape marks. Then the lion looks up at us, watching, while Dillon moans and sobs into the snow.

The lion turns his magnificent yellow eyes to me. I freeze. Is this it? Is he going for a body count? But the lion licks his lips and turns his attention to his the bigger meal instead, who had scurried a few feet away by then. No matter. The lion languidly walks toward him, his muscles bunching and sliding under his shaggy yellow coat designed for sweltering heat, doing its best in this harsh New England climate.

He straddles Dillon's pathetic wiggling figure, and sinks his mouth into the nape of his neck. Dillon screams; a desperate shriek that echoes through the cold, still forest. He shakes Dillon once more, his body flashing red, blue, red, blue.

Dillon lands a few feet from him, prone, motionless. The lion walks to him, shoulder blades rising and falling rhythmically like a metronome, counting out the solid steady beats until Dillon's final end.

He licks Dillon's face, dragging his rough tongue over the loose flap of flesh. Dillon groans and weakly tries to bat away his huge head as if he were a fly.

The lion lifts his head to the sky and roars, followed by deep rumbling chuffs that I feel in my chest. His breath hangs in the cold winter air like clouds. He seemed to be calling for his pride, announcing his kill. He stops and looks around, searching the dark edge of the forest for his kind that will never appear.

Then he bends to Dillon, clamps his wide black mouth around the column of Dillon's neck, and disappears into the forest with him.

I close my eyes and let the tears come. Dillon can't touch me anymore. He'll never touch me again. I'm free from him forever. Free from his tyranny. Free from everything he represented. And I'm free from Fear too.

The house is gone. Virginia is gone, too. But lightness overwhelms me.

I'm shivering in earnest, but it's not from cutting winds or biting cold. Chains fall away from me, chains that I had tried so hard to break. No longer will I ever let anyone have any power over me. No longer will I give in to my fears.

I had given away all my power over the years, and Dillon had taken the rest. Ruthlessly. Shamelessly. Brutally. He took from me everything that I held sacred. Something in me died along with him, but something is rising from the ashes.

Eugenia Ward is rising from the ashes.

Police burst through the door, guns pointed, sweeping the surrounds. A woman steps forward, quickly holstering her weapon and kneeling next to Ben and I. She places her hand on my back and says to her partner, "Get the EMTs. We have survivors."

CHAPTER 50

It's been two weeks have passed since my house burnt down to the ground, since I lost my sister. I stand before the ashes of our home, weak still but I'm recovering. As a matter of routine, the investigators sifted through the rubble and determined the cause of the fire. A bent gas pipe was found in my old office, pointed toward the safe room.

My house is just a blackened skeleton now. Fingers of smoke rise up from the disaster here and there. The ashes are still warm, giving off a gentle heat that stands in stark contrast to the flesh melting temperatures I'd experienced that night.

Shivering, I enter the threshold with crutches under my arms. Turns out, I'd broken my ankle, which healed wrong. The doctors had to re-break it and set it in a cast, but the prognosis was good that I'd make a full recovery.

And I make my way into the house, I see the kitchen half standing with blackened studs like a ribcage set against the blanket of white snow in the backyard. The appliances are smoked. The fridge door lays ajar. Our beautiful home has been reduced to smoke and rubble. Ashes and glass.

But the memories burn bright. Like a shadow play, I see my life reenacted by ghostly versions of Virginia and I. She's standing in the kitchen, measuring out the space for new granite countertops. She's over by the silverware drawer, pulling out a big spoon, a pint of ice cream in hand. And she's over by the coffee machine, wrestling with the small tricky drawer.

I crutch over a burned out hole in the kitchen flooring and make my way over to the machine, which is melted and broken.

I can feel Virginia standing there, lifting a cup of coffee to her lips. Not so long ago, I had stood across the kitchen bar, telling her that Amy was over.

She'd be standing here now in her terry cloth bathrobe, threatening the coffee machine with replacement, if it wasn't for my calamitous decision. I knew all along that ditching Amy would have consequences. I made the decision though. Raise up Rhenn for Jinny or let him die and raise up myself. But this . . . I didn't expect this.

Jinny had to make a similar decision. Let Amy go for me, or push Amy on for herself. We both chose ourselves. Both decisions ended in disaster.

I can't help but wonder what would have happened if we had chosen differently? If we had chosen what's best for the other person? We would both be here? Or were we both blundering down a path of inevitability?

I don't know. My heart hurts. My head hurts.

Nothing can make the pain go away. She's gone now. And I can't change a thing. Losing my sister is like a raw open wound inside of me.

My heart feels like an old callused thing, toughened up and scarred over by the loss of Mom, but broken open again now.

I know this road. I've been here before. That gives me solace. I survived last time. I will survive this time. It's a long arduous journey out of the Land of Grief. And not at all a journey I wish to travel again, but I'm here.

Jinny was flawed. She made a selfish decision based on a misunderstanding. I guess that's the part that hurts so bad. It didn't have to be this way, but it is this way.

As I make my way out of the burnt shell of our kitchen and down the hallway, I pause in the threshold of my office. The glass-paneled door had melted. Snow swirls and spirals over the ashes of my furniture. I step over the rubble and look down at my computer, broken and melted underneath a timber beam that had fallen from the coffered ceiling.

The irony makes me shake my head. I'd fought to write a new manuscript. Now, it's gone too. The guts of my computer spilled out on my burned-out blue carpet, the hard drive hopelessly melted. I want to go up to Virginia's room. Sit on her bed. Run my hand over her expensive chenille bedding and listen quietly for her voice, but the stairwell had collapsed in the fire.

Only the first few rungs survived, leading up to a cavernous hole in the roof, opening up the leaden sky.

But I need something of hers. A keepsake. That's why I came back.

With my crutches, I walk over to the living room, past the kitchen, past the five thousand dollar Hermes table; its once gleaming surface bubbled and blackened now.

In the living room, my Tiffany blue chenille chaise half-survived. It's the same one that I found Dillon lounging upon before he locked me up in the garret room, marking the beginning of Amy Mathews's end.

It's also the same chaise that Virginia liked to inhabit. I gently sit down on the edge.

Tears come. Stinging my eyes. My heart sears with pain, the re-injury of loss makes my insides feels pulpy and raw. I drop my head into my hands and cry. "I miss you, Jinny," I whisper, as memories whorl around me.

The wind curls and whispers through the ashes. And when I lift my head, I see a glimmer of sunshine touching the charred remains of our house, spangling on a something bright.

I get up and go to sparkle, so bright in a dim, dark pile of ashes, and pick it up. It's a broken shard from the Waterford trophy that Virginia had cracked on Dillon. The same one that we'd poured a bottle of champagne into.

Ha! Ha! Ha! I can feel her next to me now. I want to tell her that I forgive her and love her, despite everything. But I can't.

I rub soot off of the engraved shard with my thumb, and slip it into my satchel. My fingers brush against the pill vial that lives in my bag. And I pull it out.

It's full of my benzo buds, my little white friends that will help me through this new catastrophe in my life. Help numb the pain.

The tears slide down my face. I press my thumb and forefinger against my eyes and pull in a big shaky breath. I have to hold myself together or else I'll fall apart. Maybe I should take a pill now. Numb the pain. Numb the pain. Oh God, help me numb the pain.

I've lost everything, except for my pills. And now, I need to lose everything. I need to finally ditch my pills. I pull in a sharp breath, nostrils flaring. Am I strong enough? Can I do it?

I lift my gaze to the shaft of sunlight, still shining through a cloud break. And Jinny's words come to me.

You got this . . .

"Really?" I mumble, running my thumb over the prescription label on the orange vial, feeling emotional, but hopeful.

A hundred percent.

And I toss my pills into the rubble.

EPILOGUE

Six Months Later

"Wow," says Candace, the daytime talk show host, shifting in her well-lit seat. "Wow, wow, wow. I don't know where to begin!" She glances at the audience, safely sequestered behind dim lighting. "So Amy Matthews isn't a . . . a real person?"

Ben is in the green room. I know he's watching me on a backstage monitor. Together with a talented PR agent, we'd discussed how best to handle revealing Amy Mathews's true identity and her sudden death. Nobody likes being lied to. Nobody likes a liar.

"I mean, how did this even come to be?" Emily asks.

I like Candace. She's jovial, but astute. I'd seen her shows before; I liked her dry sense of humor. She also had some skeletons pop out of her closet some years back that had dragged her career into a rather dull light. She understands. She'll be the most sympathetic, which is why I'm currently sitting on her guest couch. She provides the ideal platform for me to handle my own little animated skeleton.

"You know," I begin, "it all happened so suddenly. I'd written this book, this vampire book that was kinda popular and,"— polite titters.

"Yeah, just a little bit," replies Candace, picking up on the mood of her audience.

"Okay, very popular. But you see, I had this problem. I had just lost my mom and . . ." I pause, thinking about her. PR guru told me to pause often for gravitas. Her voice came to me now, *breathe one two, and go.*

But this isn't a dress rehearsal. Memories of Mom are always with me, rushing to me, reaching for me, coupled with memories of Virginia. Tears, disastrous tears, sting my eyes. *Whatever you do, don't cry!* PR Guru had cautioned. *Nobody likes a crybaby.*

But I can't help it. The pain is still so raw. Every day I hear Virginia's voice saying the damnedest things, making me laugh, making me cry, making me miss Thunder Bum.

"Sorry," I murmur. "This is really hard for me."

Candace whips out a box of Kleenex from behind her chair and hands it to me. I thread a few out of the opening and press them to the corner of my eye, careful not to ruin my stage makeup.

I look out at the audience, one single nebulous entity that can make me or break me. PR Guru is back. *Just tell them a part of the truth. Nobody wants to hear every last gory detail.*

I look up again at Candace, her hair freshly frosted, her blue crystalline eyes merry and glittering, silently imploring me to, "Go on."

I take a deep breath. "Sorry, this is a little overwhelming."

Candace slaps me playfully on the knee. "Ohhhh, what's so overwhelming? We only have five *million* viewers!" She looks at me again, but here eyes aren't so merry. They're serious. Her eyes, the color of happy tropical waters, darken. *Dance,* she's telling me. *Dance, monkey, dance.*

I pull in a deep breath. Virginia is with me. I can feel her invigorating presence, telling Candace to stuff a sock in it. I smile a little. And Mom is with me, holding my hand. *You can do it, honey* . . . And in the back room, I have Ben.

"I had a terrible problem. I couldn't go out in public. I had some really bad social phobias. Have, I mean, but I'm getting a lot better." Silence from the shadows. Sympathetic? One can only hope. "And yeah, I wrote this book about vampires because during my mom's battle with cancer that's what I felt like. I felt like a dead person. And then suddenly, we got an agent. And then the book sold, you know, about four copies,"—the titters are back; Candace is back—"but I wasn't able to do the interviews. I wasn't able to do all the promotional stuff. Book signings, promotional videos. So my sister stepped in." I don't mention the part about how she engineered the stalker so she could be the face of Amy Mathews, and she paid for that blunder with her life.

PR guru approves. "And—and now that's she's gone,"—*be strong*—"well, she lives on in my books."

Candace, emotionally agile, puts her hand on my knee and said some sympathetic words that I don't hear. I'm too busy trying to hold back the tears. I smile a brittle smile, hoping she'll see my silent plea and drive our little interview vehicle over to happier terrain.

"What a story. Speaking of, I hear you have another book coming out!"

The audience erupts in applause. I breath a sigh of relief.

"Yes, yes I do. I'm finally writing under my own name now." I turn to the audience, kind of wishing I could see their faces, but not really. "But it's still me, I mean Amy Mathews. We have the same writing style."

Laughter.

"And so can you tell us a little bit about it?" Candace asks. She already knows the answer. We're playing 'toss the ball' for the viewers at home.

I straighten and wince as a sharp pain scissors up my leg. The pain carries me back to that night. The night the lion ate Dillon and set me free.

Animal control finally captured him a mile from my house and shot him with a tranquilizer dart. After his temporary stay at an animal control facility, I had him relocated to a legitimate lion sanctuary, where he grew sleek, fat, and stunning.

Then I had him flown out to Africa, where he teamed up with another bachelor male, acquired a pride, and currently lives out his days happy and free on the Serengeti. Ben and I have plans to visit him, after my ankle heals. After I get this book launch off of the front burner.

"It's a memoir," I say, feeling stronger, feeling whole. "Called *The Hunted*."

ABOUT THE AUTHOR

An American expat since 2008, Rachel has sailed over 11,000 nautical miles, rounding the Cape of Good Hope and crossing the Indian Ocean three times. After living in Sydney, Australia for a number of years, she moved up to Singapore with her husband, son, and rescue pup named Jessica Shadow Shady Lady, which unfortunately doesn't fit on a dog tag. But no matter, Shadow hates going outside anyway.

Do consider joining Rachel's Exclusive Reader's Club, where giveaways and free Advance Reader Copies of her latest releases are just the beginning.

For more information, please visit: www.rachelsquared.com.